The Class H Trilogy by Raul Ramos y Sanchez

America Libre

House Divided

Pancho Land

PANCHO LAND

A NOVEL OF A NATION'S MOST MACULATE CONCEPTION

Raul Ramos y Sanchez

Beck & Branch Publishers

Copyright © 2012 by Raul Ramos y Sanchez

Printed in the United States of America
Beck & Branch Publishers
First Edition: November 2012
ISBN 978-0-9854034-1-6
1. United States–Social conditions–Fiction. 2. Insurgency–United States. –Social conditions–Fiction. 3. Ethnic conflict–United States–Fiction. 4. Radicalism–Fiction. 6. Political fiction.

To Two-Buttons for your infinite patience

Special Features of this Edition

Acknowledgements

Like most authors, my journey as a writer has been an uphill climb. After reaching one peak, you find another summit even higher lies ahead.

At every stage of the ascent, others have guided and helped me along, people without whom I would still be in the valley wondering whether to even risk the climb.

The origins of anything of worth I've managed to achieve starts with my family. My wife, mother, sister and brother are the foundation stones of my life. I've also been gifted with a group of close friends whose caring and encouragement have for many years helped pick me up when life has knocked me down. Others I've met through my professional life also deserve recognition.

My agent Sally van Haitsma has been a guide and tireless supporter since 2005. I want to acknowledge Ralph Keyes, Kirk Whisler, Edward James Olmos, Jess Nieto, Veronica Jacuinde, Michael Steven Gregory, Julio Ricardo Varela, Scott Willis, and Reuben Martinez for their generous support.

The world of social media has also been a wellspring of support. Many thanks to my friends on Facebook, Twitter, OC Gente, Redroom, Goodreads, and Latinos in Social Media.

My work has been informed through contacts with a number of scholars including Richard Slatta, Miguel De La Torre, Henry Louis Gates, Jr., Oscar Alvarez Gila, and Franklin W. Knight. Special thanks go to John L. Woods for his skillful editing.

My deepest thanks also goes out to the readers of my work—especially those who have reached out with comments, even when our viewpoints have differed. You are the reason for the countless hours that go into this work.

PANCHO LAND

THE WITNESS

From *Witness To History,*
© 2067 by Simon Potts

As a firsthand witness to the Western Hemisphere's momentous changes during the first half of the 21st century, I have tried to record these events without currying favor among those who prevailed or seeking pity for those who did not.

Looking back at these events after five decades as a journalist, I see little difference between the two.

—Simon Potts

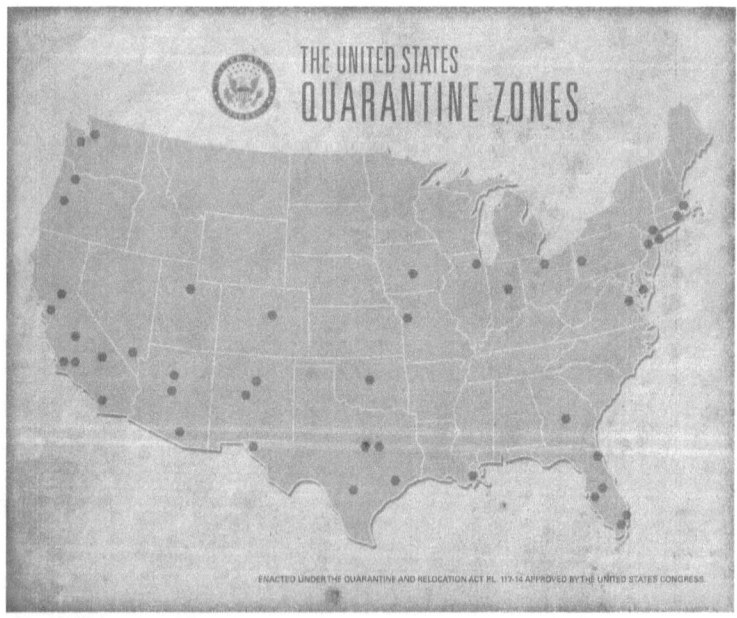

THE UNITED STATES
QUARANTINE ZONES

ENACTED UNDER THE QUARANTINE AND RELOCATION ACT P.L. 117-14 APPROVED BY THE UNITED STATES CONGRESS

THE HOSTAGE

LOS ANGELES QUARANTINE ZONE B

...drip...drip...drip...

The rhythmic beat of water falling somewhere in the darkness was Sarah's last link to reality. The steady sound gave her a focus, something to distract her from the terror of being alone in total darkness. After her last meal, The Leader had moved her to this place that could only be part of a sewer. The dank, fetid smell had convinced her of that.

Handcuffed by her left wrist to a vertical pipe, she could move only a single step in any direction. On the filthy floor around her were a mattress, a bottle of water, and a wretched-smelling pot for her excretions.

By tossing pebbles into the darkness and listening, Sarah had determined she was at the dead end of a long tunnel. In the beginning, she'd tried calling out—softly at first, then gradually louder. Her voice had echoed back unanswered.

From what she could tell, a couple of days had passed since two masked men had captured her as she jogged near her home in Santa Clarita. Being bound, blindfolded and herded over thirty miles at gunpoint by the pair she'd mentally named The Leader and Nice One had been terrifying. But this solitary horror was even worse.

Alone in a black void, her life before the two Panchos

had captured her now seemed like a dream, a time and place that had never really existed. Desperate to make her past seem real, she tried to recall the contents of her bedroom... pictures from her last visit with her dad... her collection of sports trophies... the schoolbooks on her desk...

A distant scuffling brought the terror flooding back. "Hello?" she called out into the darkness, her voice quivering. "Is somebody there?"

"It's okay, Sarah. Don't be afraid," Nice One answered from the darkness, still some distance away.

At the sound of Nice One's voice, Sarah's fear began to ebb. She knew it was strange to feel safe around one of the men who'd captured her. But Nice One's small gestures of kindness were the only comfort she could cling to in this nightmare. All the same, she did not want to show her captors how afraid she really was.

"I haven't seen you in a while," she said, trying to sound composed as the man walked closer, invisible behind the beam of his flashlight. "Actually, I haven't seen you at all, I guess."

"I just found out where you were."

"Your boss brought me here. Didn't he tell you?"

"Never mind. I brought you some stuff," Nice One said, shining the flashlight onto the mattress. Inside the cone of light, a blanket and a scuffed plastic penlight appeared. "It gets cold down here and the dark can drive you crazy sometimes."

"Thanks," she answered. "Why does it get so cold? Are we near the ocean or something?" she asked, hoping to learn where they were holding her. Judging by the time they'd walked, she was sure they were inside one of the L.A. quarantine zones, but which one?

"You shouldn't ask any questions, Sarah. The less you

know, the better it is for everybody," he said gently. "The penlight's for emergencies. Don't use it unless you have to. We don't have a lot of batteries," he said, then added, "Oh, yeah. Keep the blanket and the penlight under the mattress, okay? You're not supposed to have them."

"Will I get in trouble for having them?" she asked, suddenly anxious.

"No, I will."

"You're very nice."

"I've got to go," he said standing up. "One more thing. Don't say anything about me being here."

"Why not?"

"Remember, Sarah. You shouldn't ask questions. I'll check back on you when I can," he said before leaving.

Alone in the darkness again, Sarah turned on the penlight and moved the beam around the room, studying her surroundings. She then turned it off to conserve the batteries. To her surprise, she felt a strange euphoria.

Her terror of the dark had vanished.

THE PRODIGAL—Day 1

GLENDALE, CA

The men around her looked away as Sarah opened the top of her khaki jump suit and brought the hungry baby to her breast. During the last two hours, the others aboard the crowded bus had grown used to the only woman among them and the sounds and smells of her infant. Despite the July heat, Sarah threw the baby's blanket over her shoulder for privacy and let her two-month-old son nurse. Daniel stopped crying, his brown eyes opening slightly as he suckled dreamily.

The differences between Sarah Evans and the men on the bus went deeper than gender. While Sarah was blonde and fair with sage-green eyes, most of the swarthy faces around her revealed assorted traces of indigenous ancestry. A bigger difference still remained. Sarah had willingly boarded the bus destined for Los Angeles Quarantine Zone B. The others aboard were Class H fugitives detained outside the zones being returned to confinement. Still, Army regulations required Sarah wear the same khaki overalls issued to the detainees on the bus.

As Daniel fed, Sarah gazed at the passing landscape through the bars covering the windows of the one-time LA Metro bus. The view had changed little since they'd left the Army detainee center in Santa Clarita. Most of

Southern California had always been a never-ending strip mall sprawl, made even more monotonous by its ceaseless traffic. But now, the only movement came from the swaying branches of eucalyptus trees growing out of control, their roots piercing streets and sidewalks. To Sarah, the deserted landscape had the air of an endless cemetery.

The bus lurched violently, swerving to avoid a pothole. Sarah instinctively cradled Daniel and, unable to brace herself, fell toward the aisle.

"Careful!" the man beside Sarah called out, catching her before she hit the floor.

"I'm sorry," Sarah said as the man helped her sit upright again.

"No problem," he mumbled.

These were the first words anyone on the bus had uttered during the two-hour journey.

"You all right back there?" the sheriff's deputy at the front of the bus called out from the steel cage separating him and the driver from the passengers. Everyone aboard knew he was addressing Sarah.

Sarah's face reddened. "I'm fine. There's no problem."

The deputy slipped his thumb under the strap of the automatic rifle on his shoulder. "You let me know if anybody gives you any trouble."

"You seen that kid of hers?" the driver muttered to the deputy. "Looks like she's gotten into trouble with some Pancho already." Inside the silent bus, even those seated in the back heard him.

"Shut up, asshole," snapped the deputy.

The men seated around Sarah looked down or stared into the distance, trying to give her solitude. Sarah felt hot tears fill her eyes and fought the urge to cry. From the day of Daniel's birth, Sarah knew the path she'd chosen would not be easy. The memories of that day two months earlier were still fresh.

"You have a fine, healthy boy, hon," the shift nurse called out, pushing a gurney with Sarah's newborn into the hospital room. "His APGAR was nine."

Sitting up in bed, Sarah smiled, her bobbed hair still matted with sweat from the long labor. "Can I hold him?"

"Of course, hon," the nurse said, handing her the infant.

"He's beautiful," Sarah said, softly kissing his thick black hair.

As the infant nuzzled her chest, a wave of bliss washed over Sarah, a tingling warmth that made her quiver. This small, fragile being she'd brought into the world now depended on her completely.

Sarah stroked his tiny palm and, inexplicably, felt both young and old. The world around her seemed like a fresh new place, as if she was seeing everything for the first time; yet she also felt connected to something timeless.

The doctor had told her she might feel euphoric after the delivery but Sarah had imagined it would be like getting high. This was something far more intense than her brief flirtations with pot and pills.

She wished Pedro could see their son. She'd already decided his name... Daniel Evans Suarez. Daniel was her father's middle name. Just as important to her plans, Daniel was a name that would be the same in English and Spanish.

Sarah turned a blissful gaze toward the nurse. "When do I get to announce his name?"

"You'll do that when the birth certificate is—"

The door opened suddenly and Sarah's mother entered the room, her platinum bouffant bouncing in synch with the mincing gait of stiletto heels.

Monica Evans' mascara lines narrowed when she saw

Sarah holding the baby. "I gave you explicit instructions," she said to the nurse. "This child was *not* to be brought to my daughter after the delivery."

"Get off her case, mom," Sarah answered. "I asked her to do it."

"It's her right, ma'am," the nurse added. "State law says the child is hers—even if she's a minor."

"I see," Monica said, plucking a speck of lint from her blouse sleeve. "And does the law prevent me from having a private conversation with my daughter?"

The nurse patted Sarah's arm. "I'll be in the hallway, hon. Call out if you need me."

Once they were alone, Monica's voice softened. "Now, Sarah. I thought we'd agreed to keep the contact to a minimum. I don't think you should be getting too attached."

"Please, mom. I don't want to get into this again."

"The longer we wait, the harder it's going to be," Monica said, sitting down by the bed. "You said you'd consider an adoption. We can't put it off any longer. You've got to sign the documents right away, Sarah. The lawyer from church is on his way."

"Look, mom, I only said I'd consider an adoption because I was tired of arguing with you."

"Sarah, you're just seventeen and some very powerful hormones are affecting your judgment. Stop and think this through. You can't raise a child by yourself."

"I can work. A lot of women have raised children alone before."

"Sweetheart, I know you only want what's best for your baby," Monica said, wringing her hands. "But don't you see? Giving him to the right family is the best thing you can do for him. Pastor Avery has a list of good Christian families who are ready to take him in."

"He's mine, mother," Sarah said, tucking the baby close against her. "I don't want him to grow up around people who'll never accept him because he's Class H."

"No one has to know about his background. We can say his father's from India or something."

Sarah shook her head. "No, mother. I want my son to know who he is."

"That's ridiculous," Monica said. "If you declare that child's Class H, they'll take him away from you—or they'll send you both into a quarantine zone."

"I'm not going to tell the government he's Class H," Sarah said. "I just want *him* to know it—unless you plan on turning us in."

"Sarah, we've been over this before. Dr. Harkins explained that having sympathies for the terrorists who abducted you is normal. A lot of hostages—"

Sarah raised her palm. "Please, mom. Don't start with the Stockholm syndrome lecture again."

"I'm glad your father didn't live to see this day," Monica said, raising her eyes toward the ceiling.

"Don't go there, mother," Sarah said, her voice hardening. "We both know dad might still be alive if you hadn't thrown him out."

Monica leaned close to her daughter, eyes glaring. "Sarah, this is the child of a rapist," she said, jabbing a finger toward the infant. "Praise Jesus that you chose to give this baby life. But you can't keep it."

"I *will* keep him," Sarah said calmly, "and you can't stop me. I know the law."

"Sarah, this child was conceived in sin. Nothing good is going to come from—"

"Don't you dare talk to me about sin, mother. You think I haven't heard your all-holy Pastor Avery when he crawls into your bed after Wednesday night services? He carries on like he's still speaking in tongues but the cheap son-of-a-bitch won't even take you to a motel."

Monica rose abruptly, sending her platinum curls into a frenzy. "If that's how you feel, then you're on your own. I won't bring the half-breed son of a terrorist into my home."

"Thanks, mom. That's very Christian of you."

"I'm ashamed of you, Sarah," Monica seethed. "Someday you're going to regret this and I hope God gives me the strength to forgive you when that day comes," she said before leaving the room.

With her mother gone, Sarah looked at Daniel again and smiled. Although her mother's words were meant to frighten her, they meant nothing—less than nothing. Being with her son, getting to know this flesh of her flesh, that's all that mattered now. As she brought the baby to her breast, Daniel stirred, opening his almond-shaped eyes. *Yes, those are his father's eyes. And once Pedro knows he has a son, nothing will keep us apart.*

Since that day, Sarah had not wavered in her decision to find Pedro. Now, as the moment she'd see him again grew closer, her feelings kept swinging between elation and anxiety. From the chest pocket of her jumper, Sarah brought out a frayed strip of black cloth and held it against her cheek. Its faint earthy scent reassured her. The cloth was the last thing Pedro had touched: her blindfold.

The man in the seat next to her tapped the arm of a companion across the aisle and nodded toward the window. They were approaching downtown Los Angeles. Sarah carefully put away the blindfold and studied the buildings in the distance.

The familiar skyscrapers looked unchanged at first. But as Sarah looked closer, she saw broken glass in many of the windows and the random black smudges of burned-out fires staining the walls. As they moved closer to the center of the desolate city, the charred carcasses of cars and trucks along the street grew so thick, the bus and its Humvee escorts were forced to weave between them.

Sarah leaned her head against the bars on the window and smiled. Before long, she would see Pedro again.

NEW YORK, NY

"They're waiting for you in makeup, Simon," the associate producer said, glancing at her watch. "You're on in four minutes."

Seated behind a sleek mahogany desk, Simon Potts raised a palm without looking up. "Just a second, Connie." While the producer nervously tapped on her clip board, Potts scribbled a note on the last page of the script and rose to his feet. "Ask Ed to get these edits on the prompter, okay?"

Connie's eyes rolled. "Simon, we don't have time."

"This is breaking material, Connie," he said unfazed. "It's got to be in the show."

"All right, for chrissake," she said, opening the door. "Let's get you to makeup."

Potts followed the producer down the hallway, entered the small makeup room and dropped into one of the barbershop-style chairs.

"Lift your chin, please, Mr. Potts," the makeup artist said, applying the foundation to his face with a small sponge.

Simon watched in the mirror as she spread the ebony liquid on his forehead. "Not much call for my shade of makeup around here, is there?"

"The network made sure we ordered plenty of foundation in your color, Mr. Potts. I'd say you're a keeper."

Simon knew she was right. His weekly commentary show, *Simon At Large*, was leading the ratings in its timeslot. Eleven months ago he'd been an obscure independent filmmaker despite a Pulitzer on his résumé. The hostage crisis had changed all that. Now his face was known across the globe.

"Close your eyes, please," the stylist said before applying the final dusting spray.

The light breeze smelled of mint, a scent that reminded Potts airtime was not far away. His stomach tightened. "Thank you," he said trying to mask his nerves as the stylist finished her work.

Arriving at the entrance to the brightly-lit set, Potts stopped for a deep breath, trying to muster his composure. After nearly a year as a talking head, he was still edgy while the cameras were rolling. Today's show would not lessen his anxiety. He'd be taking to the woodshed a man he respected—and one of his best sources.

Walking into the glare of the set, Simon sat behind the anchor desk and straightened his tie just before the red light below the camera lens began to blink. They were on the air.

A photo of Ramon Garcia standing before the United Nations headquarters in Geneva appeared behind Simon as he began to read from the teleprompter.

"The Hispanic Republic of North America was founded three years ago when representatives from forty-six quarantine zones across the United States voted to form a provisional government of resistance. But today, an organization that began on democratic principles, appears to represent the will of just one man... its United Nations' representative, Ramon Garcia.

"Garcia has remained the sole spokesman for the Hispanic Republic since fellow UN representative

Octavio Perez resigned eleven months ago. The departure of Perez came amid rumors of his connection with the Latino Liberation Front, the splinter group that claimed responsibility for the gruesome deaths of seven hostages. Since that time, Garcia has apparently made little effort to replace Perez. This controversy over Garcia's leadership comes as welcome news in Washington.

A video of White House Press Secretary Marylyn Shane replaced Potts on the screen.

"The Hispanic Republic of North America is not a legitimate government and has no place in the United Nations—even in a non-voting role," Shane said into the press room microphone. "Ramon Garcia is an opportunist who claims to speak for all Hispanics. If the Hispanic rebels are voted out of the UN, the president has said he will consider joining the United Nations again."

The program returned to a closeup of Potts.

"This White House gambit raises the political stakes for the Hispanic Republic and its avowed goal of establishing an autonomous territory within the borders of the United States. The free-fire areas authorized by President George W. Nixon around several of the quarantine zones in California are an indication of Nixon's confidence in the public support of his increasingly-harsh tactics in suppressing the insurgency. By his apparent reluctance to share power, Ramon Garcia must also share the blame for this unnecessary bloodshed."

As the segment ended and the broadcast switched to a taped report, Potts tugged at the collar of his shirt. As a sympathizer of Garcia's cause, airing the report had been painful. As a journalist, he'd been left with no other choice.

LOS ANGELES, CA

The bus engine roared as it struggled up a ramp over an empty Interstate 110, its sunken roadbed marking the northwest edge of downtown Los Angeles like a dry moat. The noise made Daniel stir and Sarah gently patted his back. Lulled by his mother's touch, the infant stopped nursing and fell asleep. As she'd learned in the group home for teen mothers where she'd lived since Daniel's birth, Sarah used this time to examine her baby. Satisfied that Daniel's temperature was normal and he did not need a diaper change, Sarah leaned back in the seat and closed her eyes.

She wished her father had lived to see his grandson. His death had stolen the joy from her world. After her parents' divorce, Sarah's brief visits with her father had been precious moments of warmth in the cold home life she shared with her mother.

Her father's death of a massive coronary at 54 had surprised few who knew Henry Daniel Evans. Although Sarah had been the only hostage to survive, it was the aftermath of the ordeal that had felled the overweight and overworked deputy director of the CIA.

Hank Evans had been elated to learn his military aide at the Agency, Michael Fuller, had gone into LA Quarantine Zone B in a rogue mission to save Sarah. But during their tearful reunion at a military base just outside Zone B, Sarah had revealed a shocking truth. She and Fuller owed their lives to Pedro and his father Manolo Suarez.

Pedro had rescued Sarah from the Latino Liberation Front, the radical splinter group that had taken her hostage. After that, Pedro's father had arranged for Fuller, who had been captured by the rebels, to be released along with Sarah. But the initial news stories of Sarah's rescue covered up these facts.

The White House, eager to put a positive spin on the government's failure to save all the other hostages, had touted Sarah's release from captivity as a successful mission by the U.S. military.

Wracked by guilt about the White House cover-up, her father had gone public with the truth in an interview with Simon Potts. Although reinstated at the CIA after his account was confirmed, a heart attack had felled Hank Evans shortly afterward.

Sarah did not regret telling her father she'd been rescued by Pedro and his family. But there was a deeper, more complex truth about the incident Sarah had never revealed to her father. Her liberator, Pedro Suarez, had originally been one of her abductors—the Nice One.

She'd known Pedro for just ten days. But the experience had convinced Sarah that time was measured by the heart, not by clocks. With life and death on the line, Sarah had learned the young rebel, not much older than herself, had more courage and integrity than anyone she'd met. But their bond had gone deeper.

Despite the chasm of culture between them, she was surprised to find Pedro shared her sense of isolation. Neither felt fully accepted or had any close friends. This fact had been crystallized by one event: Their lovemaking had been the first time for both of them.

The bus entered the shadows cast by a row of tall buildings and Sarah closed her eyes, reliving the morning that had changed her life.

For eight days she'd been handcuffed to a pipe in a dank underground cell. When Pedro discovered the Latino Liberation Front had ordered her execution, he broke with them and freed her. With nowhere else to run, Pedro returned to his estranged parents. Despite the risk of reprisals, Pedro's mother and father had taken her in—and welcomed Pedro back as well.

A day later, after her first bath since being captured, Sarah sat on the bed combing out her hair, reveling in the joy of feeling clean. Simply being unbound in a furnished room was pure bliss.

Laying back on the bed in a fresh dress, Sarah stretched out, letting the smoothness of the sheets caress the bare skin of her arms and legs. She inhaled deeply, exhilarated by the act of breathing. She'd never felt so alive.

Nice One's face appeared in her mind's eye. Without him, she would still be in that dark, horrible place. She owed the young rebel her life but still didn't know his real name. A knock on the door made her sit up, suddenly embarrassed.

"I have something for you," Nice One said behind the door.

"Just a minute," she answered, smoothing out her dress and fluffing her hair with her fingers. "Come in."

He entered the room carrying a stack of magazines. "My mother said that... Wow! You sure look different."

"Do you like it?" she asked, fanning out her dress. "It's your mother's."

"You look nice," he said smiling.

"Thanks," she answered, feeling herself blush.

"I think you're going to like these," he said, holding out the magazines. "The lady who used to live here has a huge collection. They're like gold in the zones because paper is so scarce."

Sarah patted a spot next to her on the bed. "Sit down. Let's look at them."

With Sarah turning the pages on her lap, they fell into an easy conversation about the odd styles in the decades-old issues of *People* and *Soap Opera Digest*.

"Oh my God, look at that hair!" Sarah said laughing,

leaning close to him. She looked up, meeting his eyes. "Do you like my hair? It's the first time you've ever seen it washed."

"It's pretty."

"Does it smell clean?" she asked, slowly placing her head against his chest.

Sarah could feel his warm breath on her scalp. "Yes," he said softly.

Sarah felt something she'd heard about but never really known—passion. It was like a fever, or hunger, or an ache. She wasn't sure which. All she knew was she wanted to feel his body against hers.

She reached for his hand and wove her fingers into his. As their eyes met, she parted her lips, enticing him into a kiss. Closing her eyes, her old self seemed like a stranger now, someone who'd been deaf to music that had been playing all along. She'd seen how fleeting life could be—this chance to know love might be her last.

He embraced her and she lay back on the bed, drawing him down to her, longing to be touched, giving in to the desire she knew they'd both held back.

The brakes of the bus hissed and Sarah opened her eyes. The bus pulled to the curb, letting a convoy of armored vehicles pass.

For a time, Sarah had not been sure why she'd made love to Pedro that day. The memory sometimes seemed like a schoolgirl fantasy. Yet the questions had lingered. Was she trying to win his loyalty to save her life? Was she relieved to be alive and afraid to die a virgin? Had she really fallen in love with him? Now she knew all these things were true.

As the bus emerged from the empty man-made canyons of downtown Los Angeles, the first sight of their destination finally came into view: the graffiti-covered concrete wall marking the border of Quarantine Zone B. The high wall loomed malevolently above the paved banks of the Los Angeles River beyond the expanse of a long-abandoned railroad yard. The upper floors of a few multi-story buildings rose above the razor-sharp concertina wire atop the wall.

The bus slowed to a crawl then resumed normal speed as they passed a checkpoint manned by heavily armed men in brown wide-brimmed hats. They were crossing the last line of the government's defenses around the zone.

The man beside Sarah sighed dejectedly, his eyes downcast. Sarah knew he was not a Pancho—the name troops around the zones had given Hispanic insurgents. Any shred of evidence linking these men to the insurgency would have charged them with treason and put them on trial facing death by lethal injection.

No, the men on this bus had not left the zones to fight. They'd left in desperation, trying to scrounge for food, perhaps even hoping to pass as East Indians and permanently escape the misery of quarantine. But to her mother and many others outside the zones, the fact some Latinos chose to fight the government that confined them made them all terrorists.

When the bus turned onto a high viaduct over the railroad tracks and the river, Sarah caught sight of the North Gate. The large steel doors mottled with rust marked one of only two entrances into the 22-square miles of Quarantine Zone B. Built nearly five years before to deter the hostilities that had erupted between supremacist groups and Hispanic militants in Los Angeles, Zone B was the eastern part of the city's two walled enclosures. Like everyone else, Sarah knew the government had lost control inside most of the Quarantine Zones across the country less than a year after the walls had gone up.

Today, the zones were strongholds of the Hispanic resistance that U.S. troops entered at great peril. In an unwritten truce, the gates into the zones were now always left open, marking an uneasy no-man's land between government and rebels.

While Sarah stared at the distant gate, the bus came to a stop.

"Prepare to leave the vehicle," the deputy announced, leaving Sarah puzzled. The gate into the zone was still quite a distance away.

The men around Sarah silently gathered their belongings, mostly plastic trash bags stuffed with clothes and food. Sarah reached for the backpack at her feet crammed with all her possessions. Weighing nearly forty pounds, she wondered how far she'd get carrying Daniel and the pack. The time to find out had arrived.

Looking outside, Sarah saw the soldiers from the two Humvees escorting the bus emerge from their vehicles and form a corridor outside the bus door, rifles hoisted. As the detainees left the bus, they were shepherded by the troops along the viaduct that rose more than a story over the ground below. Far in the distance was their only destination: the North Gate. "Remember. We catch you outside the walls again and there won't be a ride back," she heard one of the soldiers call out to the first detainees leaving the bus.

Sarah jumped as a burst of gunfire erupted outside.

"Hey! Get down from there!" a soldier shouted at a detainee trying to scramble over the viaduct wall. Sarah was relieved to see the soldier had fired his weapon in the air. Terrified, the man dropped from the wall and continued down the causeway.

Startled by the noise, Daniel began to cry. Gently

kissing his forehead, Sarah soothed her son and laid him on the bus seat. She pulled on a knit cap and tucked her short blonde hair out of sight, then donned a pair of sunglasses. After hoisting the pack over her shoulders, she retrieved her son.

When she stepped off of the vehicle, the deputy motioned Sarah aside. "You sure about what you're doing? We can't protect you after this," he said softly.

"Why aren't you taking us closer?" she answered, shrugging to adjust weight of the backpack.

The deputy nodded toward the two Army Humvees escorting the bus. "Since the Army started the free-fire areas, all our personnel and vehicles have to stay at least 400 meters from the quarantine zones—unless they're taking part in a military operation."

"Why 400 meters?"

"That's the range of an AK-47."

Sarah swallowed hard, the danger of what she was doing suddenly very real. "I appreciate your concern, officer."

The deputy took off his wide-brim hat, his expression softening. "I've got a daughter about your age." he said. "Look, I'm not supposed to do this but if you ever need anything, you ask for me. My name is Bell, Howard Bell. Most of the guards around here know me."

"Thank you, Mr. Bell."

"You sure you won't change your mind?"

"Even if I wanted to—I couldn't," Sarah said, then turned toward the viaduct.

As she walked toward the distant gate, the straps of the backpack digging into her shoulders, Sarah's thoughts turned once again to Pedro. Was he still alive? The new troops deployed to the area had killed hundreds of Panchos over the last few months. As she'd done countless times, Sarah pushed the thought out of her mind, refusing to dwell on anything that would keep her away. Pedro had given her the most precious gift she'd ever known: her son. She longed to share that gift with him. But that longing had come with a price.

To find Pedro, Sarah had made a decision she could never change. Instead of keeping her son's identity a secret, she'd officially registered him as Class H, someone of Hispanic ancestry. Like every other Class H person in the United States, Daniel Evans Suarez was required to be confined under the Quarantine and Relocation Act enacted almost five years earlier. As a non-Hispanic parent, Sarah had a choice. She could relinquish custody to the other parent, or accompany her child into quarantine.

Even now, Sarah was not certain she could explain why she'd given up the comfort and security of life with her mother to return to the danger and poverty of the place where she'd once been a hostage. She simply knew her vivid memories of Pedro and his family were the only truly warm and caring moments she could recall before her father's death.

Like the pull of gravity, she was being drawn to them.

LOS ANGELES QUARANTINE ZONE B

The distant snare-drum chatter of an M4 drew the gaze of Jesús "Chuy" Peña to the far side of the viaduct. "You need to see this," Chuy called out, peering through binoculars from the third-floor window.

Pedro Suarez put down the wooden figurine he'd been carving and jumped to his feet. "What have we got, Chuy?" he asked after walking to the window. From the top floor of the vacant warehouse less than a block from the wall, the pair had a commanding view of the approach to the North Gate of Quarantine Zone B.

Chuy handed Pedro the binoculars. "Other side of the viaduct. Three Baldie vehicles. There's a group of men in strange uniforms headed this way."

Pedro brushed a lock of black hair from his forehead and raised the binoculars. About two dozen men in khaki overalls carrying bundles were crossing the viaduct in a ragged line. Behind them, at the far end of the causeway, a squad of Baldies huddled near two Humvees and a bus.

Pedro lowered the binoculars. "You've been on gate duty longer than I have, Chuy. What do you make of it?"

"I've never seen the Baldies do anything like this," the bearded 20-something said." It could be a trick."

In command of security at the North Gate, Pedro now faced a thorny decision. Under normal circumstances, his orders were clear. Let any Baldie units enter the zone unopposed and report on their movements. They stood a much better chance of defeating an Army sortie deeper inside the walls. But these were not ordinary circumstances.

Pedro had learned about the change in tactics during his early morning briefing at rebel headquarters from the military commander of the L.A. zones—who was also his father.

Manolo Suarez was tall and powerfully built, a man whose imposing presence alone commanded respect. Towering over the two men before him, Mano gave his orders of the day to the watch officers of the north and south gates, Pedro and Abel Solis.

"Last night we received a shipment of ammunition that needs to be dispersed and cached right away," Mano said. "Today, any Baldie units that enter the zone must be engaged and stopped at the gates. They cannot get inside and catch us with our pants down while we're burying the materiel. Do you understand?"

"Yes, sir," Pedro and Abel replied.

Pedro left the rebel's HQ hoping the Baldies would not try to enter the North Gate today.

At one time, he'd been eager for the chance to fight.

Ashamed of his father, who'd seemed weak and cowardly, Pedro had joined the Latino Liberation Front two years earlier. Known in the barrios as El Frente, the aggressive new splinter group had grown quickly, drawing recruits among the young and frustrated.

But the day El Frente ordered him to execute Sarah Evans in cold blood, Pedro abandoned the Latino Liberation Front. Instead of killing Sarah, Pedro had taken her to his father and together they'd worked with the Baldies to set her free.

Sarah's release had ended a bitter feud with his father. Nearly a year later, Mano trusted him enough to put Pedro in command over older men. Father and son now shared the same aversion to spilling blood—and the grim realization that there were times it was unavoidable.

Pedro now faced one of those times.

With orders to keep Army patrols out of the zone at any cost, Pedro had instructed his team of fighters near the gate to fire on any Baldies who entered. Were these men approaching part of some trick by the Baldies or simply innocent civilians? Pedro raised the binoculars, looking for the answer.

Most of the men were carrying bags. Could they be hiding weapons or explosives?

"Pedro, our team's going to open up on them if we don't do something," Chuy said, his voice rising with alarm. "They're going to reach the gate any minute."

Pedro anxiously scanned the group, looking for clues.

Then, at the back of the line, he found the sign he was looking for: someone carrying an infant.

"Tell them to hold their fire."

"Right," Chuy said, running for the stairs.

"Chuy, one more thing... Once these people are inside, hold them in the Strand. I want to talk to them."

The newcomers had spent time around the Baldies and Pedro realized they might have new information about their adversary. But first, he needed to be sure about his decision.

Pedro trained the binoculars on the soldiers at the other end of the viaduct. If the people now entering the zone were the spearhead of an attack, the Baldies would move quickly to support it. To Pedro's relief, the soldiers mounted their vehicles and drove away once everyone on the causeway was inside the wall.

Pedro lowered the binocs and exhaled slowly, feeling the tension drain away. Satisfied the crisis had passed, he made his way downstairs to interview the newcomers being held in the Strand, a defunct movie house across the street. When he arrived at the theatre, Chuy stopped him at the door.

"Mano just sent a runner. He wants to see you—right away.

"Did he say why?"

"No. Just that it was urgent."

"Okay. You better get back upstairs and keep an eye on things."

Chuy hooked a thumb toward the theatre. "What about the people inside? You still want to talk to them?"

Pedro shook his head. "No time right now. Have somebody take their names and put them in the common quarters on Soto Street. We'll talk to them later."

The questions for the new arrivals would have to wait.

"This way," Mano said, leading his son into the narrow alley beside a gutted restaurant.

Pedro pointed at the graffiti on the building's battered walls. "These gang placas are a warning, papá. Anybody going in here is asking for trouble."

Mano's answer startled Pedro. "I know, m'hijo. That's why I asked the Verdugos to put them there."

After walking through a side entrance of the gutted restaurant, they came to a large steel door secured by a massive padlock. Mano opened the lock, swung back the door, and flicked on a battery-powered lamp. The small room that appeared seemed completely alien in the eviscerated building. Two plush leather chairs with a reading lamp between them stood amid floor-to-ceiling shelves filled with books.

"What is this place?" Pedro asked, his eyes sweeping the room.

"This library belongs to Ramon Garcia. I'm taking care of it for him until he returns from Geneva."

Pedro ran his fingers along a row of hardcover tomes, studying the titles. They covered a wide range of topics in no particular order. "Have you read any of these books?"

"Most of them. If you want to borrow any, I know Ramon would be happy to lend them to you." Mano pulled a silver phone from his pocket, placed the device on speaker mode and gestured for his son to sit. "Right now, though, we've got to call Ramon. He said it was urgent."

"Aren't you worried the Baldies will home in on the call?"

"This phone has an encrypted signal that can't be traced." Mano smiled. "Ramon made sure of that before he sent it."

"I never knew you had this kind of phone, papá."

"You never needed to know," Mano said soberly. "And one more thing. What you hear today doesn't leave this room."

Mano dialed their delegate in Geneva and after brief greetings, Ramon got to the purpose of the call.

"I've got bad news, hermanos," Ramon said wearily. "Octavio Perez has surfaced and we could be in for some serious trouble."

Mano's face tightened. "I knew this would happen. What's Perez up to?"

"I just learned he's trying to get his hands on a suitcase nuclear weapon."

The news stunned Mano.

"We need to put Perez out of business, Ramon," Mano said after a moment. "It's time to go public with the tape."

"Perez is calling our bluff, Mano. The recording we have implicating him in the deaths of the hostages won't hold up in court," Ramon explained. "Sure, we got him to resign from the U.N. but he doesn't need to be a United Nations delegate to deploy a nuclear weapon."

"Perez doesn't have much of an organization left. El Frente's lost most of its support in the barrios. Not many people want to be tied to the deaths of the hostages."

"Perez won't need a large organization for this operation, Mano. All he needs is money. That's why he approached Claude Durand."

"Perez tried to tap Durand for money again?"

"Yes, but Perez read Durand's motives for supporting us completely wrong. Durand won't sponsor terrorism. That's why Claude came to me. He's worried Perez may find the money somewhere else."

"Is Durand sure about the nuke?"

"Perez is shrewd. He didn't say he had access to a nuclear weapon. Perez said he had connections in Russia who could give him the power to take out an American city with a suitcase."

Mano rubbed his face. "This sounds credible, Ramon," he said. "Perez is in bed with the Mexican drug cartels and they have links to the Russian mafia. With Russia's control of its nuclear weapons gone to hell, someone there might be willing to sell Perez a nuke."

"That's why we've got to stop him, Mano."

"I agree, viejo. But what can we do? We barely have the resources to keep our fight going here in the zones. How do we stop a plot in Europe?"

"We can't. But there's still a way to bring Perez down," Ramon said. "We need to leak this plot to the CIA. They're the only ones with the resources to stop him."

Pedro nervously cleared his throat. "Forgive me, Don Ramon," he said. "But isn't Perez on our side?"

"Pedro, I have no qualms turning Perez in," said Ramon. "The man is a criminal who stopped being part of our cause when he began ordering the deaths of innocent hostages. We cannot let him kill hundreds of thousands more."

"I agree," Mano said. "But how can we turn Perez in without compromising our security? We don't have our back channel at the CIA through Hank Evans anymore."

"Hank Evans? Sarah's father?" Pedro asked.

"Yes, m'hijo," Mano answered. "Evans reached out to us unofficially when Sarah was a hostage. He was desperate to save his daughter."

Pedro shook his head, surprised. "I didn't know."

"Until today, you didn't need to," Mano told his son.

"Mano, I hate it when we think alike. It makes me wonder what I'm doing wrong," Ramon said with a small laugh. "Yes, we need a new back channel at the CIA and I've already given that some thought. There's still someone in the CIA we can trust... Michael Fuller."

Mano remembered Fuller well. His security people had captured the U.S. Army captain attempting a freelance rescue of Sarah Evans. Mano had released them both, winning Fuller's trust in the process. "I agree that Fuller is the kind of man who would honor an agreement with us," he said. "But how are we going to contact him privately? His phone and email will be tapped and can be traced back to us."

"That's why I asked you to bring Pedro today."

"Ramon, are you getting enough sleep? How is Pedro going to help us reach someone who works at CIA headquarters in Virginia?"

"I've thought this through, Mano. Pedro is our key to bringing down Perez."

"I'll do whatever I can, Don Ramon," Pedro offered.

"Good. Because what I'm going to ask won't be easy," Ramon said. "Pedro, you'll need to travel to Santa Clarita, contact Sarah Evans and persuade her to put us in touch with Fuller. She can set up a personal meeting with him that can't be traced."

"You can't be serious, Ramon," Mano said. "The Baldies have brought almost an entire division to Southern California and they've designated just about everything north of the walls as free-fire areas. There's not much chance of getting to Santa Clarita alive right now."

"Papá, I've made the trip before. I know where the Baldie outposts are," Pedro said, then lowered his eyes. His mission to Santa Clarita had been a quest for a hostage on El Frente's orders. This was an opportunity to make up for that wrong. " I can do this."

"Even if you get there alive, how will you find Sarah?

The Baldies won't ignore someone who looks like you asking questions."

"Like I said, I've done this before, papá. If I dress right and don't act suspicious, they'll think I'm East Indian," Pedro said softly, trying to avoid an argument. "There are Internet cafes all over Santa Clarita. I can find Sarah online."

"Then I'll go," Mano said.

"Mano, be sensible," Ramon replied. "A man your size with swarthy skin in Santa Clarita would stand out like a drunk at a Baptist convention. Pedro can blend in. You can't."

"We could have a journalist contact Fuller," Mano said, taking a new tack. "You have a personal connection with Simon Potts. Why not ask him?"

"Fuller won't trust a journalist, Mano—especially one like Potts who's publicly supported us—even though Potts just reamed me publicly for not replacing Octavio," Ramon said with a dry laugh. "I've thought this through, hermano. Pedro is our only real option."

Mano sighed. "This is senseless. We need another plan."

After a long silence, Ramon finally spoke. "Mano, what other choice do we have?"

Folding his arms, Mano weighed Ramon's words. The danger posed by Perez was unlike anything they'd faced before. If they had any chance at all of stopping him, they had to take it—even if it meant risking the life of his son.

Mano leaned forward and placed a large hand on Pedro's shoulder. "You'll need to leave right away, m'hijo."

———

The blank marquee above the derelict movie house rose forlornly into the afternoon sky. At one time, it had been alive with the glow of a thousand incandescent bulbs and a half mile of neon tubing. But now, the only clue of its former glory was the ghostly tracing of the word "STRAND" still visible in halos of grime around long-gone neon letters. Below this twentieth-century relic, a shapely dark-haired woman in a simple cotton dress approached the theatre and paused at its boarded-up box office.

Although barely forty, Rosa Suarez could remember the Strand as it once had been, bustling with people eager to catch the latest movie. So much had changed—and so had she. She'd married Mano expecting to devote her life to her family and her faith. Then the madness had started.

The insurgency had nearly destroyed her marriage. She'd almost lost her husband to the woman who helped start the resistance. For nearly a year, Rosa had suffered without Mano in a relocation camp in North Dakota. Worst of all, she'd buried two of the four children she'd brought into this world. But with all that she'd lost, there was also something she had gained. Rosa now knew there was nothing anyone could do to avoid suffering. The only thing that mattered was how you coped with the inevitable. That, and keeping faith in God.

Today, that faith would be tested once again.

Rosa walked into the lobby and found two of Mano's men playing cards on the floor. They stood as soon as they saw her.

"Buenos dias, señora," the older one said, bowing slightly. "Chuy told us to expect you. The young woman is inside," he said, opening the movie house door.

Rosa nodded graciously. "Thank you."

Even in the theatre's dim light, Rosa immediately recognized Sarah Evans. She sat in the back row, gazing raptly at the child in her arms. Rosa recognized the baby as well. The infant had the same almond-shaped eyes as her own children, a trait passed on by Mano.

Rosa was almost close enough to touch Sarah before she looked up.

"Mamá! Oh my God!" Sarah said, her face alight as she rose to her feet. "I'm so happy to see you!"

Rosa took the young woman's face in her hands. "I never thought we'd meet again, m'hija," she said, stroking the girl's cheeks. Then Rosa brought her hand to the child's forehead. "But I can see why you're here."

"This is Daniel," Sarah said, gently passing the baby to Rosa. "He'll be two months old next week."

Rosa smiled. "He's beautiful," she said, taking the baby in her arms.

"How is Carlos? He's probably talking by now."

"Yes, and he's not like his father and brother. He talks way too much," Rosa said smiling. "That's why I left him with a neighbor before coming over."

"How did you know I was here?"

"When Chuy told me an Anglo girl with a baby was asking to see Pedro, it wasn't hard to figure out who it might be."

"When will Pedro be here, mamá? I can't wait for him to see his son."

Rosa settled into one of the theatre seats. "Let's sit down and talk for a while, Sarah," she said, patting the seat beside her.

Sarah remained standing, her face suddenly pale. "Did something happen to Pedro? Is he..." her voice trailed off, unable to say the words.

"No, Pedro is alive. Please, m'hija. Sit."

"All right," Sarah said nervously.

"Pedro is away right now, so Chuy came to me. You see, Chuy did not want to leave the message that a young woman with a baby was looking for Pedro... with Pedro's wife."

For an instant Sarah stared in shock, then her eyes slowly closed. Hands trembling, Sarah covered her face, trying to hold back the tears.

Rosa patted Sarah's arm. "Let the tears go, m'hijita. Don't try to fight it. There's no way to avoid this pain. It has to run its course."

"I worried that Pedro might have been killed. But I never imagined this," Sarah said, chest heaving. "I thought he loved me, mamá," she said. "How could I be so stupid? I gave up everything to raise our son together."

A pang of guilt tore at Rosa. When Pedro had asked if he should marry Isabel after her brother's death, Rosa had encouraged him.

"None of us expected to see you again, Sarah," Rosa said. "We thought you'd return to your life out there and never come back. If Pedro had known about your child—"

"You're just trying to make excuses for him," Sarah cut in her face hardening.

"You're hurting right now, Sarah. Being angry is part of the healing," Rosa said tenderly. "You've been wronged, m'hija. Be angry but don't hate. Hating is just punishing yourself and expecting it to hurt someone else."

Sarah's tears stopped but the despair in her eyes remained. "I don't know what to do now. I registered Daniel as Class H. We can't go back—and I won't leave him."

Rosa stroked the baby's hair. "This is my grandson, Sarah. You both have a home with Mano and me for as long as you like."

"What about Pedro's wife?"

"You've had a painful shock, m'hija. She's in for one as well. You'll both survive."

After stacking the last of the empty crates in the corner of the bedroom, Isabel rolled her neck and stretched, aching but contented.

Despite being different sizes, she'd piled the ammunition crates as neatly as she could. This was their bedroom, after all, and a woman had to keep her house in order. The biggest crate with the Chinese-looking writing was at the bottom with the two French ammo boxes above it. The smallest one, with the backward-facing Russian letters, she'd placed on top. Over the last six hours Isabel had taken all the bulk ammunition that had arrived in those crates and loaded the bullets into the AK-47 ammo clips now stockpiled tidily on the floor.

After wiping her brow, Isabel got back to work. She still needed to stuff the clips into the bandoliers the fighters of the Hispanic Republic of North America would carry into battle.

Isabel hoped Pedro would be proud of her progress with the ammo when he got home. Although he was the son of the top military man in the L.A. zones, Pedro did not expect any special favors. The same went for his wife. They both worked harder than most for the cause.

Isabel knew few women in the barrios liked this kind of chore and some even thought she was strange for doing it. But she'd grown up an orphan with a brother who'd been the mero of a street gang and later became a leader of El Frente. Living with a warrior was the only life she'd known and the small house she shared with Pedro was as much a weapons storehouse as the home of newlyweds. But she had other plans for the house—and for herself. She'd already added a few touches to cheer the place; flowers when she could find them, colorful baskets woven from salvaged electrical wiring, and discarded plastic shower curtains fashioned into window coverings.

Someday she hoped to add a baby crib—once she could convince Pedro.

Being with Pedro was all she'd ever wanted. She'd fallen in love with him not long after they'd met. He was so different than her brother's other vatos who'd tried to impress her with their bragging and crude talk. Tall and polite, Pedro had been quiet to the point of being shy. But strangely, Pedro's unshakable calm made her feel safer from harm than any of the blustering machos in her brother's gang.

As a husband, Pedro was kind and considerate, but he could be distant at times. Isabel worried that the responsibility he carried at such a young age made him feel isolated. Still, she would have been satisfied with her life but for one thing. The traitor who had killed her brother was still not avenged.

Isabel glanced at the picture of her brother she kept on a plastic milk crate by the bed. Taken on the day he'd gotten the large tattoo of a winged angel on his chest, Angel Sanchez posed shirtless, eyes shining with pride, his face hard and unsmiling.

The framed snapshot was the only photo in the house. Rebéldes and their families did not keep images of themselves. Under the needle law, photos could become lethal evidence. But Angel was dead and had never been captured. His photo would implicate no one.

Each day, the ache of Angel's death followed Isabel like her shadow. One of their own people had taken Angel's life, stirring whispers that brought shame to his memory. Isabel had pledged to God that she would expose the traitor who had killed her brother. The day would come when she would clear Angel's name and wash away his shame in blood.

But today she had other tasks. So she focused on her

work, grateful for its distraction.

While filling another bandolier with the assault rifle clips, she heard the familiar squeak of the back door. "I'm coming," she called out, putting down the canvas pouch. Hoping to look pleasing, she unraveled the braid that kept her hair out of the way as she worked. With her black tresses now cascading sensuously over her shoulders, she walked to the kitchen.

Standing at an open cabinet, Pedro was taking down portions of chicken jerky wrapped in corn husks from the shelf.

"I have to go," he said without looking at her.

"When?" Isabel asked, touching his arm. She'd learned long ago while living with her brother never to ask a rebélde where he was going.

He turned to face her. "Right away. It's important," he said, then caressed her cheek. "I'm sorry."

"How long?"

"Three days. Maybe more."

After he removed a water canteen made from a discarded juice container from the cupboard, Isabel slipped her arms around his waist and pressed her willowy body against him.

"Sure you can't spare some time for your wife before you go?" she asked, raising her chestnut eyes to meet his.

Pedro kissed her then gently pulled away. "I wish I could, mi amor. But this is urgent," he said, filling a small backpack with the supplies. "I'll be back as soon as I can." He then kissed her forehead and left.

Isabel sighed and walked to the living room where she pulled back the plastic curtains covering a small alcove. On a low table in the small recess was a ceramic statuette. The white robed figure with a skeleton's face and hands held the grim reaper's scythe and a globe of the earth. Two unlit candles flanked offerings of an apple and a shot glass of tequila. Beside them was a set of rosary beads.

After making the sign of the cross, Isabel knelt before the shrine and lit one of the candles. "Santa Muerte, I call upon you in the name of the Father, the Son, and the Holy Spirit to keep my husband safe from danger." She then lit the second candle. "Santa Muerte, I beseech thee to bless us with a child."

Taking the rosary, Isabel began the long chain of prayers the beads represented.

Isabel's knees were aching by the time she completed the cycle and put back the rosary Father Ignacio had given her. The old priest had said the funeral mass for her brother and was one of the few pastors who tolerated the worship of Santa Muerte. Isabel offered a final prayer of thanks for his kindness.

After making the sign of the cross once more, Isabel blew out the candles, closed the curtains to the shrine, and returned to work. As she'd learned sharing a home with her brother, life with a rebélde was always the same. You had to forget that each time you said goodbye might be the last.

LANGLEY, VA

Sonya Bailey glanced at her reflection in the large window, making a last check of her beret. The hat's embroidered shield with a single silver bar was lined up perfectly over her left eye, exactly by the book. Her new boss would be arriving shortly and this was not the time to look sloppy—especially for an Army officer who less than two years ago was trying to decide what to do with a bachelor's degree in sociology.

A short man with thinning hair appeared in the

doorway of the small office. Sonya rose from the guest chair, stood at attention, and saluted. "Lieutenant Bailey, reporting for duty, sir," she said crisply, trying to hide her surprise at finding her boss in civilian clothes.

"Relax, Lieutenant," the man said. "I'm not Major Fuller."

"Sorry. I just assumed..."

"That's all right. The only outfit more screwed up than the CIA is the Army. Whoever sent you over this morning didn't bother to check Fuller's schedule. He's in a briefing until eleven with all the other bigwigs around here." The man extended his hand. "I'm Jeff Drury. I live in the cube right across the hall. I report to Fuller, too."

Bailey found Drury's grip mushy as she shook his hand. "Hello," she said, trying to keep her voice neutral. Something about the drifting gaze of his pale yellow eyes made her uneasy.

"Look, with all the bosses up on the sixth floor, there's not much going on around here. Would you like some coffee?" He smiled broadly and cocked his head toward the door. "There's a break room around the corner."

Bailey weighed the invitation. She'd had guys throw themselves at her just for returning a smile. It came with the territory of being tall and shapely. Being a black woman seemed to embolden a lot of guys, too. But she'd handled the come-ons before—and Drury did not look particularly imposing. In any case, her boss would be out for the next two hours and Drury might give her the skinny on this new post. "Some coffee sounds good," she said, trying to keep the tone neutral.

Drury grinned and led her down the hall. "This half of the floor is Domestic Operations," he said, sweeping his hand like a tour guide. "I've been with the Agency nine years and when I started, the CIA only operated overseas.

Things ran pretty well back then. But it's been a fricking nightmare since they decided to bring the whole security circus under one tent." Drury shook his head in disgust. "They said it was supposed to 'create synergy in our security resources.' What a crock. What we really got was more caseloads, less staff and a pay freeze for the last three years."

"What do you do here, Mr. Drury?"

"Please," he said, waving his hand dismissively. "I'm just a Tech Ops geek. Call me Jeff."

Drury looked a little old for such a modest position to Bailey. Maybe his willingness to openly criticize his superiors had something to do with that. "How long have you been working for Major Fuller?" she asked as they entered the break room.

"Nine months, right after Fuller was promoted." Drury led her over to a table in the corner, out of earshot from a woman at the vending machines before continuing. "Fuller's not the most popular guy around here," he said softly, sitting down. "He was Hank Evans' go-to guy and a lot of people were really pissed when Evans went public about the hostage rescue. That embarrassed the hell out of the White House and made the CIA look disloyal."

Bailey had followed the headlines of the hostage crisis and knew her new boss had been involved. But Drury's inside view of the incident was eye-opening. "I remember when the White House reinstated Evans and threw the old CIA director under the bus," she said. "Her name was Burns, right?"

"Byrne," Drury corrected.

"So what happened?"

"Well, with Evans back in charge, he got Fuller promoted and assigned him as Senior Military Advisor for Hispanic Intelligence. Since Evans croaked, the top floor's treated Fuller like a dunsel. He doesn't do much except attend briefings. But they won't transfer him because they're afraid of another media fiasco."

"I'm confused. If Major Fuller doesn't have much to do, why would they assign me as his adjutant?"

"Lieutenant, you're telling me no one at the Pentagon asked you for reports on Fuller when they gave you this assignment?"

"No. Far as I know, the post is just part of my standard duty rotation."

"Of course, Lieutenant," Drury said with a smirk. "I shouldn't have asked."

At that moment, three floors above them, Major Michael Fuller stirred restlessly in the plush swivel chair of a large conference room. At the front of the semi-circular array of seats, CIA Director Jim Tanaka advanced another electronic slide onto the screen behind him.

"I'm very pleased to report the rate of insurgent body counts keeps showing an upward trend in California since we launched the pilot on the free-fire area initiative," Tanaka said, his laser pointer tracing the rising angle on a projected graph. "Based on this success, we now plan to expand the free-fire areas to all forty-six quarantine zones. We expect a tipping point within the next six months as the attrition rate removes the incentive for rebellion."

Fuller studied the faces around him. Was he the only CIA staffer appalled by this new approach to the insurgency?

An eleven-year Army veteran, Fuller had served two combat tours in Southern California. He'd lost comrades and gotten familiar with several hospital ceilings courtesy of the Panchos. All the same, Fuller was certain implementing free-fire areas and charting their progress by body counts was a brutal folly that would undermine the effort to end the Hispanic insurgency—no matter how popular it was with the public.

However, Fuller had no doubts why these measures were popular.

The wanton slaughter of seven teenage girls taken hostage by the Latino Liberation Front last year had stirred demands for retribution against all Hispanics—especially after the gruesome photos El Frente had released appeared in the media.

In response, the administration of president George Whitehead Nixon had redeployed three divisions of elite troops from the Middle East into duty around all the. quarantine zones—with great media fanfare.

The new troops were better trained and equipped than the National Guard and local law enforcement units already in place around the zones. Not surprisingly, the number of insurgent battlefield kills had increased. But the body counts were also bolstered by court-ordered executions under the Terrorist Arraignment Act.

Widely known as the "needle law," the TAA charged anyone convicted of supporting the insurgency with high treason—including spouses and families. The punishment was death by lethal injection. As a soldier in harm's way, Fuller had seen firsthand how the Terrorist Arraignment Act had failed in quelling the insurgency.

Unlike conventional adversaries who surrendered when the situation was hopeless, the Panchos fought ferociously to the last bullet knowing they faced certain death if captured. The law also prosecuted Pancho defectors, robbing government forces of valuable intelligence. Most damaging of all, each unnecessary death created more hatred among Hispanics toward the government and produced more recruits for the Panchos.

Rather than quelling the insurgency, the White House

was fueling a vicious circle of violence—primarily to appease public opinion.

"The latest polls show support for the Terrorist Arraignment Act has increased to seventy-four percent," Tanaka said dryly, pointing at another slide. "That compares with fifty-two percent support at the same time last year. We've also seen a nine percent rise in the government's approval rating on handling the insurgency since we began our media campaign questioning the legitimacy of the HRNA leadership."

Fuller looked out the conference room window at the placid Virginia countryside six floors below. The Agency, like other halls of power, reduced reality to numbers. The people in these lofty places lived in a world of abstract statistics, immune to the bloodshed and misery created by their decisions.

As the meeting ended, a fleeting thought made Fuller grimace. After eleven years in uniform, his role had been reduced to that of a eunuch in a harem of advisors whose most valued purpose was to flatter the conclusions of their superiors.

Trying to shake off the gloom, Fuller headed for the stairs. A little exercise might help. Four floors later, he emerged from the stairwell feeling less dejected.

Approaching his work station, Fuller caught the first glimpse of his new adjutant through the large window of his office facing the interior of the building. *So this is the mole the Pentagon has assigned to me*, he thought. It was almost flattering.

The bio he'd received on Sonya Bailey was not impressive. No special technical or language skills. No geo-political credentials. No combat experience. However, her former commanders had given Bailey high ratings for intelligence and initiative in her posts as an aide-de-camp. *The perfect résumé for a spy*, he thought, lips curling into a sneer. Standing next to Bailey, Jeff Drury was busy chatting her up. One look at Bailey made it clear why. Even the stodgy Class B uniform could not conceal her seductive contours. Beneath the black beret, Bailey's ebony eyes glowed in a tawny, heart-shaped face.

Sending a beautiful young woman to spy on him certainly made sense. Fuller had never married or had a relationship longer than a one-night stand. *Maybe they think this old warrior monk is longing for the ladies*, he told himself.

But what he really longed for were the days when his service to his country had made a difference.

LOS ANGELES QUARANTINE ZONE B

Pedro had waited until it was fully dark to leave, but not a minute longer. His forced march to Santa Clarita would take most of the night—if he was lucky enough to avoid any Baldie patrols.

After emerging from a tunnel under an abandoned factory a quarter mile beyond the wall, Pedro peered outside, looking for Baldies. The derelict industrial zone looked clear. Avoiding open spaces, he made his way north through the labyrinth of angled streets and irregular buildings, a perfect landscape to escape detection.

Crossing railroad tracks, Pedro entered a warren of small, abandoned homes. Most had been looted, their doors thrown open and windows smashed, debris scattered in the small yards. Moving in the relative safety between the closely-spaced houses and overgrown trees, Pedro found himself with time to think.

The journey to Santa Clarita was a trip into his past, a mission that mingled the lives of two people he'd never expected to see again: Sarah Evans and Michael Fuller.

Striding through the silent darkness, Pedro's mind drifted back to their last moments together nearly a year ago.

His father had brought Sarah and Fuller to what had once been the ninth hole of a long-abandoned golf course inside Zone B to release the blindfolded pair. Pedro had led Sarah while Mano guided Fuller.

"You can take off the blindfolds now," Mano told them.

Sarah removed the black cloth from her eyes, squinting at the glare. "I almost forgot what the sky looked like."

Pedro took the blindfold from her hand. "I'll burn this when I get home."

"No, I'd like to keep it," Sarah said, taking the blindfold back.

Fuller dropped his hood and removed his blindfold, handing it to Mano. "My part of the deal is done."

"Here you are, captain," Mano said giving Fuller the transponder.

Fuller pulled out the transponder's tab, extending its antenna. "We have about five minutes before the chopper arrives, Suarez. Care to tell me why a man like you would turn against his country and his comrades in uniform?"

Mano stared into the distance, then looked back at Fuller. "For the same reason the American colonists turned against the British," he said, then glanced toward Pedro. "And for the same reason a son rebels against his parents. Sometimes they forgive each other when it's all over. We'll see."

"I hope you're right," Fuller said.

Sarah stepped closer to Pedro and touched his cheek. "I wish we could have met some other way."

Pedro nodded and looked down. He knew saying anything more would only prolong the pain.

The four of them stood in silence then, knowing their lives had intersected for a brief time but there was little chance they'd ever meet again. After a while, the throbbing of a helicopter rose in the distance. As the craft drew closer, the wind from its rotors made them stagger, whipping their hair and clothing.

With the chopper nearly on the ground, Fuller faced Mano. "I met a man of honor today," he said saluting.

Mano returned the salute. "Likewise, captain."

Sarah held Pedro's face in her hands, looking into his eyes. "I won't forget you," she said, then turned and ran toward the craft.

That parting had been a turning point in Pedro's life. Reunited with his family after his time with El Frente, he'd settled into the path his parents had expected of him, a dutiful son following his honorable father. His marriage to Isabel was a natural part of that path. Isabel had needed him, a lost soul alone after the death of her brother. And he needed Isabel, a devoted wife who accepted the hard life of a rebélde without complaint. Still, the taint of guilt haunted the relationship. Although it remained unspoken, Pedro and his parents understood the union was an atonement for their role in the death of Isabel's brother.

Even so, Pedro loved his wife and would never leave her. But at this moment, the thought of seeing Sarah again excited him in a way Isabel never had. It shamed him to admit it. But he could not escape the truth in his heart.

Pedro's thoughts of the past ended abruptly as he reached the first critical point in the journey.

Now over a mile from the border of the zone, Pedro stood on a wooded ridge alongside a high school. Before him was the first stretch of open country he'd encountered so far: the barren slopes of Ascot Hills Park. The crescent moon cast a sheen of tarnished silver on the rolling landscape of the three-quarter mile tract.

Making a beeline through the park would save valuable

time. But it also would leave Pedro exposed to any Baldie patrols moving through the area. There were risks either way. Looking for a better vantage point to assess the danger, Pedro walked along the crest of the tree-lined ridge.

The moment of indecision would prove costly.

The way to his house looked different tonight, but Mano was not sure why. They'd lived in the nondescript one-story ranch almost two months, a long time by his standards. In that time, he'd walked along Fresno Street enough times that even under the moonlight he knew the dark shapes on the wall of the corner bodega were a fading mural of Jesus on the cross. The hand-painted image took on a new meaning tonight. He, too, might sacrifice a son to save countless strangers.

Should he have refused to send Pedro? Was his honor so precious that it was worth the life of his son? Mano walked along the empty street knowing this was a torment he would bear alone. He never spoke to Rosa about their clandestine operations. The less she knew, the better it would be for all of them. So Pedro's absence would remain a painful mystery he could not explain to his wife—unless they found his body, which was not likely.

Adding to his sense of dread was a rare message from Rosa asking him to come home right away. Whatever she had to tell him could not be good.

Mano could see the double-gabled outline of their small house now, black against the indigo sky, the dim light of a soy oil lamp leaking from the window shutters. On the sidewalk outside the house, he stopped.

Facing Rosa would not be easy. They'd already lost two

children to this war. Now Pedro might join Elena and Julio as victims of the bloodshed. By force of will, Mano steeled himself. He could not let Rosa see his pain. She'd suffered enough.

As Mano unlocked the door, he heard female voices inside. Walking into the kitchen, he was stunned to find Rosa and a fair-haired young woman bathing an infant in the sink. After a moment of disbelief, he recognized Sarah Evans.

Rosa smiled as she wrapped a towel around the baby and brought the child to him. "It's time you met your grandson, Mano."

Private Burris rubbed his temples, trying to ease the pain as he scanned the nighttime landscape. The new thermal-detection night vision gear their unit had been issued worked way better than the old model. But after staring through the monocular for a while, it gave him a headache.

"Sarge, you got any aspirin?" he asked the soldier half asleep against a sandbag inside the small two-man observation post. Erected six days ago at the high point of a city park north of L.A.'s Quarantine Zone B, the post was a crudely-built circle of Hesco barriers, refrigerator-sized blocks of wire-reinforced fabric filled with dirt.

Sergeant Wilkins opened his eyes slightly. "Do I look like the fucking infirmary to you, Burris?" he muttered. The young sergeant then managed a faint smile. "Here, shithead. Give me the goggles. I'll relieve you."

"Thanks, Sarge," Burris said as he stepped down from the observation platform and removed the night vision device from his helmet.

Wilkins snapped the ENVG onto his own kevlar and climbed onto the platform. "When the Dalton Gang relieves us in the morning, ask *them* for some aspirin. Those fuckers run a regular black market—and their biggest customers are the Panchos." The dodgy reputation and wide brimmed hats of the local sheriffs' deputies pressed into guard duty around the zones had earned them the nickname "Dalton Gang" among the troops.

Since they'd arrived in Southern California three months ago, the elite troops redeployed from the Middle East had changed the tactical environment around the quarantine zones. Battle-hardened and well-equipped, the soldiers had regained control over much of the abandoned areas outside the quarantine zones in Los Angeles, San Diego and Bakersfield.

Observation Post Ascot, the small fortification manned by Burris and Wilkins, was one of 18 newly-built defensive structures around the zones the Army hoped would permanently contain the Panchos inside the walls.

Burris slumped against the wall, still rubbing his temples. "Did Manelli tell you about the kids?"

"What kids?" Wilkins asked while his eyes swept the area toward the zone through the night vision device.

"Manelli's torn up about it," Burris said. "His squad was taking fire and he tossed a frag grenade into the house they thought it was coming from. When Manelli went inside, they found two dead kids. Said it damn near made him puke."

"Manelli's a pussy, Burris. My sister knew one of the girls they grabbed in Dallas. The Panchos didn't have a problem shooting her and six other girls in the head and posting their pictures online. Think I give a shit if some of their kids get wasted by accident?"

"You know that wasn't really all the Panchos, right? The Latino Liberation Front killed those girls."

"Who gives a fuck? The bastards who killed those girls

are in there somewhere," he said, pointing toward Zone B.

"It's not that simple, Sarge. We need to make distinctions between—"

"Hold it! I've got a heat trail."

Burris jumped onto the platform. "How many?"

"Just one guy, about 400 meters away on the hill over there by the school. He's moving through the trees on the ridge." To Burris, the trees were a black shape against the violet sky. But through Wilkins' ENVG, the white hot outline of a man blinked in and out as he moved between the trees.

"Is he one of ours?"

Wilkins dialed the transponder recognition setting on the ENVG. The telltale green glow of a friendly was missing. "Nope. He's not wearing a transponder. Call the CO and tell him to scramble the Quick Response Force."

Burris retrieved their field phone and reported the sighting to their commanding officer. "CO says our QRF will be here in ten minutes," he told Wilkins.

"Not good enough. Give me the phone."

"You sure you want to do this, Sarge?" Burris said, handing him the handset.

Wilkins nodded and spoke into the phone. "Sir, our target is moving toward a ridge to the west. In ten minutes he could be out of our line of sight. Request permission to engage the target under the free fire area rule, sir."

"Are you sure he's not friendly, Wilkins?" the CO said over the phone.

"I'm sure, sir. I checked the transponder."

After a long pause, the CO answered. "You have permission to engage the target."

"Roger that," Wilkins said and handed the phone back to his comrade.

Wilkins raised his M4 to a firing position and brought the ghostly figure on the far ridge into his sights. Aiming through the ENVD monocular was tricky. At 400 meters, they'd need to spray and pray. The tracer bullets they'd been issued for night duty would help. "Burris, lay your fire down where you see my tracers going. We're going to light this Pancho up."

Wilkins squeezed the trigger, releasing a series of three-shot bursts.

———

Pedro saw a stream of pink-white flashes streaking toward him from a hilltop in the park. Instinctively, he dove behind a tree. The thud of bullets striking earth and wood were followed by the far-away woodpecker echo of automatic rifles.

Branches rained down on Pedro as a deadly stream of lead traveling faster than sound shattered the trees around him and made the ground tremble with their impact.

Pedro rolled into a crouch and leaned against the narrow tree, putting as much of his body as he could squeeze behind its meager shelter. The hail of bullets kept coming.

His pulse racing, Pedro fought the panic thrashing in his chest. He could not stay on this ridge. The Baldies had zeroed in on his position and it was only a matter of time before a bullet found its mark. Leaving by stealth was pointless. His only chance was to reach the cover of the downhill slope some thirty meters behind him.

Like a sprinter leaving his blocks, Pedro launched himself from a crouch. Breath churning, heart pounding, he ran with abandon as the streaking tracer rounds buzzed like angry bees around him.

A few strides from safety, a searing, dog-bite pain gripped his right leg. Pedro howled and stumbled to the ground, his momentum sending him tumbling down the other side of the ridge. A merry-go-round of trees, sky and ground spun before him as he rolled down the slope, unable to stop. Then everything went black.

Pedro opened his eyes, uncertain where he was. The growl of engines in the distance brought him back to his senses. He wasn't sure how long he'd been out. But it had been long enough for the Baldies to close in.

He tried to stand but fell, the pain in his leg too intense. Delicately, he probed his right thigh and felt a wet gash inside the fabric of his trousers. The bullet had gone clean through. That much was good. But he was bleeding, a patch of dirt below him was already muddy with blood.

The roar of the engines grew louder. With his carving knife, Pedro cut strips of fabric from his trouser leg and fastened a tourniquet above the wound. He rose again, keeping the weight off his right leg, and managed to hop a few steps until he was leaning against a tree.

Hopping, falling, rising, crawling, Pedro retreated desperately toward the houses. The vehicles were close now, their snarls filling the air. About fifty meters ahead of him, the shelter of the houses beckoned. He could easily lose the soldiers amid the homes, even moving at a crawl. Or he could lay low for days if necessary. He'd brought enough food and water. But that wasn't likely. He knew from experience the Baldies would not commit large numbers of troops to find a single man. Even with their new reinforcements, they were spread too thin.

But he needed to get out of the open where the Baldies could easily spot him.

When the sound of the engines stopped, Pedro knew he

was running out of time. The Baldies were dismounting. At least he was no longer bleeding and leaving a trail they could follow.

Gritting his teeth against the pain, he ran for the houses, each step on his right leg a jolt of agony that brought tears to his eyes.

When he reached the first house, Pedro looked back. Voices drifted toward him from the other side of the ridge along with the squawk of a radio. He stumbled ahead, seeking more distance from his pursuers. His right leg throbbed mercilessly each time it carried weight.

Several houses later, Pedro found a godsend: the remnants of a canister vacuum cleaner. Propping the sweeper head under his armpit, the plastic tube became a crutch that kept the weight off his leg. After several halting strides, he was nearly at full walking speed.

Sheltered by the houses and trees, Pedro headed for home awash with relief. He'd escaped the Baldies on the ridge and was confident he'd evade them getting back. But his buoyant mood was short-lived.

As the surge of adrenaline subsided, Pedro realized that he'd managed to escape with his own life. But his mission to save many more lives had failed.

———

When Sarah saw Mano take her son in his arms, she knew that coming back here had not been a mistake. Cradling the baby in those large hands, Mano gently pressed Daniel's forehead against his own, a timeless benediction that transcended religion. The tender gesture from the burly man brought tears to Sarah's eyes.

"What's his name?" Mano asked, his eyes growing moist.

Sarah wiped her cheeks. "Daniel Evans Suarez."

"Does Pedro know?"

"No," Rosa answered. "Sarah arrived this morning. But Pedro left the zone before anyone could get word to him."

Sarah watched Mano's face tighten with pain. "Is something wrong?" she asked anxiously.

Mano answered slowly, measuring his words. "Pedro... might be gone for a while."

"How long?" Sarah asked, her voice rising with alarm.

Rosa put her arm around Sarah's shoulders. "M'hija, I learned long ago there are some things it's best not to ask a rebélde."

"That's what you told me when I was a hostage. But I came here on my own this time."

"It's still the same, Sarah," Rosa said softly. "Inside the zones, we're all hostages."

Mano looked into his grandson's half-open eyes for a moment, then kissed the baby and handed him to his wife. "Rosa, I need to speak with Sarah alone."

Rosa nodded then turned to Sarah. "M'hija, I've been hoping for some time alone with my grandson. Do you mind?"

Sarah nodded. "Take him, mamá."

Stroking the baby's hair, Rosa retreated down the hall with Daniel.

"It's bad news about Pedro, isn't it?" Sarah asked once Rosa was gone.

Mano rubbed his chin. "Every time a rebélde leaves the zones it's dangerous, Sarah. But that's not why we need to talk," he said gently. "You need to go back to Santa Clarita—as soon as possible."

"No," she said defiantly. "If you don't want me here, I'll go live somewhere else. I'm not going back."

Mano shook his head. "It's not that I don't want you here, Sarah. There's something very important you have to do in Santa Clarita," he explained. "We need you to contact Michael Fuller and ask him to come and see you."

Sarah's eyebrows rose in surprise. Then her eyes narrowed. "I won't let you use me to draw Mike into a trap."

"Sarah, we set you and Fuller free. Why would we want to capture him again?"

"He's a major now. He's more important."

"No, we're not trying to trap Fuller. We need you to get a message to him. He'll be in no danger if he meets you in Santa Clarita."

"Why don't you contact him yourself?"

"A man in Fuller's position at the CIA has no private communications. Any way we try to contact him could be traced."

Sarah looked away and sighed. "I'm sorry. I can't help you."

"Sarah, this is important. A lot of people could die if we don't reach Fuller."

"This doesn't make any sense. How did you know I was coming? Why didn't you try to reach me before?"

Mano shook his head. "I'm sorry, Sarah. I can't—"

"Yeah, yeah, I get it," she said, rolling her eyes. "It's better if I don't know."

Mano looked into her eyes. "Sarah, you have to trust me."

She saw Pedro in those eyes—and the eyes of her son. "Suppose I agree. What do you want me to do?"

"We need to get you to the North Gate right away and send you out under a white flag. You can tell the Baldies that you've changed your mind and want to go back," Mano said, rising to his feet. "I'll explain what you need to tell Fuller on our way to the gate."

Sarah did not move. "I told you. I can't do this," she

said, looking down. "I had to accept Class H status to keep Daniel. I can't leave here anymore than you can."

Mano exhaled slowly. "That complicates things," he admitted. "But we've left the zones before. We'll get you identity papers and a cover story. The Baldies will take someone who looks like you back to Santa Clarita without many questions."

"And Daniel? How will my cover story explain him?"

"The baby would be a problem. You'll have to leave him with Rosa. She'll find a wet nurse."

"I won't do that," she said, turning away.

"Sarah, I wouldn't ask unless it was important," Mano insisted. "If we don't get in touch with Fuller, a lot of innocent people could die and even more will suffer— including Daniel."

"I want to help. But what you're asking..."

"Sarah, we've thought this through and we have no other options. You're our only hope to get in touch with Fuller."

Sarah stared at the floor, her eyes distant. She'd never imagined coming back here would turn out like this. Her dream of raising her son with Pedro had vanished. Instead, she was being drawn into a conflict she'd wanted to avoid. *Someday you're going to regret this*, her mother had warned. Had she been right?

Sarah refused to believe it. Her life was here now and she had to make the best of it. This was not what she'd expected, but the family that had saved her life now needed her help. Then a thought surfaced that lifted her mood. *Maybe helping Pedro's cause will help win him back.*

Her gloom fading, Sarah recalled something that made her smile. "I don't have to go back to Santa Clarita to call Mike," she said, eyes suddenly gleaming. "One of the deputies on the bus that brought me here this morning offered to help. His name is Bell. If I can get in touch with him again—"

A knock on the front door stopped her.

"Wait here. I'll see who that is," Mano said and left the kitchen.

Ignoring Mano's warning, Sarah quietly followed him down the hall, staying in the shadows.

Under the faint light of an oil lamp in the living room, Sarah watched Mano pull a pistol from his trousers and peer through the peep hole in the door. Putting the gun away, he opened the door and waved a young woman inside. She was short with a lithe figure and a long braid of dark hair trailing down her back.

"Is something wrong, Isabel?" Mano said softly, gesturing with his palm to keep her voice down.

"Pedro wants you to know he couldn't get where he was going. He said you'd know what that means."

The mention of Pedro's name stabbed at Sarah's heart. This had to be his wife.

Mano exhaled slowly, apparently relieved. "Where is he now?"

"At our house. He was shot in the leg and sent me since I could get here sooner. Don't worry. I've already sent for the medic."

"How bad's the wound?" Mano said, suddenly anxious.

"Not serious. Looks like the bullet didn't break any bones. From what I can tell, it passed through—"

The wail of a baby rose from the back of the house. Turning toward the sound, Isabel saw Sarah in the hallway. Realizing she was discovered, Sarah stepped into the living room.

"It's... uh... we have a guest," Mano said awkwardly.

The two women locked eyes, immediately sensing a

rival. The icy glares remained unbroken as the baby cried out again.

Moments later, Rosa appeared, tenderly cradling the wailing infant. "I think our grandson's hungry and wants his—" Rosa stopped as she noticed Isabel.

Isabel looked at the infant, her face livid. "Your grandson? Whose child is this?"

Sarah took the baby from Rosa. "Mine," she said, chin rising with pride.

"Who are you?"

Rosa stepped between the young women. "Isabel, I hoped there would be a better time to explain all this, but there's never a good time for painful news, m'hija. We only learned about Sarah's baby today," she said calmly. "Sarah lived in our house for a while—about a year ago, before you and Pedro were engaged."

"I don't understand, señora. What was this gabacha doing in your— " Isabel stopped, her face hardening. She glared at Sarah, suddenly aware of her identity. "El Frente was sloppy not to finish off all the hostages," she said coldly.

"I know this is a shock, Isabel," Rosa said, stepping closer to her daughter-in-law. "You need to let go of the hate—for your own good."

"Someone killed my brother while *she* was here," Isabel said, thrusting her chin toward Sarah. "I know she's connected with that somehow."

"You're angry, Isabel. I understand that," Rosa answered softly. "But you have to believe me when I say that Mano and I have always looked out for you."

"Señora, what I can't believe is that you have a whore and an enemy in your house."

Rosa managed a soft smile and gently stroked Isabel's

arm. "Sarah's child is our blood, Isabel. Mano and I are not going to turn away our own." Rosa then touched Sarah with her other hand. "Sarah has no place else to go. She chose to be Class H to keep this child and she's here to stay. None of us can change what's happened. We can only deal with things as they are now. From this point on, our family will have to live together, if not in harmony, at least in peace."

Looking at Isabel's cold stare, Sarah wondered how long that peace would last.

Gilbert Ochoa zipped up the military medic's bag and hoisted it onto his shoulder. "Like I said, Pedro. You're very lucky."

"If I was lucky, the bullet would have missed," Pedro said, reclining against a pair of corn-husk pillows on the bed.

Ochoa laughed softly. "Be thankful you have your father's build. That bullet would have found bone on a man with less muscle mass."

Pedro held out his palm. "Thank you for coming so quickly, Gilbert."

"De nada, hermano," the medic replied shaking his hand. "You've lost a lot of blood and that's something I can't replace. So stay in bed. Get some rest and eat. You've got a good wife. Let her take care of you. I'll be back tomorrow to check on the sutures."

After Ochoa had gone, Pedro lay back in the bed and closed his eyes. Unbidden, the thought that had tormented him since he'd been wounded returned. *I've failed*, he told himself. *I've failed our cause and my family.* Now, with the pressure of survival gone, a new thought surfaced. How would his father take the news? The answer made him sit upright.

Papá's going to leave for Santa Clarita. Pedro knew it was a futile gesture that would likely cost Mano his life. But he also knew his father. Mano would go anyway. *I need to stop him*, he realized and rose from the bed. His first step brought on a jolt of pain that nearly felled him. Woozy, he braced himself against the wall and began to get dressed.

While pulling his pants over the bandaged leg, Pedro heard the front door open. Hobbling out of the bedroom, he found Isabel in the living room. She sat in a rusting metal lawn chair, face buried in her hands.

Pedro gently touched her shoulder. "Mi amor... What happened?"

Isabel pushed his hand away. "My brother taught me never to ask a rebélde about anything they do for the cause," she said, wiping tears from her face. "That's why I never asked you about the gabacha hostage. All I knew was that you and your father helped set her free. Now I find out there was more between you."

Her words startled Pedro. Something did not make sense. His father would not have revealed anything about the mission to Santa Clarita, even to his family. "My father told you something about Sarah Evans?"

"Don't hide behind your father. I want *you* to tell me about her."

Pedro's jaw clenched. This was dangerous ground. Sarah's rescue harbored two secrets his parents had kept from Isabel—and both were devastating. First, Isabel did not know her brother Angel had led the kidnapping of the hostages for El Frente. Worse still, if Isabel ever learned Angel had died in a shootout with Mano during Sarah's rescue, Isabel might blame his father for Angel's death. Pedro's lingering feelings for Sarah only complicated things. "Isabel... you know I can't talk about that," he said finally.

"No!" she said rising to her feet. "That's not going to work anymore. I want to hear about her from *you*."

"What did my father tell you?"

"He didn't have to tell me anything," Isabel said, her face knotted with anger. "I saw Sarah at your parents' house tonight... and that puta gabacha was there with your son."

———

"Sarah's gone to bed," Rosa whispered to Mano entering the living room.

Mano rose from one of their two prized upholstered chairs. "Good. I'm going to see Pedro."

Rosa shook her head. "Sit down, mi amor," she said softly. "I know what you're thinking. You're going to let Pedro know he has a son. Believe me, Isabel has already told him and it's better if those two deal with that alone. All you're going to do is make matters worse."

Mano realized Rosa was right—in ways she could not know. Once Isabel told Pedro that Sarah was with them, Pedro would realize his mission to Santa Clarita was no longer necessary. Knowing Pedro, there was a chance he would have tried to go again. "Maybe you're right, querida," Mano said, sitting down again.

Rosa walked behind her husband and began kneading his brawny shoulders. "Dios mio, what a day" she said wearily. "Who would have guessed we'd be grandparents overnight?"

Mano nodded, mulling the consequences of Sarah's arrival. Their plan to stop Perez was now much closer to reality. He would call Ramon tomorrow and share their good fortune. But Sarah's presence also posed a danger to his family.

"Sarah can't stay here, querida. I've talked to her and she's agreed to go outside the walls tomorrow to deliver a message. When she comes back, we'll need to find another place for her," Mano said softly.

Rosa stopped rubbing his shoulders. "What? You can't be serious."

Mano stood and faced his wife. "You saw what happened with Isabel tonight. Having Sarah in our house is going to make Isabel suspicious. She's going to ask questions about her brother." Mano rubbed his face. "I should have told Isabel what happened the day Angel died."

"Isabel was in shock, Mano. She'd lost the last member of her family on earth. Even though you tried to spare Angel, she would have blamed you for his death."

"And you think she'll blame me any less if she finds out now?"

"Leave the dead in the ground, Mano. Isabel doesn't need to know who killed her brother or how he died. What difference will it make?" Rosa said, her voice rising. "It's not going to bring him back."

"Keep your voice down," Mano said, trying to calm his wife. "I have nothing but sympathy for Sarah, mi amor. But my gut tells me she's going to bring trouble to this house."

Rosa locked him a cold stare. "Her child is your blood, Mano, and she's part of your family now. If you turn away Sarah and our grandson, I'm going with them."

Underscoring her scorn, Rosa pulled the collar of her tattered robe tighter against her chest and turned toward the hallway. She did not see Sarah silently close the door to her room in the darkened hall.

THE PRODIGAL—Day 2

OUTPOST BRAVO, CA

A wave of nostalgia enveloped Michael Fuller as he stared through the helicopter's window at the layout of Outpost Bravo several hundred feet below. The neatly-parked vehicles alongside the orderly rows of barracks reflected a purity of purpose now missing from his life. His duty had been clearer during the years he'd served in this backwater garrison in Southern California. Now he was returning to the post higher in rank but less certain of the value of his duty. *Is that inevitable?* he wondered.

One thing was sure. He was glad to have the clout to swing a cross-country trip aboard a military jet and a chopper in less than a day. Few U.S. Army majors had that kind of juice. But a galling fact remained. Finding time for the trip would have been much harder if he'd been doing something important. He'd even toyed with the idea of bringing Bailey along before quickly dismissing it. The urge to travel with a spy just for the company was borderline pathetic.

As the LUH touched down, Fuller saw a lone figure waiting for him on the helipad. Dressed in a tan and black law enforcement uniform, the man held down a wide-brimmed hat against the wind of the rotors.

After thanking the crew, Fuller stepped out of the craft

and walked to the lawman. "Deputy Bell," he said. "I'm Major Fuller."

"Hello, Major," the deputy answered, nodding in respect. "She's waiting for you in the gym like you asked."

"I appreciate you letting Sarah call me. I know this arrangement was... unconventional."

"She's a gritty kid, going in there alone with a baby and all. I figured she could use some help."

Fuller glanced at the slope-roofed gym about twenty paces away. "Would you mind waiting here while I talk to her?"

"Will this take long, Major? My shift ends in an hour and I need to make sure she gets back inside while I'm still on duty. I'm willing to bend the rules for the kid but I can't release someone who's Class H."

"Of course. I'll make sure she returns to your custody as soon as possible," Fuller said before turning toward the gym.

The building had special place in Fuller's career, although it was not one he remembered altogether fondly. The gym's tan paint had faded some since the day almost four years before when he'd secretly met Sarah's father inside. During that late-night briefing, Hank Evans had drawn Fuller into the murky world of spooks by recruiting him for a black mission to capture Manolo Suarez. Since then, it seemed the rebel leader's life and his own had become intertwined.

As Fuller walked into the gym, the clank of the metal door echoed through the empty, vaulted space.

Sarah sat on the front row of the bleachers. "Mike!" she called out with a smile before running to him. She was thinner than the last time he'd seen her and looked older than her seventeen years. But even in worn jeans and a work shirt, she was still pretty enough to turn heads.

"Thanks for coming," she said pressing her head against his shoulder.

"You made this sound pretty important," he said after parting from her hug.

She looked at him expectantly for a time. "Well, aren't you going to ask me the big question—why did I come back here?"

"Your mother called me when she found out you'd registered Daniel as Class H. I had good idea then what you planned to do," he said. "Sarah, I probably know better than anybody what you went through as a hostage. If you decided to come back here, your reasons must have been very good—and very personal."

"You and dad are the only ones who ever trusted me."

"I think you earned that trust," Fuller said, then looked at his watch. "But we haven't got much time. The deputy outside has to take you back soon."

"You're right, Mike," she said, nodding. "The reason I asked you here is not about me. I have a message for you from Ramon Garcia."

THE PRODIGAL—Day 3

EAST FALLS CHURCH, VA

The cyber café was empty except for the college kid behind the counter with his nose in a textbook. Dressed in civvies and bleary eyed after his return flight, Michael Fuller paid in cash for a large coffee and an hour's worth of web time.

Choosing a terminal in the corner of the room, Fuller navigated to the URL Sarah had given him, a bulletin board on a bird watchers' website. Sarah had said he'd find a message from Ramon Garcia at the site under the username *Songbird*. Once there, Fuller entered the password Sarah had relayed. The screen went white for an instant, then revealed a plain text message.

> *We have learned the Latino Liberation Front may soon have a suitcase nuclear weapon. Because our resources cannot match yours in preventing its deployment, we are ready to provide you with the identities and whereabouts of those involved. However, for our protection, this must be done through unofficial channels. You must not reveal our role in this to anyone. A man within our ranks you've already met assures us your word will be enough for us to trust you. But we cannot be sure others in your government will not betray us. If you are willing to help under these terms, reply to this message immediately. The threat is imminent.*

Fuller stared at the message, suddenly wide awake. He

read the note again, unwilling to form a judgment until he'd weighed all the possibilities. This could be some kind of trap or an attempt to distract them from another operation. But if Garcia's offer was true, the risks were too great to ignore. One thing was certain. The conditions of the offer put him in a quandary.

If he agreed to Garcia's terms, he risked his career— and possibly a jail sentence. Fuller also knew the message from Garcia was untraceable. So reporting the contact to his superiors would leave his side with little more than a hazy threat. The most logical option was simple. Reply to Garcia, get the information on the LLF and pass it on to his superiors.

But that left the matter of his word.

Fuller knew "the man within our ranks you've already met" was Manolo Suarez, the Pancho leader who'd saved his life. *Can I betray Suarez after giving him my word?*, he asked himself. Fuller hated to admit it, but he trusted the Pancho leader to keep his word more than some on his own side.

Stroking his chin, Fuller pondered the decision. Then, almost on their own, his fingers tapped out a reply.

Send the information. I agree to your terms.

Fuller logged off with a sobering realization. Following his conscience would not be easy. He was a pariah being watched by superiors eager to replace him. But for the first time in a long while he had a chance to serve his country again.

Despite the exhaustion, he left the café with an eager stride.

LOS ANGELES QUARANTINE ZONE B

"This is your home now, Sarah," Rosa said, leading her into the kitchen. "We don't have much, but whatever we have is yours."

"Thanks," Sarah answered as she gazed around the small kitchen, bewildered. All the cabinet doors had been removed—to be burned as fuel, Sarah imagined. To her surprise however, the shelves were full. But the items they contained looked nothing like the brightly-labeled food packages Sarah would have expected in a normal kitchen. Instead, she saw an assortment of bundles wrapped in corn husks alongside a motley collection of improvised containers—discarded product packaging, recycled cans, and plastic jugs, even computer and electronic product casings.

Rosa walked past a blackened one-time electric range with the ashes of a wood fire in its oven and gestured toward a set of metal shelves near the back door. "I keep prepared food over here... dried fruit, chicken-jerky, peanuts, things Mano can take if he has to leave suddenly. Help yourself when you're hungry," she explained. "I keep the staples over here—cornmeal, beans, chilies," she said, waving her had. "We get fresh vegetables, eggs and chicken on most days but without a refrigerator, I buy them in the market each day. And this is where I keep the soy milk for Carlos. You'll want to know where it is once you've weaned Daniel."

Sarah looked at her son as Rosa spoke. Daniel yawned, oblivious to the new surroundings. Sarah stroked his hair, envying the luxury of his innocence. The world she'd left three days ago already seemed like a vague memory in this strange, uncertain place. Still, mamá's words were reassuring. She had a home here now. But that was not the reason she'd come back.

"Do you think Pedro wants to see his son?" Sarah asked softly, looking at the floor.

The hint of a smile crossed Rosa's face. "I think you know the answer to that," she said. "He sent word to me through Chuy yesterday while you were out with Mano. Pedro wants to see Daniel—and talk to you."

Her eyes brightening, Sarah touched Rosa's arm. "When?"

"Well, m'hija. That's the complicated part," Rosa said, frowning. "Pedro has a right to see his son. But that's not going to make Isabel very happy." She paused, looking out the window. "I hate going behind Isabel's back. But I'm worried there's going to be a blowup if she's there when you see Pedro. So this has to be done quietly. You cannot tell anyone—especially Isabel. You understand?"

"I won't say anything, mamá. I promise."

"All right. I'll take you to Pedro's house later this morning. Isabel goes to the market every day before lunch. We'll go there then." Rosa made the sign of the cross and turned her gaze upward. "Forgive me, señor. I know this isn't right. But I don't know any other way."

MCLEAN, VA

The sign above the four cubicles read FOR GUESTS ONLY. Fuller ignored it and sat down at one the compartments. He doubted anyone on the hotel staff would have the balls to question an Army officer in uniform using the lobby's public internet access—especially a hotel less than an hour's drive from a half dozen defense facilities.

This stop on his way to CIA headquarters would probably make him late for work. *Tough shit. This takes priority.* Four hours had passed since he'd sent his message to Garcia. With the time in Geneva reaching early afternoon, the rebel diplomat should have responded by now. After logging into the message board on the bird watcher's website, Fuller saw the reply button was active. Pulse quickening, he clicked on the link.

> *Former UN delegate for the HRNA Octavio Perez and his aide Miguel Cardona are close to acquiring a nuclear weapon for the Latino Liberation Front. We believe the weapon will come from criminal elements within Russia. Perez and Cardona were last seen in Lyon, France two days ago.*

Garcia's message continued for several more paragraphs listing the hotel where the men had stayed in Lyon and their last known addresses in Geneva along with photos of each.

After studying the message, Fuller was disappointed. The rebel leader's comm was pretty skinny. He'd given Garcia his word not to share the source of this intelligence. But that didn't mean he had to accept Garcia's information as true. He scanned the web page and found what he wanted: an instant messaging function. Opening the dialog box, Fuller began to type.

> How do I know you are not setting us up for a trap?

Fuller was relieved when the dialog box blinked, indicating Garcia was drafting a reply.

> *We have as much at risk as you. If these emails lead to any kind of criminal activity, they are legal evidence that would convict me in a court of law anywhere in the world. We need to trust each other.*

> Fair enough. But I still need to know more.

> *I will tell you whatever I can.*

> Who last saw Perez and Cardona in Lyon?

> *Perez approached one of our donors asking for money to purchase the nuke.*

> Who is the donor?

That is confidential.

You asked me to trust you. Now you have to trust me.

There was a delay in Garcia's reply. Evidently, this was not an easy decision, which meant Garcia was likely telling the truth. Finally, the rebel's answer appeared.

Claude Durand

Fuller had read about Durand, one of those eccentric billionaires with a hard-on for do-gooder causes. The connection made sense.

Tell Durand to invite Perez back for more discussions. I can have a team ready to tail Perez when he shows up to meet with Durand.

I will inform Durand and send you the location of their meeting.

Let's communicate again in four hours. Agreed?

Agreed.

After using the hotel's wireless printer connection to make copies of the data on the suspects, Fuller left the lobby feeling like a moocher. *They'll never know it, but the Fairfax Envoy Hotel probably helped save a lot of lives today*, Fuller consoled himself as he drove away.

LOS ANGELES QUARANTINE ZONE B

The open air market on Whittier Boulevard was alive with a mid-morning crowd shopping for the day's meals. No longer used by vehicles, this section of Whittier had evolved into a bazaar offering the growing number of goods produced inside the zones at a motley array of stalls and storefronts. Out of sight but available with the right connections were the black market items smuggled in from the outside, usually through the local cops guarding the zones.

The scent of frying lard mixed with the din of voices

from the bazaar drifted toward Isabel as she walked toward Whittier, less than a block away. The restless beehive drone of the marketplace usually charged her up. But today Isabel was oblivious to the sound. Her thoughts were consumed by the arrival of the gabacha and her son.

Rosa and Mano were smitten by the baby and not thinking straight, she was sure of that. *Will the gabacha's bastard turn Pedro's head too?* The question tortured her like an aching tooth which she could not resist probing. Making the torment worse were the many times she'd failed to entice Pedro into giving her a child. *The blonde bitch got what should have been mine*, she thought bitterly.

"Roasted peanuts here! Cacahuate aqui!" shouted a vendor on a bike cart pedaling past Isabel, headed toward the market.

The peanut seller's call broke Isabel's trance. She would deal with the problem of the gabacha later. For now, the need to put food on their table for another day came first. And the chore was far from easy. Haggling with the market's hard-assed vendors always took way too long and left her nerves jangled.

At a stand selling beans, Isabel struck a quick bargain for a half pound paying more than she should have but too distracted to care. "Where's your bag?" the merchant asked, pouring a scoop of pintos onto an ancient balance scale.

"Carajo," Isabel muttered in disgust. With all her worries about the gabacha, she'd forgotten her canvas market bag. "I'll be back," she said and turned for the short walk home.

Rounding the corner onto her street, Isabel stopped, stunned by the sight outside her house. Rosa and a woman in a knit hat and sunglasses carrying a baby were approaching their stucco ranch. Isabel was not fooled by the disguise and immediately recognized the gabacha. Ducking into the entry of an apartment building to avoid being seen, Isabel watched Rosa unlock the front door and lead Sarah into the house.

Isabel's eyes narrowed, glaring with rage. *Rosa's bringing the gabacha into my home.* The words echoed in her head like an angry taunt. *She's bringing that whore into my house.*

Isabel broke into a run.

Striding toward the house, exhaling fury with each breath, the image of her actions began forming in her mind. She would get her gun, drag them both outside by the hair and...

The thought of hurting Rosa made Isabel stop. There was no way she could harm her mother-in-law. Rosa had taken her in after her brother's death when she had nowhere else to go. More than anyone else, Rosa had supported her marriage to Pedro. If Rosa was bringing the gabacha to her house, there might be a good reason why. Maybe there was hope—maybe Rosa had a plan to make Pedro forget the green-eyed whore.

Instead of bursting into the house, Isabel walked to the side yard, keeping out of sight from those inside, and knelt below the open bedroom window, pretending to pull weeds. She would listen to what was going on before she'd pass judgment on her mother-in-law.

"Come in, quickly," Rosa said, unlocking the front door. "The neighbors know who I am. But somebody might start asking questions if they see strangers."

Sarah entered the house unsure what to expect. Although sparsely furnished, the living room was oddly attractive with its bright plastic curtains and a colorful assortment of baskets woven from electrical wire hanging on the walls. "The place is kind of nice," she said grudgingly. "I'm surprised."

"We haven't got time for a decorating tour, m'hija," Rosa said smiling. "Pedro is waiting for you in here," she said, leading Sarah down a short hallway and opening the door.

After ushering Sarah inside the bedroom, Rosa left them alone, closing the door behind her. Pedro was propped up on the bed, supported by cornhusk pillows that rustled softly as he leaned forward to adjust his bandaged leg. His bare chest shone in the light from the window revealing a lean, sculpted torso.

For long seconds, they stared at each other in silence. Then Sarah shifted the baby aside, reached into the pocket of her shirt and held out her blindfold. "I told you I'd never forget you."

"You should have," Pedro said, his voice hoarse with emotion.

Sarah covered her face and wept. In the reunion she'd imagined many times before, she would be holding Pedro tightly now, her head buried in his chest. Instead, they stood across a room divided by an icy wall of circumstances. "I thought everything would be the same between us when I came back."

"I never thought I'd see you again," Pedro said, looking away.

Sarah took a step closer. "I'm here now."

"We can't change what's happened, Sarah," he whispered. " I wish we could."

Sarah wiped her cheeks with the blindfold, trying to compose herself. She needed to be strong for Daniel's sake. "Well, no matter what's happened, this is still your son," she said putting the baby in his arms.

Pedro held the infant gently against his shoulder and

Daniel began nuzzling his neck. "Thanks for bringing him," he said, his eyes welling with tears.

"I think he recognizes his father," Sarah said stroking the baby's head. "His name is Daniel."

"My mother told me."

"He has your eyes. Even your mom says so."

Gazing at the baby's face, Pedro nodded. "Hard to deny he's part of our family."

"From the moment he was born, bringing Daniel back to you was the only thing I wanted to do." She let her caress on the baby's head slide to Pedro's bare shoulder. "My time here with you... that was the most alive I ever felt."

Pedro placed his hand over Sarah's. He then slowly removed her hand from his shoulder. "Sarah, no matter how we feel... we can't do this," he said, looking into her eyes.

His words pierced her heart.

And yet she knew he was right. At that moment, Sarah understood why she loved Pedro. He would do the right thing—even when it hurt. "I'm sorry," she said, stepping back from him. "When your mother said you wanted to see me, I thought there might be a chance..." she said, voice wavering. "I get it now. You were just being polite."

"Not exactly," he said, meeting her gaze. "I owe you an explanation ... about Isabel."

Sarah turned away. "I don't want to hear it."

"Please, Sarah. You need understand," he said. "I didn't want you to go. But you belonged in your world, not here with me. After you left, I tried to forget you." He paused and closed his eyes, searching for the right words. "Isabel needed someone. She didn't have any other family after her brother was killed... although it was an accident, it was my fault he died."

"How was that your fault?"

"It's not important. I'm telling you so you understand why I married Isabel," Pedro answered. "I can't say any more about it." He exhaled slowly, closed his eyes and held Daniel out to Sarah. "I think you better go. Isabel will be back soon."

Sarah took the infant from Pedro's arms. "When can I see you again?"

"Leave it to my mom. She'll figure something out."

Unable to meet Pedro's eyes, Sarah's gaze drifted to the photo on the steel milk crate by the bed. The unsmiling man in the picture looked familiar but Sarah could not place him. All the same, his face stirred up feelings of dread. "Who is that?" she asked, nodding toward the photo.

Pedro was silent for a moment. "You don't need to know," he said finally.

"I get that answer a lot here."

"Please. You have to go now. I'll see you again."

———

Crouched outside the window and listening to the conversation, Isabel leaned her head against the stucco wall and wept silently, crushed by Pedro's parting words. He wanted to see the gabacha again.

What she'd just heard had been like the day she'd identified her brother's body, a horrible truth that was impossible to escape.

The person she'd trusted most had betrayed her.

Pedro was not only still in love with the gabacha, he'd been responsible for the death of her brother. Then, twisting the knife in the wound, Pedro had told the gabacha he'd married out of pity.

Isabel's fingers dug into her hair and squeezed, hoping

the pain would blot out the shame. Even the death of her brother had not hurt like this. Then she heard the front door open. Rosa and the gabacha were leaving the house.

Taking cover behind a bush, Isabel watched in a cold fury as they walked away. *The Suarez family has played me long enough*, she thought bitterly. *They're all liars and posers.* Pedro would pay for this—his parents and the gabacha, too.

She thought of going into the house for her gun. But it was a foolish idea with too many risks. Someone would stop her before she could get to the others. No, she would bide her time and have her revenge on all of them at once.

The only questions were the time and place.

ANNECY, FRANCE

The small Peugeot sedan traversed the narrow cobblestone street winding like a gorge through the timeworn medieval buildings. Tires rumbling on the uneven pavement, the car came to a stop at a dingy hotel. A heavy-set man in a business suit waiting under the faded awning of the Hôtel du Canal Vert glared sourly at the driver, then laboriously squeezed inside the tiny car.

"Pinche madre, Miguel! Where did you get this fucking roller skate?" Octavio Perez said, settling into the passenger seat.

Miguel Cardona lowered head. "Sorry, jefe. You told me to watch our money," he said. "This was all the rental company had left except for a Mercedes."

Perez haughtily waved his hand, dismissing the matter. "All right. You fucked up. I'm not going to let it ruin my mood," he said, a tight smile forming on his face.

Cardona raised his head, eying his boss. "Good news with the North Koreans?"

"The chinos came through with the money," Perez said grinning broadly.

Cardona's eyes widened. "All of it?"

"Not quite," Perez said, patting Cardona's shoulder. "We'll still need to rely on you for travel expenses, hermano."

"Maybe not," Cardona replied.

"What are you saying?"

"Durand wants to talk to you again," Cardona said smiling. "I got the word from one his people."

"How soon does he want to meet?"

"Right away."

Perez slapped his thigh, smiling with glee. "So the puto frog changed his mind, eh? Good! Here's what we're going to do." Reaching into his pocket, Perez produced a folded sheet of paper. "This is the number of the Swiss bank account the chinos gave us. It's black money so nobody has to worry about it being traced. You contact the Russians and have them deliver our little nest egg," he said. "Meantime, I'll set up a time to see Monsieur Durand about giving us more money." Perez winked at Cardona. "Who knows? We might even have enough left over to sample some of the French pastry around here," he said, grabbing his crotch.

Cardona looked away, ignoring his boss's posturing. They had a lot left to do. "Can I use some of the money to set up the website? Those untraceable URLs don't come cheap."

"Si, hermano," Perez said, his eyes gleaming. "We're on a hot streak, Miguel. If Durand comes across with the money, we'll have enough for *two* bombs," he said, slowly rubbing his hands together. "Then we'll give the gabachos a real taste of war."

After driving to a truck stop on the D.C. beltway on his lunch hour, Fuller logged in at a by-the-minute web kiosk and found a message from Garcia waiting for him.

> *Durand will meet with Perez at the Café de L'Isle in Annecy, France at 1400 local time.*

Smiling, Fuller typed his reply.

> A surveillance team will be deployed to the location. Tell Durand to ask Perez for proof of the nuke before he will pay. That may lead us to the bomb. Send me everything Perez says to Durand.

Hooah. The trap's been baited, Fuller said to himself shutting down the web connection. *Now I need to set the spring.*

Back in his office twenty minutes later, Fuller rang up CIA Director Jim Tanaka on the inter-office voice line.

"What is it, Major?" Tanaka said impatiently.

"Sir, I'm requesting permission to deploy a surveillance team to eastern France in the next two hours."

Tanaka's dry laugh made Fuller wince. "Putting aside the fact that you're bypassing all the proper protocols," he said, "isn't this a little outside your normal scope of duties?"

"I understand my request is irregular, sir. But I can assure you it's vital to our national security—and urgent."

"Major, I shouldn't have to remind you that our assets are stretched pretty thin right now."

"The deployment won't last more than twenty-four hours, sir."

"And what makes this surveillance so urgent?"

Fuller hesitated, reluctant to show all his cards. "We've got a lead on some Pancho activity that could be serious. I know you're busy, sir. But if you have the time right now, I can come to your office and brief you with all the details."

Fuller held his breath, hoping he'd played this right.

Had he gone through channels, a surveillance request from an Army major could have easily been put on the back burner by a mid-level CIA chief. But Fuller knew he was no ordinary Army major to a political appointee like Tanaka—especially when it came to the Panchos. The CIA Director would tread lightly around him, hoping to avoid another media fiasco like the White House had suffered with his old boss Hank Evans.

After a long pause, Tanaka finally answered. "That won't be necessary," he said, "Tell Miller in Overseas you can have the team."

GENEVA, SWITZERLAND

At a small desk in his apartment, Ramon Garcia anxiously rubbed his temples as he spoke into the bulky satellite phone. "Did Perez give you any clues on where he got the money, Claude?"

"Perez told me he has new friends in Asia who are funding his operation," Claude Durand answered over the encrypted connection. "He asked me to fund a second project. Perez seemed to think I'd be more eager to support him now that he has other backers."

"Did you ask him for proof of the device?"

"Perez said I'd read about the proof in the papers."

Ramon exhaled slowly. "Hopefully, we'll intercept him before that happens," he said, not sounding convinced.

"Ramon, you know I believe in your cause. But a lot of the people I do business with do not. If word of my financial support becomes public, I'm going to deny it—and that will be the last time I'll be able to help you. I hope you understand."

"We'll do as you say, Claude. You're a generous friend of the people," Ramon said, ending the call.

Ramon turned on his laptop and navigated to the bird watching website. He needed to alert Fuller right away. The situation with Perez was worse than he'd expected. Octavio's "new friends in Asia" pointed to North Korea, a regime that would not balk at hitting the U.S.—if they could avoid retaliation. Perez's plot gave them exactly that opportunity. Worse yet, Octavio's "proof in the papers" comment could only mean one thing: He already had his hands on the nuke.

Ramon hurriedly typed out the message and hit the send button, plagued by a gnawing thought. If Fuller had failed to put a tail on Perez after his meeting with Durand, any hope of stopping Octavio was gone.

LOS ANGELES QUARANTINE ZONE B

Rosa entered the living room and found Mano reading to Carlos while the three-year-old sat in his lap, gleefully embellishing the story. "And the cow went *way high* over the moon," Carlos said, sweeping his small hand in an arc above his head.

"This one, he's going to be a politician," Rosa said laughing softly. "Unlike his father and brother, he actually *likes* to talk." Rosa reached for the child. "Come on, Senator. It's time for bed."

"Can he stay up a little longer?" Mano asked. "I haven't spent much time with him lately, Rosita."

"I don't want to sleep," Carlos added, pouting.

"Mano, you already have him up way past his bedtime. I can't believe how you're spoiling—" Rosa stopped as a realization struck her. Mano did not want to repeat the same mistakes as a father he'd made with Pedro. "All right, ten more minutes. But no more arguments from you, counselor," she said, wagging her finger at Carlos. "I'll go finish cleaning the kitchen and come back."

When she returned, Carlos was asleep in Mano's arms. The sight made Rosa sigh. Carlos was Mano's second chance to be the father he could have been with Pedro. But Mano had never shown his love in a way a child could understand. Only now was Pedro beginning to realize the depths of his father's love.

"I'll put him to bed," Mano whispered before quietly leaving the room. Rosa was grateful for the understanding and joy Carlos had brought to their family. The situation with Daniel was altogether different. She loved her grandson but his arrival had brought a festering conflict to their family that Rosa needed to resolve. Fortunately, she had an idea that might restore the peace.

When Mano returned to the living room, Rosa unveiled her plan.

"We need to baptize Daniel," she told her husband.

Mano rubbed his forehead. "Rosita, that could get complicated. You think it's that important?

"I'm not going to risk the eternal soul of our grandson, Mano," Rosa said, hands on her hips. "Besides, it'll be good for our family. Having Daniel baptized will help Isabel accept what's happened. She respects the church, Mano. I'm counting on that. And Sarah will feel she and Daniel are being accepted too. I've already talked to Father Ignacio and he's agreed."

Mano raised his large hands in surrender. "I know better than to argue with you when I see that look."

"Good, because I'm going to tell Isabel tomorrow."

"What about Sarah? When does she find out you're asking her to raise a Catholic son?"

"Right now," she said, leaving the living room.

Rosa tapped lightly on Sarah's door.

"Come in," Sarah said.

Entering the room, Rosa found Sarah seated on the bed holding Daniel, her eyes red and swollen. "You don't look so good, m'hija. What's wrong?"

"I tried to feed Daniel but I don't have any milk."

"That's not unusual," Rosa said, stroking Sarah's shoulder. "My milk dried up a few times while I was nursing Carlos. Stress will do that."

Daniel whimpered weakly and Sarah cradled the baby against her. "This is the second night it's happened, mamá," she said, closing her eyes. "If I can't feed Daniel... I'm going to lose him."

"Listen to me, Sarah," Rosa said gently. "Stop worrying. I have a remedy to bring back your milk. You wait here."

Walking into the kitchen, Rosa began searching the cupboards, not really sure what she was looking for. She knew of no remedy for a mother's lack of milk. Sarah's real problem was the strain of her new life. Worrying about Daniel would only make things worse. The best thing she could give Sarah was hope.

A jar of dried fennel caught her eye. *That should work*, Rosa thought as she began a fire to heat some water. After preparing a tea from the fennel, she added a pinch of salt to the steaming cup and carried it into Sarah's bedroom.

"Drink this, m'hija," Rosa said, handing Sarah the cup ceremoniously.

Sarah took a drink and grimaced. "What is it?"

"It's a cure women have used for generations. Drink it down, m'hija. Tomorrow morning, you'll have milk. You'll see. In any case, you're not going to lose this child, Sarah. We'll find a wet nurse for him if we have to."

Sarah's face warmed into a smile. "Thank you, mamá," she said, taking another sip.

"Sarah, there's something else you need to give your son besides milk," Rosa said, stroking the baby's head.

"You need to provide for his soul." As Sarah finished the tea, Rosa explained the baptism ceremony, what was expected of her and where it would be held. "You brought your child back here so he could be raised among his own. This is part of his culture, Sarah."

"Will Isabel be at the baptism?"

"Yes, m'hija. Isabel is part of our family," Rosa said, then gently nudged Sarah. "And just between us, I think her being there will be good for everyone. Isabel needs to see that you and Daniel are part of our family too. But this isn't about her—or you either, for that matter. It's about your son's soul. Will you do this for him?"

Sarah looked at her baby pensively, weighing the question. "I wish I had your faith, mamá. I'm not so sure. But if you think the baptism is best for Daniel, I'll do it," she said finally.

Rosa patted Sarah's knee and smiled. "You won't regret it, m'hija. I promise you."

GENEVA, SWITZERLAND

Seated alone in the closet-sized space, connected to wires dangling from his body, put Ramon Garcia uncomfortably in mind of a man awaiting execution by electric chair. The cramped interview room's throne-like chair faced a remote-controlled camera and a television monitor almost close enough to touch. On the monitor, Ramon could see a live broadcast of *Simon At Large* being beamed in from New York. As the show cut to a commercial, a German-accented voice spoke into Ramon's earphone.

"You're on the air in one minute, Mr. Garcia."

"Thank you," Ramon answered, taking a sip of the designer water the Swiss network page had given him before confining him to the tiny room.

Alone for the last ten minutes, Ramon had once again mulled the opportunities of this television interview with Simon Potts. Uppermost in his mind was how the air time could help prevent Octavio from deploying the nuke. So far, he'd come up with zero. He'd also considered a different angle on the problem, one that was far simpler but not nearly as noble: how he could deflect the blame from the Hispanic Republic if they failed to stop Perez.

"We're on in ten seconds, Mr. Garcia. Please stand by," the voice in his earphone said. Watching the monitor, Ramon saw the shot of Simon Potts in the studio switch to a split-screen and his own image appear beside Potts, superimposed on a photo of the United Nations headquarters at the Palais des Nations.

"Joining us today from Geneva, Switzerland is the non-voting delegate to the United Nations from the Hispanic Republic of North America, Ramon Garcia. Welcome, sir."

"Thank you, Simon."

"Mr. Garcia, following the introduction of free-fire areas around several U.S. quarantine zones last week, Vice President Melvin Bates made some remarks that many considered inflammatory. I'd like to play the recording and get your reaction."

On the monitor, Ramon saw Melvin Bates address a swarm of reporters thrusting microphones toward him as he walked. "I think the free fires areas are a good idea but they don't go far enough in stopping these Hispanic terrorists. I think we should be enforcing the needle law in situ."

When the split screen view of Simon and Ramon returned, Potts said, "Mr. Garcia, as I'm sure you know, in situ enforcement of the Terrorist Arraignment Act, which most people call the needle law, is a euphemism for legalizing battlefield executions. Coming on the heels of the free-fire areas, the vice president's comments seem to signal the Nixon administration plans increasingly punitive tactics in dealing with the Hispanic liberation movement. Some have said your reluctance to find a fellow delegate at the U.N. shows a lack of commitment to democratic principles and that's giving the White House a free pass to employ these harsh measures with very little public outcry. How do you react?"

Ramon forced himself to smile. "Simon, you characterize the vice president's comments as part of a concerted effort from the White House. But you could also argue that this is a calculated move by a politician serving his own agenda."

"What makes you think the vice president is not following the White House lead?"

"Melvin Bates is an ideological extremist that the Nixon team put on the ticket to win far right votes. As a congressman, Bates was the architect of the quarantine zones and the needle law. When Nixon was in Congress, he opposed both measures. Since moving into the White House, the Nixon people have tried to put a muzzle on Bates, but they've not always been successful. Bates is a loose cannon and I don't think he speaks for everyone in the United States government. We have our extremist elements, too. I think the greatest danger both sides face is letting the extremists take control of events."

As Potts cut away to another commercial, Ramon managed a genuine smile. At least he'd accomplished one of his goals for the broadcast.

THE PRODIGAL—Day 4

LANGLEY, VA

When Michael Fuller approached his office, he found Sonya Bailey waiting for him outside the door.

"Good morning, Major. I have the overseas deployment reports ready, Bailey said smiling. "Would you like to review them this morning?"

"Not now, Lieutenant," Fuller said curtly.

Walking past her, Fuller noticed Bailey's shoulders slump. Disappointing an attractive woman was the last thing he wanted to do. But the news he'd gotten from Garcia at the truck stop web kiosk on his way to work could not wait.

After entering his office, Fuller closed the door and dialed CIA Director Tanaka. "Our surveillance has uncovered something big, sir. I should brief you right away," he said into the voice-only phone.

"Major, you're testing my patience," Tanaka answered. "I have a *scheduled* briefing in ten minutes. Can't this wait?"

"I wouldn't ask if it wasn't urgent, sir."

Tanaka exhaled audibly. "All right. Come up to my office. I'll give you five minutes."

The director did not look up from his laptop as his secretary ushered Fuller into the spacious top floor office. "Please proceed with your briefing, Major."

"Sir, we have good reason to believe the Latino Liberation Front has a portable nuclear weapon and they intend to use it against us. The deployment could take place in as little as three days."

"What?" Tanaka said, eyes rising from the keyboard. "Where did you get this?"

"It would be best for our government if the source remains black, sir," Fuller answered. He was betting Tanaka's fear of publicly embarrassing the White House would protect his word to the Panchos.

Tanaka nodded. "All right. Let's assume your source is reliable. What are the plans to deploy the nuke?"

"I have two suspects, both are currently under surveillance in Annecy, France. It's likely the weapon will be brought into the country through Octavio Perez or Miguel Cardona. Here are their dossiers," he said, handing Tanaka two thin files.

Tanaka skimmed through the documents. "I've heard of Perez, of course. But there isn't anything in these reports to link either of these guys with a nuke. Has anyone seen the bomb? Do you have any other sources that can confirm the story?"

"I have every reason to believe the information is reliable. That's all I can tell you without exposing our government to some difficult public explanations." Fuller paused, giving Tanaka time to think. "But if you insist, I can tell you—"

Tanaka waved his hands, cutting him off. "That won't be necessary, Major." Tanaka rose and walked around his desk to Fuller, lowering his voice. "Major, this is one hell of a burden you're putting on me. If I go to the president with this, he's got to move to DEF-CON 2. Besides throwing the country into a panic, the press is going to say he's grandstanding for his party's mid-term elections. I'm going to need more proof before I take this to the White House."

"We don't have a lot of time, sir. If we drop the ball, a lot of people could die."

"This country is under threat every day, Major. Unless you give me something more substantial, I can't act on this."

Fuller's face hardened. "Director, I've just given you written evidence of two men who pose a threat to the United States with a weapon of mass destruction. If you're wrong about this, the president is going to have a hell of a lot more to explain than a public relations issue." He stepped closer to Tanaka, staring hard into his eyes. "We've only got three days..., *sir*."

Tanaka dabbed at the sweat forming on his forehead. "All right, Major. I take your point. But I'm not going to put the president's reputation at stake on your word alone. So here's what I'm going to do," he said, regaining his composure. "You will conduct this investigation— with my approval on any deployment of assets you decide to make."

"I see," Fuller said with a tight smile. "So if anything goes wrong, I take the blame."

"Your cynicism is very unseemly for a man in uniform, Major," Tanaka answered. "Are you refusing to take responsibility for the investigation?"

"No, sir. I'll do it."

"Good. How do you want to proceed?"

Fuller exhaled slowly, gathering his thoughts. "We need to start with a round-the-clock tail on the two suspects in France. In the meantime, we should put the CBP on full alert. Perez or Cardona will probably try to bring in the nuke in as cargo. So we need Geiger counter teams ready to sweep all our seaports. Just to cover all the bases, we should also deploy Geiger counters at every international airport that doesn't already have them. That's just the beginning. We should also—"

Tanaka raised his palm, cutting him off. "Just a minute, Major. Let's not get too carried away. We'll start with the tail on the two Panchos in France and see where that leads us." Tanaka glanced at his Rolex, then said, "I'll have the work schedules cleared for Bailey and Drury. They'll be permanently assigned to you until further notice. You'll have access to one of the situation rooms if you need it."

"But, sir. This threat is—"

Tanaka opened the door. "That will be all, Major," he said, nodding toward the hallway. "You show me some hard evidence and I'll make sure we're ready."

LOS ANGELES QUARANTINE ZONE B

Kneeling before her shrine, Isabel slowly lit a candle. "Santa Muerte, I ask for your guidance. Please show me the way to avenge my brother's death. I promise to—"

A knock on the door interrupted Isabel's prayer.

Isabel rose from her knees, covered her shrine and peered through the living room curtains. Her mother-in-law stood on the porch.

Opening the front door a few inches, Isabel addressed Rosa drily. "Pedro is sleeping, señora. You should come back later."

"I'm here to see *you*, m'hija," Rosa said smiling. "Can I come in? We can talk in the kitchen so we won't disturb Pedro."

Isabel waved her inside. "Come in," she said looking away, trying to mask her contempt.

Once in the kitchen, Rosa placed a bundle wrapped

in plastic bags on the metal dining table. "I brought you something," she said. "Go ahead and open it."

Unwrapping the bundle, Isabel found a large can of peaches. "Thank you, señora," she said quickly.

"I know peaches are your favorite. I snapped these up when I saw them at the market this morning."

"You didn't need to bring me this gift."

"Sit down, m'hija. We need to talk," Rosa said, taking a seat at the table. "I know it's hard for you to accept it, but our family's had a gift too," she said, touching Isabel's sleeve. "Sarah's child is your husband's blood. If you want to be happy, you need to recognize that, m'hija. Hating Sarah and her child are not going to do you or Pedro any good. You and Pedro will have children some day and Daniel is going to be their brother. Don't you see? Daniel can be a blessing to all of us if we open our hearts."

Isabel stared at Rosa, wondering if this woman really believed what she was saying. *Your family betrayed me and my brother*, Isabel answered silently. *Why should I accept the gabacha and her bastard just to please you?* "I'll consider what you've told me," she said aloud.

"That's good, m'hija. I'm happy to hear it because I've planned something that I think will bring our family closer together," Rosa said smiling. "I've asked Father Ignacio to baptize Daniel and I want you to be there."

Isabel felt the bile rise in her throat but managed to control her rage. Her brother had taught her that remaining calm against an enemy was the surest way to win. "When?" she asked, her voice tight.

"Tomorrow, eleven o'clock at Holy Trinity."

Trying to keep her composure, Isabel breathed evenly. The thought of having the gabacha's bastard baptized in her parish made her burn with shame. *Poor Isabel*, they'd say. *Pedro put the horns on her for sure.* Isabel rose, walked to the counter and slowly opened a drawer, her fingertips caressing the smooth handle of a butcher knife. She could dispatch Rosa now and finish Pedro while he slept. Then her brother's voice came to her. *Make them all pay*, Angel said softly. *Make them all pay*.

As if guided by her brother, a plan for revenge began to unfold in Isabel's mind. Closing the drawer, she faced Rosa again. "Will all of the Suarez family be at the baptism?"

"I haven't told Pedro yet. I was hoping you would."

Isabel smiled for the first time since Rosa's arrival. "I'll make sure he's there, señora."

THE PRODIGAL—Day 5

LANGLEY, VA

Fuller had the day's first cup of coffee almost to his lips when the phone rang. Seeing Jeff Drury's extension on the ID display, he put down the mug and pressed the speaker button. "Any news from Annecy?" he asked anxiously.

"I think we've got something, Major. One of our surveillance guys is trailing Miguel Cardona. He's in a taxi with a suitcase. Looks like he's headed for the Geneva airport."

"The timing's right on schedule. This could be it, Jeff. Can you get us a list of the destinations for all outbound flights leaving Geneva International today?"

"Will do."

"Any chance he's got the nuke in the suitcase?"

"If he does, it'll never get past airport security. The Swiss are pretty thorough."

"What's the name of our guy tailing Cardona?"

"Snow... Nicholas Snow."

"Make sure Snow finds out where Cardona's going and gets on the same flight. We can't let this guy out of our sight."

"Got it."

"Anything new on Perez?"

"Business as usual. He still hasn't done anything

suspicious."

"Looks like Perez is going to let his aide do the heavy lifting. Let me know the minute Snow finds out where Cardona is heading."

Ninety minutes later, Drury called back. "Snow overheard Cardona check in for a flight to Toronto. We've got a problem, though. The plane is full and the Swiss Airlines clerk refused to give Snow a seat."

"Get me that clerk on the phone."

"It's too late, Major. The flight's in the air."

Fuller slammed his palm on the desk. "Shit," he said, jaw clenched.

"What do you want to do?"

Fuller closed his eyes, trying to control his anger. "Get the situation room ready and call Bailey in—and call your wife, too. Tell her you may not be home for a while. I'm going to get in touch with Tanaka."

When Fuller relayed the news to Jim Tanaka, the director was still unconvinced. "You've got a Pancho on a plane to Toronto. That's it. No hard evidence of a weapon of any kind. I need a more credible security threat than that before I get the president involved, Major."

"With all due respect, sir. I think you're making a serious mistake."

"Major, this matter has political implications I'm better qualified to assess. We need to protect the president from a major public relations blunder. As serious as this threat may seem to *you*, I can't rule out the possibility we're being deliberately misled. Unless you can give me more reliable information, I see the political repercussions as a bigger hazard."

"Will you at least authorize me to deploy an EODN team?"

"You want to give me that in English? I don't keep up

with all the military mumbo-jumbo."

"It's a six-man unit trained to disarm nuclear devices. They operate totally black. No one will know who they are or what they're doing."

"All right. Taking some quiet precautions can't hurt."

"I'll have an EODN team put on alert. Now that Cardona's on the move, I'll be conducting the operation from the situation room on the second floor. We'll have someone pick up his trail in Toronto."

"Fine. Call me if you get something more tangible."

Like a mushroom cloud? Fuller wanted to say but held his tongue.

Arriving at the second floor situation room, Fuller found Drury tapping on the keyboard of the workstation controlling the data feeds to the large display screen on the wall. "Everything's fired up, Major. Where do you want to start?"

"What kind of assets do we have in Toronto to pick up Cardona's trail?" Fuller asked, settling into one of the high-backed chairs around the central table. He hated to admit it but it felt good to be back in a position of command. The situation room was more than an array of state-of-the-art communications equipment. Every message sent to the field from here was a top priority directive.

"Let me check," Drury answered, his fingers tapping the keyboard. The plasma screen blinked into life and a map of Canada appeared. Drury's cursor moved over Toronto and a screen popped up with the names and contact information for the three CIA agents in the area.

"Get the local honcho on the line," Fuller ordered.

Drury double-clicked on the phone link for the Toronto team leader. After two rings, a confident voice from the overhead speaker said, "Mark Petty."

"Petty, this is Major Michael Fuller at Langley. I have an priority one assignment for your team."

MID ATLANTIC, 45,000 FT.

The flight attendant leaned forward offering a glimpse of cleavage as she handed the Pinot Noir to the handsome young man in 17B. "Can I get you anything else?" she asked, smiling coyly.

Miguel Cardona recognized the enticement in the phrase—and was tempted by the invitation. But this was not the time. "No, thank you," he said smiling.

Gazing out the window at the gathering dusk, Miguel tried to clear his mind. He took a long drink of the wine, hoping it would help him sleep during the nine-hour flight. He needed to be rested and alert when he arrived in Toronto.

The most important deed of his life was almost here. His name would become a part of history, joining the pantheon of men who'd reshaped the Latin world: Bolivar, Zapata, Juarez, Guevara... and soon, Cardona.

Would his mother and father understand? Probably not. He was grateful to his parents for all they'd given him—manners, an education, his monthly stipend, even his green eyes and European features—although they'd be shocked to learn all these had become assets for his cause.

His parents had sent him to Berkeley hoping he'd return to Mexico as a professor of North American history. Instead, he'd lost all traces of an accent while discovering the political philosopher who would change his life: Jose Antonio Marcha.

Miguel had abandoned his bourgeois ambitions and dedicated his life to his people after Marcha's writings opened his eyes. Unlike most in his social class, he'd come to love the people Mexico's elite called nacos, a racist term used to belittle the bulk of their landsmen—the short, brown people descended from the land's indigenous cultures. He'd learned to love the nacos because Marcha had taught him that in the eyes of the gabachos he was no different.

He knew his parents didn't really know or understand him. They supported him financially, replenishing his credit card every month. But they had no idea what he was trying to do for their people. They'd learn soon enough.

LOS ANGELES QUARANTINE ZONE B

Standing beside the Corinthian columns of Holy Trinity church in her best dress, Rosa scanned the street both ways and anxiously shook her head.

She opened one of the church's tall wooden doors and a shaft of sunlight preceded her, illuminating the small group gathered in the dimly-lit vestibule. Mano and the elderly Father Ignacio were closest to the door. Behind them were Pedro on crutches and Sarah holding Daniel, along with the godparents to-be, Chuy Peña and his wife Gloria.

Arms folded tightly across her chest, Rosa approached them. "Isabel said she'd be here. Give her some more time."

"We can't wait any longer, querida," Mano said, stroking her shoulder. "The padre has another baptism after ours."

"Then we'll have to come back another day," Rosa insisted. "Isabel needs to be here."

Mano rubbed his forehead, torn by Rosa's request. Unknown to his wife, he'd arranged for a half-dozen Rebéldes to discreetly provide a security screen around the church. This personal indulgence was something he did not want to demand of his people again. "Rosita, I want to make you happy. But we need to—"

Mano stopped as two sharp whistles echoed toward them from the back of church.

Pedro and Chuy eyes met Mano's as they recognized the security team's warning signal. Mano's stomach tightened as the thumping of a helicopter rose in the distance.

"Should I see what's happening outside?" Chuy asked, trying to keep his voice calm.

"Go," Mano said, nodding his head toward the front doors. As Chuy sprinted away, Mano addressed the others in a steady voice. "It's probably nothing but we need to move to a safer place." As always, Mano had devised an emergency plan, a habit ingrained in him since his days as the security director for La Defensa del Pueblo, the community group that had been the cradle of the rebellion in Southern California.

"Take Pedro's crutches," Mano said to Rosa as he walked to his son. "Put your arm around my neck, m'hijo," he said to Pedro, lifting him until his wounded leg was off the ground. "Follow me," Mano said to the rest, leading them toward the back of the church.

As the sound of the helicopters grew louder, seven pairs of eyes filled with dread rose toward the ceiling.

━━━━

U.S. Marine Lieutenant Don Holt leaned out the door of the Blackhawk, scoping their landing zones as the two-choppers ferrying his platoon closed on the church. The intel on this operation was pretty damn sketchy and that gave Holt a pain in the gut. After getting a tip from the Dalton Gang on the location of the Panchos' top military leader in the area, Captain LaSalle had gone cowboy and sent his platoon into the heart of Zone B without alerting the brass. That meant they really didn't know dick about what to expect.

What little he knew about the mission, Holt didn't like. Their rules of engagement called for being cops instead of soldiers; they could shoot only if fired upon and were limited to non-lethal flashbang grenades. Although these were standard ROE for densely populated areas, Holt hated to see his Marines hamstrung. But as the leader of the only airmobile-trained platoon in the area, no one had asked his opinion.

The lethal twinkle of muzzle flashes appeared from the buildings below as they made their landing approach. Leaning back inside the craft, Holt tapped the chopper's door gunner on the arm and yelled over the noise of the rotors. "Open up with the '50. We're going in hot."

The throbbing of the choppers was deafening by the time Mano and the group reached the sacristy at the back of the church. The chatter of gunfire erupted outside, a din Mano recognized as the helicopters' heavy machine guns in an uneven duel with his fighters' pistols. A cold chill traveled down Mano's spine. The Baldies were about to land.

Lowering Pedro into a chair, Mano signaled the others to stay back and opened the door leading outside. Staying under cover, Mano carefully peered into a paved courtyard about twenty paces wide. They had to get out of the church. If the Baldies managed to surround the isolated building, there would be no escape. Their only hope of safety lay in the apartment complex across the courtyard. Once inside the apartments, they could evade the Baldies in the maze of connected buildings and reach the safe house Mano had arranged for an emergency. From there, they would send for reinforcements if necessary.

"Two Baldie choppers have landed," yelled Chuy, rushing into the sacristy from inside the church. "Our people are trying to hold them off but we're outgunned."

"We need to reach those apartments," Mano said, pointing to the doorway across the courtyard. "Everybody get ready to run on my signal."

"Are you sure, Mano?" Chuy asked. "It's going to be risky crossing that open space."

"It's more dangerous to stay," Mano answered. "Chuy, when I give the word, you go first and set up covering fire from the doorway. The rest of you will run when I tell you... and keep running until you're all the way inside the building. Understand?"

"Got it," Chuy said as the others nodded.

Mano glanced outside. The area looked clear. "All right, Chuy... Go!"

As Chuy sprinted across the courtyard, Mano waved for the others to join him by the door. "Padre, you'll go next... Rosa, you and Gloria help Sarah with the baby... I'll follow you with Pedro."

"I wish God had blessed me your courage, my son," Father Ignacio said trembling.

"I'm as scared as you are, padre," Mano said, patting the old man's shoulder. "I've just had more experience hiding it."

Mano watched as Chuy reached the apartment doorway, drew his pistol and took a firing position. Glancing back at Mano, Chuy gave him the thumbs up sign. "Let's move!" Mano called out.

Running in an awkward crouch, Father Ignacio made his way across the courtyard with the women and baby close behind. Mano lifted Pedro onto his shoulder. "Come on, m'hijo," Mano said. "We don't want to keep the family waiting."

Father Ignacio was nearly halfway to the apartments when Chuy began firing toward Mano's right. Looking in that direction, Mano saw two Baldies take cover behind the corner of the church. With any luck, Chuy would keep the soldiers pinned down until they could make it to safety.

Then their luck changed.

The priest, startled by Chuy's gunfire, stumbled to the pavement. Following close on his heels, the women tripped over the old man, sending the entire group down in a heap.

"Go help them!" Pedro said to his father, untangling from Mano's arms.

Mano had made more life-and-death decisions under fire than he could remember—but never a harder one. "I'll come back for you," he said, letting go of his son. But as Mano charged ahead, another member of his family was about to change the equation.

Staring over the sights of an AK-47, Isabel watched Mano and the others from a second floor window overlooking the courtyard.

The moment she had been waiting for was not turning out as she'd expected.

Her day of revenge had arrived at last and she'd wanted to savor it. But the thrill of vengeance had never come. Even worse, she'd dreamed of Pedro's death last night and felt wounded by his loss. But she would not give in to weakness. Angel had been strong, never showing pity or remorse. She would honor her brother's memory and live by his example.

Angel would have been proud of her cunning in tipping off the Baldies—and in choosing this hiding spot. Although she hoped the Baldies would capture or kill the Suarez family inside the church, if they managed to escape it would happen below her, through the exit toward these apartments. Sure enough, there they were, all of them in one place—easy targets under the sights of her rifle. From her hidden perch she could finish them all and no one would ever know.

So why haven't I pulled the trigger? she asked herself.

Trying to work herself into a rage, she replayed the conversation she'd overheard through the bedroom window between Pedro and Sarah. The words seemed to have no meaning, like a movie in a foreign language.

Below her, she watched Mano leave his son behind and blanket the others with his large body, trying to shield them from the bullets. This was not what Isabel had expected. Did Mano deserve to die? Her brother had told her how many lives Mano had saved—including Angel's.

And Pedro? What had her husband done to deserve a death sentence? His only crime had been lying to her about the accidental death of her brother. Was he really her enemy?

When the Baldies began firing again, Isabel had her answer.

———

The Baldies taking cover at the corner of the church both leaned out at once—one high and one low—each firing a long burst from their M4s toward Chuy. With two targets at once, Chuy knew he was outgunned. Heart thudding in his chest, he ducked behind the doorway as a hail of bullets struck like hammer blows against the concrete wall. Sticking his head out to fire back at the Baldies now would likely cost him his life.

Although out of sight from the Baldies, Chuy could still see Mano and the others in the courtyard. "Stay down!" He yelled to Mano, while reloading his pistol. "The Baldies have the doorway covered."

Then, as if coming from a guardian angel, someone above him opened fire with the distinctive bark of an AK-47. *Please, señor. Let it be one of ours*, Chuy prayed as he leaned out from the protection of the doorway and opened fire toward the Baldies. To Chuy's relief, the Baldies had once again ducked behind cover.

"We're clear, Mano! We're clear!" Chuy yelled, waving for the people stranded in the courtyard to advance. "Hurry!"

Seizing the momentary advantage, Mano helped the priest and women to their feet and quickly ushered them past Chuy into the safety of the apartment building. Pedro was still hobbling in the courtyard when the Baldies massed their fire again. This time, there were four soldiers shooting from the corner of the building.

About five paces from safety, Pedro dove for the ground as a hail of bullets pocked the concrete wall of the apartment. Chuy ducked inside as Mano arrived at his side, his own pistol at the ready. "Rosa's taking the others to our safe house. Your wife is safe," Mano assured Chuy.

Chuy nodded in thanks.

"You need to get out of here," Pedro called out to them. "Throw me a gun and I'll hold them off."

Before he could answer, Mano heard footsteps behind him. He turned in time to see Isabel charge past him into the courtyard at a run, firing her AK-47 toward the Baldies. Mano reached for her, trying to keep Isabel behind the cover of the doorway but she eluded his grasp.

Isabel was cut down after just three steps, her slender body knocked backward by the bullets that ripped through her, leaving pink trails of blood and flesh.

Chuy watched in shock, frozen by grisly spectacle. Mano and Pedro were transfixed in horror as well. Their spell was broken by a heavy *clunk* as a cylindrical flashbang grenade landed on the pavement in front of them.

A blinding white flash consumed Chuy's world. An eye blink later came a detonation so loud it struck him like a punch to the temple. Staggered, Chuy fell back against the wall, coughing as a gray cloud enveloped him. When the smoke cleared, the world started to make sense again.

Fortunately for Chuy, the corner of the doorway had protected him from the brunt of the Baldies' non-lethal grenade. The other two Rebéldes had not been as lucky. Pedro was unconscious, bleeding from the ears and sprawled in the courtyard. Mano was on his back, trying to raise himself but too disoriented to move.

"First squad, move in!" Chuy heard in the distance. The Baldies were closing and Chuy needed to buy time. Sticking his pistol around the corner of the doorway, Chuy fired off an unaimed flurry of rounds. That would buy him a few precious seconds—maybe enough time to save Mano. Helping Pedro was hopeless. If he emerged from cover to reach Pedro, the Baldies would cut him down as they had Isabel.

"Come on," Chuy said, tugging on Mano's heavy frame, "we need to get out of here." As he laboriously dragged Mano deeper into the safety of the building, Chuy looked back at Pedro, still unconscious on the pavement. *Adios, hermano. It was an honor fighting at your side*," he said silently.

Nearly an hour after Fuller and Drury had set up shop in the situation room, Sonya Bailey arrived dressed in civvies. "Sorry I couldn't get here sooner, sir. I was on my way to Baltimore when you called."

"Stand by, Lieutenant," Fuller said before looking at his watch. "We may need you to make a food run soon."

"Yes, sir," Bailey answered, taking a seat at the table.

Despite all the other demands on his attention, Fuller could not ignore the way Bailey's jogging suit clung to the curves of her body. Lust aside, Bailey's arrival gave Michael Fuller a new puzzle to ponder.

If the lieutenant was indeed a Pentagon spy, her presence might actually be an asset. Should things go south on this operation, at least the Pentagon would have a witness to document how the Nixon people had failed to protect the country. He had nothing to hide—except his pipeline to the Panchos. In the meantime, Bailey would at least be useful as a gopher if this turned into a marathon session.

"Major, I just got an email confirming that our Toronto team has an agent ready to intercept Cardona at the airport at 1900 hours," Drury reported.

"Thanks, Jeff," Fuller answered. "Deploy the rest of the local team to cover the Port of Toronto. I'm betting the bomb is coming in by boat."

"I think you're right, sir," Bailey added. "There's no way they'd get a nuke past the air cargo detectors. Does our Toronto team have Geigers?"

"No, we already checked."

"I know of some Geigers at Quantico. I can requisition them and call a commercial carrier for delivery. We can probably get them there in four hours."

"Do it," Fuller said, pleasantly surprised. Maybe the

young lieutenant might be useful for something more than fetching coffee and sandwiches.

A short while later, after a flurry of phone calls, Bailey emerged from one of the adjacent glass-walled rooms. "The Geigers are on the way, Major," she reported.

Fuller nodded. "Good work, Lieutenant."

"Sir, what's your take on Cardona's target?" Bailey asked, taking a seat at the table.

"It's got to be Manhattan... high profile... heavy population density. You couldn't come up with a better target for a small nuke. Problem is, we'll have to wait until Cardona crosses into the U.S. before we nab him."

"I take it the Canadians are still being pissy about extradition?"

"Absolutely. Their PM likes Nixon, but Parliament acts like his great uncle is still the president."

"That's going to make it tougher."

"Yeah. I've been trying to figure out where Cardona will cross the border," Fuller said, gesturing to the map of upstate New York on the wall plasma. "I doubt he'll go west around Lake Ontario and cross at Buffalo. There are only three bridges across the river there and they all have checkpoints. He'll probably head east of the lake and cross somewhere in the rural areas around the Adirondacks. Only two of those roads have border checkpoints. In any case, we've already alerted the Border Patrol. They're putting out a bulletin on Cardona for every checkpoint in upstate New York."

"Do we have any assets in the area we can deploy?"

"Jeff's already checked. We have only one agent in Syracuse, but there's a National Guard motorized battalion on stateside rotation in Albany. We'll use them to set up roadblocks on the unguarded roads. I've got a call in to their CO."

Bailey pointed to the photo of Miguel Cardona inset on the plasma screen. In his early twenties with chiseled features, sandy hair and green eyes, Cardona looked more like a WASP Ivy Leaguer than a Latino radical. "We should circulate Cardona's picture, sir. If the Border Patrol and the Guardsmen are looking for a guy they think looks Hispanic, they're probably going to miss him."

Fuller nodded in agreement. "I remember when the Panchos infiltrated our camp with a black Latino back at Outpost Bravo. The sooner our side figures out that Hispanics come in every color, the fewer chances we have of getting sucker punched."

TORONTO, CANADA

Pulling his wheeled carry-on case, Miguel Cardona exited the jetway and merged into the stream of bodies flowing through the terminal. After traveling with the herd for several hundred meters, he made his way into a men's room.

Entering one of the stalls, Cardona took off his navy sports coat, opened his case and pulled out a pair of sweat pants, a red nylon jacket, sunglasses, and a ball cap. Slipping these items over his clothes, he walked out of the stall, leaving the suitcase behind.

Melting back into the moving crowd, Cardona walked to the escalators and rode the one heading down. He waited for a moment and then took the escalator back up, watching for anyone behind him doing the same. Convinced no one was following him, he walked outside and got into a taxi.

LANGLEY, VA

The embarrassment in Petty's voice was evident over the situation room's speaker. "I lost him... I lost Cardona at the airport, sir," he said haltingly. "I followed him into a restroom and found his coat and carry-on case in one of the stalls. He must have changed clothes."

Fuller's face flushed with anger, but his voice stayed calm. "Thank you, Petty. We'll let you know if we need anything else," he said and disconnected.

Drury buried his face in his hands. "We're screwed."

"We need possibilities, right now, not pessimism," Fuller said, pressing his hands together tightly.

After a long pause, Bailey said, "Credit card records?"

Fuller rubbed his chin, mulling Bailey's idea. "You really think Cardona would use a credit card, Sonya?"

"No way," Drury said, his voice deriding. "This guy's too cagey. Why wouldn't he just use cash?"

Bailey smiled. "For the same reason you wouldn't. He probably doesn't have it. Cardona may be smart, Jeff, but he's not loaded. He bought an economy ticket, remember? The dossier on Cardona said he depends completely on his parents for money. Perez pays him nothing. I think he'll use a credit card—and it'll be his own. It takes some serious coin to set up fake identities."

"I have to agree," Fuller added.

"Even so," Drury insisted. "That still leaves us with hundreds of credit card issuers and thousands of vendors to check around Toronto."

"I admit it's a long shot, but what else have we got?" Bailey countered.

Fuller nodded approvingly. "Let's cross-check all the credit card issuers against hotels and rental car companies in the Toronto area. If we look in the most likely places first, we'll improve our chances of finding him."

Drury rolled his eyes. "That could take all night, Major."

Fuller patted his tech officer's shoulder. "Then you better get started right away."

LOS ANGELES QUARANTINE ZONE B

Sarah walked to the apartment window again and looked out toward the weed-choked patio. There was still no sign of the men.

"Sit down, m'hija," Rosa called out to Sarah, patting the floor beside her. "Save your energy. We may need to move again."

Holding Daniel in her lap, Gloria spoke to the baby in a playful voice. "Tell your mámi to relax, little man. She doesn't need to get all worried."

But worried she was. Sarah could not shake the feeling that the soldiers' raid had somehow been her fault. "Why are we waiting here?" she asked Rosa. "Why don't we just go home?"

Rosa answered her with the patience of a kindergarten teacher. "Home may not be the safest place to go right now, m'hija. If the Baldies came for us in the church, they might know where we live, too. We have to wait until our people make sure it's safe to go back home," she explained. "Come on. Sit down."

Sarah nodded, suddenly understanding why one of the young men in the safe house had led Father Ignacio away. The soldiers would be looking for a group of people and a priest. Sarah settled next to Rosa. "I don't know how you stay so calm."

Rosa smiled. "I was like you at first, back when Mano got involved in all of this. But there's something you learn after a while. No amount of worrying has ever stopped a bullet."

Leaning her head against Rosa's shoulder, Sarah closed her eyes. She'd expected her life would be difficult inside the zones. But how much longer could she face the threat of death every day? Then she recalled something that made her feel ashamed. She'd made a choice to live here. Pedro and his family had not.

Sarah heard footsteps outside and rose to her feet as the door opened. Chuy and another young man carried Mano into the room, struggling to support his large frame.

"Mano's just shaken up, señora," Chuy said to Rosa as they carefully laid the big man on the floor. "He'll come around in a minute."

"Where's Pedro?" Sarah asked, her voice breaking with emotion.

Chuy lowered his head. "The Baldies have him. He was still in the courtyard when they threw a stun grenade." Chuy looked up, nearly in tears. "I'm sorry. I could only save Mano."

"I know you did the best you could, Chuy," Rosa said, then turned away, palm pressed against her lips.

"There's more bad news, señora, " Chuy said, eyes downcast. "Isabel showed up during the firefight... She was gunned down by the Baldies."

"It's my fault," Sarah said, her face twisted with pain. "The soldiers came because I was here."

Rosa drew Sarah to her. "No, m'hija. Don't blame yourself. Only God knows why these things happen."

"I'll go to the soldiers and bring Pedro back," Sarah said suddenly. "I'll tell them how he saved me and Mike Fuller."

"No..." Mano said hoarsely still lying on the floor, eyes beginning to open.

Rosa knelt beside him as every face in the room turned toward the rebel leader. "What are you trying to say, mi amor?"

"The Baldies... they won't believe you, Sarah," Mano said slowly sitting up. "They'll ask too many questions and make things worse."

Sarah moved closer to Mano. "There's got to be something we can do."

"I want Pedro back as much as you do, Sarah," Mano answered, rising unsteadily to his feet. "But we can't put more people in danger trying to save him."

Unexpectedly, a memory from her time as a hostage filled Sarah's mind. She was back in the dank, pitch-black underground cell, scared and disoriented. She'd lost all hope. The only question left was how her life would end. *Pedro is feeling the same right now*, she realized.

When Sarah next spoke, she felt as if they were someone else's words. "Tell the soldiers I'm a hostage and you'll trade me for Pedro. You can give me that fake identity you talked about," she said to Mano. "If Mike Fuller backs up the story they'll believe it."

Mano rubbed his face, troubled by the idea but sensing her plan might succeed. "The cover story won't work if you have Daniel with you."

"I know," Sarah said, looking at the floor.

"Sarah, if something goes wrong, the Baldies will send you to jail," Mano added.

"I don't care."

"Don't let her do this, Mano," Rosa pleaded.

Sarah gathered her strength for what she had to say next. "I don't want to stay here anymore," she said to Rosa. "Daniel will be better off if he grows up here and doesn't know anything about me. I want to go home."

THE PRODIGAL—Day 6

DETROIT, MI

The Border Patrol guard leaned closer to the silver Impala's window, comparing the photo on the Canadian passport with the driver's face. "Your reason for visiting the United States, Mr. Branch?"

"Business," the young man behind the wheel answered.

"How long do you plan to stay?"

"Three days, ma'am."

The guard handed back the young man's passport and driver's license. "Enjoy your visit," she said and waved for the next car in line.

Cardona was well into the tunnel toward Detroit before a smile spread across his face. He'd done it. He'd made it across the border. The forged passport had been painfully expensive but had worked flawlessly.

Octavio had insisted on taking every precaution. "Remember," he'd told him, "you are the matador and the gabachos are the bull. Use their size and their power against them. Flash the cape to get their attention and then let them charge at air." That's why Miguel had flown into Toronto and changed clothes at the airport, then rented a car and driven almost 300 miles to cross the border in Detroit and then south to Toledo. Although the likelihood he'd be followed was slight, they were taking no chances.

The only weak point in their plan was a minor one: using his personal credit card. But without his money, there would have been no operation. So this was a risk he'd have to take—a small price to pay for immortality.

It was nearly one in the morning. when Cardona pulled the silver Impala into the parking lot of the Regency Motor Lodge near downtown Toledo and checked into the low-end motel. The five-hour drive from Toronto had been uneventful—exactly as he'd hoped. Lying in bed in the threadbare room, Miguel felt exhausted but could not sleep. *Tomorrow will be a day of fate,* he told himself, *a day for a monumental deed.*

OUTPOST BRAVO, CA

When Pedro regained consciousness, the throbbing pain at the base of his neck was the only element in his universe. Disjointed images of the firefight outside the church drifted into his mind, gradually bringing him into the present. His eyes fluttered open, scanning the dimly-lit space around him but unable to focus. Finally, as his vision cleared, he took stock of his surroundings.

He was in a communal shower room, lying shirtless on the floor, his face against the hard coldness of ceramic tiles with the lingering scent of disinfectant. He tried to move but realized his hands were bound behind his back around a pillar. The only light source came from an open doorway about five paces away. As he struggled to sit up, a shadowy figure near the doorway called out. "The Pancho's coming to, Captain."

A bright lamp shone suddenly in Pedro's face, making him squint, as the captain entered the room. Pedro could see the boots and legs of the officer's camo fatigues but the rest of the man remained in shadow.

"You speak English?" the captain asked in an accent that Pedro suspected was from a big East Coast city.

Pedro stared straight ahead in silence.

"Corporal, if this Pancho doesn't answer me in five seconds, put a bullet in his head," the officer said in a steady voice.

Unconsciously, Pedro's eyes shifted toward the shape of the guard near the door.

"So you do speak English," the captain said with a small laugh. "Belay that order, Corporal. I think we can come to an understanding with this gentleman. What's your name, amigo?"

After Pedro again refused to answer, the officer tried a different tack.

"Your people left you behind, amigo," the captain said. "Seems to me, you don't owe them shit. You tell me where we can find Manolo Suarez and I'll ask them to go easy on you."

Pedro held back a smile at the officer's crude ploy. Even if he'd considered for a second betraying his father, he knew the needle law made no exceptions. A death sentence awaited him, regardless of anything he said.

"I know what you're thinking," the captain said softly at first, then with growing intensity. "You're going to die anyway so why talk, right? Well, let me tell you something, amigo. We may have regs against torturing prisoners these days but I've got guys in my unit who've lost friends to terrorist pricks like you. And they'd like nothing better than for me to bring them in here and go out for a smoke. After that happens, believe me, you'll wish you were dead. So, how about it? You want to start by telling me your name?"

Pedro still refused to speak.

"All right, then," the captain said, stepping back from

Pedro. "Corporal, get a mop and bucket ready. It's going to get real messy in here," he said before turning out the light and leaving.

LANGLEY, VA

Fuller refilled Drury' coffee cup from a large silver thermos. "This jug's done," he said, rising from the table. "I'll go put on a fresh pot."

"Let me do that," Bailey offered.

"Don't bother, Sonya. I'm beyond caffeine," Drury said, looking up from the terminal, his eyes bleary. "Major, it's close to two in the morning. I need some sleep."

Fuller locked his tech officer in a hard stare. "Look, Jeff. I don't think I'll ever sleep well again if that bomb explodes somewhere in this country. We've got to come up with something."

"You're right. I'm sorry," Drury said wearily. "We should be getting the results back from the latest batch of card records soon."

Fuller turned to Bailey and said, "Cardona should have reached the border by now. You think the roadblocks scared him off?"

"That's possible. But at least we're keeping him out of Manhattan... and it buys us more time to track him down."

The chime of an incoming e-mail riveted their attention. "It looks like the transaction records are here," Drury said. "Let me get the attachments on the big screen." A moment later, a long list of names and account numbers appeared on the wall plasma. "We've got over eleven thousand credit card transaction in this batch. Cross your fingers or finger your crosses. I'm going to run the search query."

Drury typed *Cardona, Miguel* into the search box, sighed deeply, and clicked *Run*.

For an instant, the screen went black. When it blinked back on, a single record in the long list was highlighted. "Hot damn! I think we finally got something!" Drury shouted. He double-clicked on the highlighted record and details of the transaction appeared on the screen.

"What's it mean. Jeff?" Fuller asked, unable to decipher the cryptic mix of computer code, real words, and abbreviations.

"Cardona rented a new Impala in Toronto just over eight hours ago. Length of rental is five days. We've got the license number, color, and the VIN."

"Good work," Fuller said, slapping Drury on the back. "Let's get this information out to the field. It's going to be a hell of a lot easier to find Cardona now."

Bailey scratched her head. "Something about this seems fishy. If Cardona is hard up for money, why would he rent the car for five days?"

"To avoid raising suspicions," Drury offered.

Bailey shook her head. "I don't think so. If Cardona had expected us to track his car rental records, he wouldn't have used his own card. No, if he rented the car for five days, I think it's because he needed it."

Fuller's eyebrows furrowed. "I don't like where this is going, Sonya."

"I don't either," Bailey answered. "But when you consider that Cardona hasn't tried to cross a border that's only two hours away and still chose a five-day rental, I think there's a good chance he may be headed somewhere besides New York City."

"Jeff, put up the map of the Great Lakes again." After the image appeared on the big screen, Fuller said, "We've got every entry into New York State covered around Lake Ontario. But what if he rolled west over Lake Erie to Michigan?"

"Detroit... " Bailey said, tapping her lips, considering the idea. "It's not Manhattan. But it's still a big target."

"That's got to be his play," Fuller said, nodding. "Jeff, get me the chief of the Border Patrol in Detroit. I want the surveillance videos of all the traffic crossing the border into Michigan for the last ten hours."

"He's probably sleeping, Major."

"Well, wake his ass up. I'm not in a mood to be polite right now."

After a heated discussion with the sleepy Border Patrol director, Fuller got what he wanted. The Border Patrol would issue an alert for Cardona and provide the traffic surveillance videos within the hour. The digital recordings, angled to capture license plate numbers, were posted to a secure FTP site. Drury then copied the videos into a pattern recognition program that would examine the thirty hours of tape from two different checkpoints looking for the license number of Cardona's Impala. Despite being totally automated, the process would take almost three hours.

Fuller looked at the clock over the main screen. The digital display read 0312. "Not much we can do here until the computer's finished processing those tapes. You two go home and be back here at 0600 hours. I'll mind the store."

Drury yawned and slowly rose from his chair. "See you later," he said, walking wearily out of the room.

"Think I'll stay, sir," Bailey said to Fuller after the two of them were alone. "I don't think I can sleep anyway."

"Suit yourself, Lieutenant," Fuller said. "I'm going for a drive. Getting away from this place might clear my head. And we could use some fresh ideas." Although telling the truth, Fuller had a second motive for leaving. He wanted to check with Garcia for any new information, something he did not dare from any computer system inside CIA headquarters.

Bailey met his eyes. "Mind if I join you?"

From somewhere deep in his libido, Fuller suddenly imagined checking into a room with Sonya and slowly undressing her... the feel of her thighs against his... her hot breath rasping in his ear... He rose abruptly from his chair. "I don't think that would be... uh, productive," he said awkwardly before leaving the situation room.

Ten minutes later, Fuller entered a public Internet kiosk at an I-495 rest area and logged into his web link with Garcia. The message waiting for him left him conflicted and dismayed.

> We are awaiting confirmation that you have successfully tailed Perez and Cardona. In the meantime, another crisis has emerged.
>
> The son of your warrior colleague was captured in a U.S. Army raid at a church in LAQZB today. Your colleague asks for your help in releasing his son. He makes it clear this would be a personal favor and is not conditional to our cooperation in stopping Perez and Cardona. The daughter of your dead coworker has offered herself for a hostage exchange to save the father of her child. Will you help?

Damn you, Garcia. This is too much, Fuller said silently. He was ass-deep in an operation to stop a nuclear attack and now the Panchos were asking him to help free Suarez's son. *These text messages aren't going to work anymore*, Fuller realized. There were too many questions he needed to ask Garcia and not enough time to wait for written answers.

Fuller looked at his watch. The time in Geneva was just after nine in the morning. Garcia would be awake. Rising from the Internet station, he walked a few steps to a pay phone in the empty rest area. After memorizing the number printed above the dial pad, he returned to the terminal, typed in the number and added...

Urgent that we speak. Call this pay phone in the next ten minutes. The call will be secure if you use a public phone.

As Fuller waited for the call, a chilling thought entered his mind. *At what point will I be crossing the line into treason in order to keep my word?*

GENEVA, SWITZERLAND

Checking his vu-phone from the back seat of the chauffeured Audi, Ramon read Fuller's message. So the major wants to talk, he noted. That's encouraging.

Spotting a telephone booth along the Rue des Bains, Ramon asked the driver to pull over. *This morning's meeting with the Belgian legation will have to wait,* Ramon thought as he got out of the car. Inside the minimalist metal and glass-walled booth, Ramon dialed the number. After one ring, a deep male voice answered the line.

"I don't like where this is headed."

"Believe me, I don't either." Ramon replied. "What's the situation with our two suspects?"

"Cardona flew into Toronto but we lost his trail there."

"Shit," Ramon muttered. "Any way we can help?"

"You have any assets in Canada? Someplace we can look for him?"

Ramon mulled his answer. "No," he said after a pause.

"You expect me to believe that?"

"Look, I just revealed a weakness of ours. I could have sent you on a goose chase to mislead you about it. But we don't have time for that.

"You're right about not having much time. So why did you dump the kid's capture in my lap?"

"You don't have to help. Your warrior colleague insisted we make this request unconditional."

"Good. Because I'd have no qualms about turning your ass in if you tried to blackmail me."

"I understand."

"What was he doing when he was captured?"

"At a church for his son's baptism. We think somebody ratted out his father and the son wound up getting caught."

"So what do you expect me to do about the kid?"

"If you tell the commander of the unit that captured him the CIA needs a Pancho for a hostage exchange in a black operation, they'll probably release him to you. We can say the girl's a diplomat's daughter. That would explain why you'd want to trade the boy for her."

"Let me get this straight. You're asking me to lie to the people on my side to save somebody on yours—and you're asking me to do it in the middle of an operation that could cost God knows how many American lives if it fails?"

"Exactly—but keep this in mind. The father of that 'someone' on our side saved your life."

After a long pause, Fuller answered. "All right. I've got a couple of hours until our next move. I'll make some calls and find out who's holding him. I'm not promising anything beyond that. Let's talk again in four hours. I'll post the number online for you to call beforehand," he said before ending the call.

Walking back to his car, Ramon wondered what Pedro's chances were to survive. Right now, it looked like very long odds. But their chances of stopping Cardona and Perez looked even worse.

LANGLEY, VA

"Yes, I'll be in touch about the prisoner," Fuller said into the desk phone as Sonya Bailey entered the situation room. "I have to go now, Captain," he said quickly before hanging up.

"Prisoner?" Bailey asked, handing him one of three coffees from the take out tray she was carrying. "Have we got another lead on Cardona?"

"It's most likely a dead end," Fuller said, accepting the cardboard coffee cup. "I see you're back early."

"Yeah, I tried to sleep but I'm too wired. A long, hot shower helped, though."

Sonya's words conjured the image of her naked and glistening. The salacious thought only added to his sense of guilt.

Lying to the CO of the unit holding Pedro had shamed him. But Garcia had been right. The Marine captain had seemed in awe at being part of a black operation with the CIA. The officer had followed Fuller's orders about a hostage exchange without question. The problem now would be coordinating the hostage exchange without tipping off Bailey and Drury—and still finding Cardona in time.

When Drury arrived a short while later, he accessed the computer program with the analysis of the license plate videos. "Major," he said, face suddenly pale. "Cardona's vehicle crossed the border into Detroit just before midnight."

"He's a cagey bastard," Fuller said, rubbing his chin.

"We ought to tell Tanaka," said Drury.

Fuller shook his head. "No, Tanaka's going to say we haven't got anything new. We're on our own on this one."

"Should we deploy the EODN team?" Bailey asked.

"Good idea, Sonya. Have the EODN team flown to Detroit and arrange for ground transportation. We need to alert our own assets there as well. We're over six hours behind this guy... and we haven't got a lot more time," Fuller said gravely. "Jeff, I need you to—"

"I know. I know," Drury moaned, slumping into his

chair. "I'll start the credit card searches for hotels and restaurants around Detroit right away."

OUTPOST BRAVO, CA

Pedro heard footsteps in the corridor. A hour had passed, maybe more, since the officer had left. Taking deep breaths, he tried to steel himself, determined not to weaken. No matter what they did to him, he would concentrate on his son. He needed to think about how ashamed Daniel would be if his father ever betrayed his family.

The officer turned on the lamp and walked into the cone of light, revealing a ruddy, freckled face under the kevlar helmet. The name patch above his right pocket read LaSalle. *I'm not leaving this room alive*, Pedro realized suddenly and swallowed hard. His only regret was that he would never know his son.

The officer's hard laugh chilled Pedro. "Amigo, I know your people like to gamble, bet on chicken fights and shit like that," the captain said. "But if I was you, I'd never place another bet again. Because all the fucking luck you'll ever have in this life has been used up."

THE PRODIGAL—Day 7

TOLEDO, OH

Miguel Cardona lifted his head from the pillow and looked at the clock again. Glowing blue in the darkness of the motel room, the digital numerals advanced silently to 5:46. Conceding that sleep was impossible, he rose, showered, and dressed. After a complimentary breakfast of stale pastry and instant coffee in the lobby of the three-story motel, Cardona put the room's plastic passkey on the counter and walked outside.

Toledo was coming to life as traffic from the suburbs moved haltingly past the Regency Motor Inn into the central business district. Cardona studied the long line of cars creeping past the offices and small shops lining the street and smiled. Soon the population of downtown Toledo would be swollen with suburban workers. They'd chosen the time and place of their target well.

Attacking a minor city in the center of the States had been his idea. He'd convinced Octavio it would strike fear into the hearts of the gabachos more deeply than bombing a major coastal city. No one in the U.S.A. would ever feel safe again, he'd argued. And with a lightly guarded seaport, the operation would be easier to execute in Toledo as well. Finally, the city had no Quarantine Zone, avoiding loss of life to their own.

Walking four blocks, Cardona entered the EconoCar office at the end of a strip mall. Twenty minutes later, he drove away in a dark green Taurus.

LANGLEY, VA

"That's the last batch of transaction records, Major," Drury said, staring numbly at the monitor. "Detroit's a dry hole. I couldn't find a damn thing for Cardona's card at any hotel or restaurant."

Fuller looked at his watch. Drury had been searching just over three hours. "Why did the Toronto search take so much longer?"

"We know Cardona's credit card issuer this time around."

"Are you sure about Detroit, Jeff?"

"Yeah. I'm sure."

Fuller rose and pointed to the plasma map. "Then we need to widen our search. The next big city is Cleveland. It's about a three-hour drive around the lake from Detroit."

"Lansing, Flint, and Toledo are closer," Bailey said, studying the map.

"You can throw out Lansing and Flint," Fuller countered. "They don't have seaports. Toledo's a possibility, though. It has a port on the Maumee River." Fuller rubbed his temples, weighing the decision. *It's time to go all in*, he realized. They didn't have time to cover both cities. As a military officer, he'd choose Cleveland. It was farther away but a bigger target. He'd accept the risks. But Cardona was not military, he was a spy. And there was a spy in the room.

Fuller turned to Bailey. "Cleveland is bigger. Toledo is closer. Which would you choose if you were Cardona?"

"I'd get the hell out of Dodge as soon as possible,

Major," she said. "From Toledo, I could jump back across the border in an hour."

Fuller nodded, his mind made up. "All right. Let's start with Toledo, Jeff."

Drury tapped on the keyboard for a few seconds, then groaned. "There's a fly in that soup, Major," he said, shoulders slumping. "We don't have any assets in Toledo."

"Dammit!" Fuller said, then quickly composed himself. "Sorry, Jeff. That's not your fault. Sonya, send down some agents from Detroit. And have them bring Geigers if they have them."

TOLEDO, OH

Cardona lowered the window of the Taurus, handed the Port Authority guard a bill of lading and said, "I'm here to inspect a shipment."

The aging guard slid his bifocals toward the end of his nose and scanned the document. "You got any ID?"

Cardona handed him the Canadian passport and the guard gave it a cursory glance.

"Fill this out," he said, handing Cardona a visitor's log-in sheet on a clipboard.

After Cardona had completed the form, the guard handed him a key. "Your shipment is in warehouse Ell. It's about a quarter mile down on the right," he said, pointing to a row of rusty, weed-lined metal buildings facing the river.

Cardona parked the Taurus near the back entrance to the warehouse, unlocked the padlocked door, and went inside. His heart raced as he walked along the cluttered rows of crates and shipping containers. In a dark corner, Cardona found the shipment he was looking for, a crate of Chinese pipe couplings labeled BRC1992.

Hands sweating, Cardona pried open the wooden crate

and carefully dug through the plastic couplings until he found a hard vinyl briefcase wrapped in a packing blanket. He looked warily around the empty warehouse, then entered the combination that unlocked the case.

As he lifted the lid, the dull gleam of brushed stainless steel shone from the face of the bomb. The surprisingly simple array of dials and buttons matched the drawings he had memorized. His fingers trembled as he ran them over the weapon. Under his hand was a power few men on earth had ever unleashed.

Before locking the briefcase, Cardona removed the automatic pistol and two ammo clips secured on the inside of the lid and tucked them into the pocket of his nylon jacket. Struggling to keep his composure, he carried the bomb to the car and placed it in the trunk. Twenty minutes later, he was back in downtown Toledo.

LANGLEY, VA

"I've got something, Major!" Drury called out, pointing to his screen. "Cardona checked into a motel in Toledo last night!" Fuller and Bailey rushed to look over Drury' shoulder as he typed furiously on the keyboard. "There's more... he checked out of the Regency Motor Lodge this morning at 7:25."

"That was over an hour ago. Our Detroit team should be in the area by now," Bailey noted.

"Jeff, send our Detroit guys to the hotel right away. I want to question the manager and anyone who may have seen Cardona."

"You want to bring in the locals as a backup?"

"No. If we have uniforms around, it might spook Cardona. But I want you to dispatch any assets we have within an hour's drive to Toledo." Fuller wheeled in his chair to face Bailey. "Bailey, let's move the EODN team in there, too."

Bailey nodded and said, "I'll check with the Port Authority and see if they've spotted Cardona's car around the docks anywhere."

"Good idea."

Twenty minutes later, a call arrived from one of the Detroit agents. The plasma screen identified her as Senior Agent Ashley Vail. Fuller pressed the speaker button. "Go ahead, Vail."

"We found the suspect's silver Impala in the parking lot of the Regency Motor Lodge, sir."

Fuller looked stunned. This was not what he'd expected. "Have you questioned anyone at the hotel?"

"No, sir. We noticed the car as we pulled in."

"Hold on a minute, Vail," Fuller said and muted the connection. "What do you make of that, Bailey?"

"Two things... Cardona could be on foot somewhere in the area. Or the bomb could be in that car and he's already bugged out."

Fuller reconnected the speaker. "Do you have a Geiger, Vail?"

"Yes, sir."

"Good. I want you to park near the Impala and sweep it—but don't make it obvious. Cardona could still be in the area. While you're doing that, have your partner question the staff—very discreetly."

"Understood, sir. I'll call when we have something," Vail said and disconnected.

Fuller kneaded his hands. "If they find anything more radioactive on that car than a glow in the dark dial, I'm calling Tanaka." *He can't keep burying his head in the sand much longer*, he said to himself.

Vail called again eleven minutes later. "I swept the car,

sir. No signs of unusual radiation."

Fuller swallowed hard, relieved yet bewildered. "All right, Vail. Stake out the car for now and let us know what you come up with after questioning the staff."

"Will do, sir."

Fuller stared at the ceiling. *Could Tanaka be right?* he wondered, rubbing his hands. *Is this a dodge to distract us?* No, it wasn't likely. If the Latino Liberation Front was scamming him, they would have made it easier. Cardona wouldn't have changed clothes at the airport. He would have headed straight for Manhattan, too. That was the obvious play. This operation had to be real.

Fuller looked at the clock on the plasma display. It was nearly 10:00. "That car's been sitting there for over an hour and a half. How far could Cardona walk in that time?"

"Seven or eight klicks," Bailey answered.

"Jeff, give us a look at Toledo at that scale, will you?"

As Drury zoomed in on the view of the Great Lakes, Bailey said, "Why assume he's still on foot?"

"Of course!" Fuller said excitedly. "Bill, get a list of car rental companies within ten kilometers of the hotel and check for Cardona's card. That son of a bitch has probably switched cars."

"Getting the list of rental car companies is easy, Major," Drury said. "But I'll still need to get clearance and run separate scans on each car company to check for Cardona's card."

"How long will that take?"

"About a half hour."

Fuller looked at the clock. He had fifteen minutes until his next call to Garcia. "Get started on the credit card checks, Jeff." Rising from the table, Fuller walked to the door. "I'm going to call Tanaka again," he said before leaving the situation room.

Walking briskly, Fuller made his way out of the building and into his car. With any luck, he'd have time to check with Garcia and call Tanaka before Drury was done.

GENEVA, SWITZERLAND

At two minutes before the hour, Ramon checked the private message board of the bird watchers site on his vu-phone again. This time, he found a nine-digit phone number waiting for him. *This Fuller's a man of his word,* Ramon noted as he walked to a public phone at the Cornavin train station and dialed the number.

After a single ring, Fuller answered in a tense voice. "We've tracked down Cardona to Toledo, Ohio. Any leads on where he might go in the area?"

"I'll check with our people in the Cleveland zone. We'll contact the Detroit zone too. If anybody's seen him, I'll leave you a message on the website."

"We don't have time for that. If you uncover anything, call my cell from a public phone," Fuller said and gave Ramon the number.

"You've got cojones, I'll give you that. Any word on our boy in California?"

"The hostage exchange is set. Take the girl to the North Gate at noon Pacific Time. The switch will take place in the middle of the viaduct. One person from each side will accompany the hostages."

Ramon knew the spot well. The viaduct gave both sides an unobstructed view with no place for anyone to hide. "My compliments on your choice of location. Who'll make the delivery for your side?"

"Your prisoner's being held by a Marine unit. One of their officers will escort him."

"Anything else?"

Fuller's voice lost its edge. "Yeah. I asked them to have the kid blindfolded for the exchange. I figured he might try to resist if he knows who's being traded for him."

"Your warrior colleague is a good judge of character. You're a man of honor, sir."

Fuller laughed dryly. "Don't send me any medals. My side might not quite see it that way."

TOLEDO, OH

Cardona steered the Taurus into the entrance of the five-story garage and took a ticket from the automated kiosk. Ignoring the many vacant parking slots on the lower levels, he continued up the ramp until he emerged into the sunshine of the roof. Studying the expanse of empty spaces, he pulled the car into the corner nearest the center of the downtown district.

Cardona had learned from the Russians that a surface burst would limit the bomb's effectiveness. But from a rooftop five stories above the ground, the fireball and blast wave would travel farther, increasing its destructive zone and spreading the radioactive fallout over a wider area.

Selecting a parking space along the edge of the roof, he stepped out of the car and opened the trunk. Keeping the trunk lid partially closed to block the view from the high-rises around him, he unlocked the briefcase.

Cardona began to sweat as the magnitude of what he was about to do weighed on him. He set the timer for three hours and paused. Once he engaged the red toggle to arm the weapon, there would be no turning back. The fate of tens of thousands of human beings would be sealed.

Breathing heavily now, Cardona's finger lingered over the red button. Most of the people who would die in three hours were innocent. But many innocent people had died on his side as well, he reminded himself. He struggled for moment, unsure if he could bring himself to do this. Then, a quote from Marcha surfaced in his mind... "Wars are won by moral men who can kill in cold blood."

Cardona flipped the toggle switch, closed the trunk, and locked the car.

On his way back to the Impala parked at the motel five blocks away, he dropped the keys to the green Taurus into a street-side trashcan.

Agent Ashley Vail opened the car door and emptied a styrofoam cup of coffee onto the pavement. "Jesus H. Christ," she said grimacing. "This isn't coffee. It's watered-down cat piss." A tall, buxom blonde with a penchant for low-cut sweaters, Vail's girly looks belied her salty vocabulary and a reputation as one of the toughest field agents in the region.

"You want an e-bar?" her partner asked, extending a foil-wrapped package from behind the wheel.

"Not without something decent to wash it down," she answered, closing the door. "This motel is a shithole. The staff couldn't tell us diddly-squat about Cardona and then they serve us this god-awful coffee. I haven't had coffee this bad since... Hey, check this guy out," she said, nodding toward a figure approaching the hotel parking lot. Crossing the street was a Caucasian male of average height and build—making a beeline for the silver Impala. As the man drew nearer, Vail recognized him from the dossier photos. "That's Cardona. Cover me. I'm going after him," she said, emerging from the car.

Vail wandered toward Cardona, avoiding eye contact, feigning a search for a room number. When her quarry was beside her, she dropped her keys.

As Cardona looked down, Vail grabbed his wrist, twisted his arm and kicked him in the knee, forcing him face-first to the pavement. Pressing her Glock against the base of his skull, she calmly said, "Hold very, very still, Miguel."

"Get off me, bitch!" Cardona screamed as he reached into the pocket of his jacket with his free hand. When Vail saw the hand emerge with a pistol, her years of training took over. She instinctively pulled the trigger on her weapon. A hollow pop echoed through the parking lot as the top of Cardona's head exploded, leaving a red fan-shaped smear on the blacktop.

"Ashley! Are you OK?" her partner asked, running up to her.

Vail slowly lowered her eyes, rocking slightly on her knees. "Oh, God," she whispered, "I fucked up."

LANGLEY, VA

"I don't think a dead Pancho carrying a forged passport proves a hell of a lot," Tanaka said over the receiver on Fuller's desk phone. He'd returned to his office to have this conversation with his boss in private.

"There's more than that, sir. Cardona tried to evade us by changing clothes at the airport. Then he drove over 200 miles from Toronto to cross the border in Detroit."

"I'll admit your suspect's behavior appears suspicious. But put yourself in my place, Major. How in the hell can I convince the president we have a national emergency based on that?"

"Sir, I'll stake my career that Cardona is involved in a plot to deploy a nuclear weapon—and there's a good chance it could already be armed and ticking."

Tanaka sighed. "All right, all right. I'll alert the

president. But I'll give it to you straight. I'm not going to recommend we issue any public security alerts until we get better information," he said before hanging up.

Fuller walked back to the situation room fuming over Tanaka's latest rebuff—and trying to suppress his guilt for withholding his source. Entering the room, he found Drury and Bailey waiting for him on their feet.

"Cardona had another car, Major," Drury said soberly. "I just got back the last search on his credit card. He rented a Taurus four blocks from his motel at 0800 hours."

"It gets worse," Bailey added. "The Port Authority in Toledo said a man named Robert Branch driving the same Taurus inspected a shipment from China just after 0900. Branch is the name on Cardona's forged passport."

Fuller felt his throat tighten. The second car was almost certainly the delivery vehicle for the bomb. Now only two questions remained. Had Cardona deployed the weapon? And if he did, where was the vehicle?

"Jeff, put out a description of the car to all our assets in the field," Fuller ordered.

"I already did."

Fuller nodded approvingly. "How many agents do we have in Toledo right now?"

"Nine, counting the teams from Cleveland and Columbus."

"Have them use the motel as the center point for the search. They can fan out from there. Cardona arrived on foot and that Taurus has to be somewhere within walking distance."

"Our EODN team is heading south on I-75," Bailey reported. "They should be in Toledo in twenty minutes."

"Station them at the motel. That's our base."

"Yes, sir."

"Sonya, how much time do you think Cardona would

give himself to get out of the area after arming the nuke?"

"It's an hour's drive across the border through Detroit. I'd add another hour for the possibility of getting stuck in traffic. So I'd say a minimum of two hours."

Fuller checked the plasma screen for the time. Vail had shot Cardona just about two hours ago. "Shit," he said, his mouth suddenly dry.

LOS ANGELES QUARANTINE ZONE B

The rebel guard shack stood ten paces inside the North Gate, a ramshackle hut of scavenged corrugated metal propped against the high concrete wall. Within the shack, Sarah waited wordlessly, holding her sleeping son as the heat of the noonday sun radiated from the walls. The stifling air weighed on her, draining her of any feelings.

Close enough to touch in the cramped space inside the shack were Mano, Chuy and Rosa. They stood silently in the oppressive heat, their eyes hollow and turned away. There was nothing left to say. Talking now would only increase the pain, or worse yet, cause someone to have a change of heart.

Chuy checked his watch and broke the silence. "It's time."

Sarah looked at her sleeping child, trying to etch every detail of his face into her memory. She then gently pressed her lips against Daniel's forehead and passed the child to Rosa.

"Sorry, but we got to make this look real," Chuy said, holding out a short length of electrical wire.

"I understand," Sarah said, placing her hands behind her. As Chuy began wrapping the wire around her wrists, Sarah stopped him. "Wait," she said, reaching into her shirt pocket for the familiar strip of black cloth. After slowly placing the blindfold over her eyes, she tied it off. "Okay, you can finish now," she said as her tears began to soak the fabric.

"Ve con dios, m'hija," Rosa whispered to Sarah as Chuy led her out of the shack.

Guided only by the sliver of sight below her blindfold, Sarah walked slowly as Chuy held her arm. When they stopped, Sarah knew they must be near the center of the viaduct. "Can you see him?"

"Yes," Chuy whispered. "Don't say anything. He might recognize your voice."

Sarah felt her knees weaken as she caught a glimpse of Pedro's shoes under the blindfold, his gate still hobbled by the bullet wound.

"Welcome back, hermano," she heard Chuy say to Pedro, their voices drifting as Chuy led him away. "You have to keep the blindfold on until we get inside the wall or the deal is off."

Her knees suddenly weak, Sarah stumbled. But a hand out of the darkness caught her arm,. "It's okay. You're safe now, Miss Jacobs," a male voice said, leading her away.

After reaching the other side of the viaduct, Sarah's hands were freed and her blindfold removed. The first face Sarah saw was a heavily freckled soldier. "I'm Captain LaSalle, Miss Jacobs. Glad to have you with us," The officer said smiling. "If you'll please follow me, Major Fuller has arranged for your flight back to Washington."

TOLEDO, OH

At the corner of Superior and Adams, Vail slowed her unmarked sedan and noticed signs for three public parking garages amid the tall buildings lining both sides of the block. Her team had been searching nearly an hour for the dark green Taurus and she knew there was not much time left.

Vail pulled into the closest garage and after taking a ticket, raced through the four-floor underground facility, tires squealing at every turn. Coming up empty, she sped to the exit, flashing her CIA badge at the startled attendant as she exited without paying.

Back on the street, Vail accelerated toward the next garage but a traffic signal stopped her in the middle of the block. As the pedestrians filed past her car, Vail's hands began to shake.

Shooting Cardona had been the worst blunder of her career. But she didn't have time to dwell on that now. She'd even blown off the cops at the scene, quickly asserting her immunity to local investigations. Still, there would be hell to pay—and finding Cardona's car might help redeem her.

When the light turned green, she steered the car across the street and entered a free-standing five story garage. Rushing past the rows of parked vehicles, she made a final hard turn and reached the roof.

There, parked alone in a corner, was the dark green Taurus.

LANGLEY, VA

"I've got a call from Agent Vail," Drury reported. "She sounds excited."

Fuller rose from his chair. "Patch her into the speakers, Jeff," he said, suddenly animated.

"I found it! I've found the car!" Vail shouted. "It's in a parking garage on—"

A shrill whine from the speakers in the situation room replaced the agent's voice. Fuller, Bailey, and Drury covered their ears as the screeching grew unbearable.

"What happened?" Drury asked, rubbing his ears as the sound died.

Fuller stared at the floor. "That was the electromagnetic pulse. The bomb just detonated."

TOLEDO

TOLEDO—Day 1

From *Witness To History*,
© 2067 by Simon Potts

The one-kiloton bomb instantly leveled six square blocks of downtown Toledo. For a two-mile radius, a shock wave moving at the speed of sound bowled over small buildings, uprooted trees, swept away vehicles, and crushed every living thing in its path. Anything that managed to survive the shock wave was incinerated by the heat flash that followed one second later. For an instant, the entire twenty-one-foot depth of the Maumee River was turned into steam.

The glow of the fireball was seen on the outskirts of Detroit, over fifty miles away. As far east as Sandusky along the Lake Erie coast, waves up to four feet reached the shore. Within one hundred miles of the epicenter, electrical power, telecommunications, radio, TV, and GPS signals were all disrupted by the bomb's electromagnetic pulse.

A cloud of radioactive dust formed over Toledo and began drifting east on the prevailing winds, carrying it over Lake Erie and threatening the northeast U.S. and Canada.

Casualty figures for the city of 300,000 were still a guess immediately following the explosion. One thing was certain. This was the most devastating attack ever launched against the United States. Those who survived the ordeal found it hard to believe the bomb dropped on Hiroshima, Japan, had been fifteen times more powerful.

Minutes after the blast, the Latino Liberation Front claimed responsibility for the attack through a temporary website that stated: "The crimes against our people have been repaid today."

—Simon Potts

SANTA CLARITA, CA

From the passenger's seat of the Marine Corps Humvee, Sarah Evans watched the vehicle turn from 13th Street onto the tarmac of the military airstrip. Built just a few miles from her childhood home only two years before, Brewer Air Base took up most of a two-mile stretch of farmland in Santa Clarita sown with cabbage and asparagus for as long as Sarah could remember.

"You'll be on your way back to your family before long, Miss Jacobs," the soldier behind the wheel said. He then pointed to a four-engine jet being fueled near the control tower. "That's your bird right there."

Sarah nodded and turned away.

Since she'd learned Pedro had been captured, her sole focus had been on arranging the hostage exchange that would set him free. The drive from L.A. had given her time to ponder what came next—something she'd refused to dwell on until Pedro was safe. Her options were not encouraging.

At first, the answer had seemed simple: reveal her real identity to the Marines who had "rescued" her. Being Class H, they'd eventually return her to Quarantine Zone B where she'd be reunited with Pedro and Daniel—even if she spent some time in jail. But then Sarah remembered what that would mean for Mike Fuller. His career would be ruined for arranging the fake hostage exchange. She could not do that to her father's friend. Her only hope now was that Mike had a plan for her once she got to Washington.

The Humvee pulled up to a small building near the airport control tower marked POST COMMAND in stenciled letters. The soldier turned off the engine, stepped out of the vehicle and spoke to Sarah through the window. "Please wait here, Miss. I need to check in with the base CO," he said before entering the building.

A few minutes later the soldier returned, his face ashen. "You need to come inside, miss. All non-essential flights have been cancelled."

A drone of tense voices met Sarah as she entered the command post. The room was alive with an air of crisis as over a dozen people talked into phones, tapped at keyboards, or huddled in small groups. The soldier led Sarah through the maelstrom to a door opening into a locker room.

"The CO said for you to wait here until he figures out what to do with you."

"What's going on?"

"There's been an attack back East and we've gone to DEFCON 2. I'm sorry but I need to report to my unit right away," the soldier said before leaving her alone.

Sarah slumped onto the narrow bench between the lockers, stunned. She'd been around her father's work enough to know this situation was not normal. The attack back East must have been something big. If the Panchos were involved, it would surely pose a threat to Pedro and her son. Then she remembered Rosa's words. No amount of worrying has ever stopped a bullet. Whatever this crisis was about, with the soldiers around her distracted, it could be an opportunity.

She rose and walked to the end of the row of lockers. Her pulse quickened as she saw a heavy metal door with an exit sign above it. A smile spread across her face as she tried the handle and found the door unlocked.

QUARANTINE ZONE B—LOS ANGELES

Chuy led Pedro past the guards posted discreetly outside the light blue bungalow and opened the safe house door.

"I'll wait out here," he said waving Pedro inside.

Mano rose from a rusting metal lawn chair as Pedro limped into the living room. "Sorry we had to keep you isolated, m'hijo," he said, embracing his son.

Pedro clapped his father's broad back then stepped back and smiled. "Glad I checked out clean, papá," he said. "The Baldies had plenty of chances to plant a tracer on me while I was knocked out by the grenade. But I don't think they expected to let me go."

"What do you mean?"

"The officer who interrogated me was about to get rough and went off to get some goons. But when he came back, something had changed. That's when I found out they were swapping me for one of their own. I didn't know we were holding any Baldies."

Mano rubbed his face and dropped back into the chair. "Sit down, m'hijo," he said waving toward a chair. "I've got some things to explain."

Pedro listened, his face hardening with each word, as Mano described how Sarah had volunteered for the hostage exchange. When his father was done, Pedro shook his head. "You shouldn't have let her do that."

"What other choice did we have? It was the only way both of you got out alive."

"What about the needle law? They'll charge her with treason."

"The Baldies think they swapped you for a diplomat's daughter. As far as they know, Sarah Evans is still inside Quarantine Zone B."

"We need to bring her back... for Daniel's sake."

"That may not happen for a while, m'hijo," Mano said, putting his large hand on his son's shoulder. "Ramon called a while ago with more bad news... We couldn't stop El Frente in time... They nuked a city in Ohio."

SANTA CLARITA, CA

The images on the shopping mall's videoboard let Sarah know just how serious the attack back East had been. Gone from the mall's large animated sign were the usual flashy ads for clothes, groceries, gym memberships, and ballroom dance lessons. In their place, a U.S. flag waved somberly while text messages crawled slowly across the bottom of the screen ... CONDOLENCES FOR THE VICTIMS IN TOLEDO ... GOD BLESS AMERICA ... PANCHO, WE WILL NOT FORGET ...

The last message confirmed her greatest fear. The rebels of the quarantine zones were being blamed for the attack. She was not sure where Toledo was or what had happened there, but it seemed likely her son and the people who mattered most to her might soon be the targets of vengeance.

Since leaving the airstrip, Sarah had noticed other gestures of support and mourning in her old neighborhood. U.S. flags of every size dotted the streets, flying from poles at half mast, hung from windows, and streaming from passing cars.

There were also signs of fear. The parking lot of the Saveway supermarket was a noisy snarl as people rushed to stock up on essentials. At the gas station on the corner, vehicles were lined up around the block waiting for their turn at the pump.

Most disturbing of all was the outpouring of revenge. NUKE THE QUARANTINE ZONES read a hand scrawled sheet taped in the window of a martial arts studio. A sign outside a pizza shop said PAY BACK THE PANCHOS NOW.

Her anxiety rising, Sarah picked up the pace of her steps. Her mother's house was now only four blocks away. Entering the residential area near her childhood home, Sarah saw a half-dozen young people huddled around an

SUV parked along the curb, listening to the radio.

"...the death toll remains unknown at this time as rescue crews and medical teams from across the nation converge on Toledo," Sarah heard the radio announcer say as she neared the group.

One of them, a young woman about her age, stared hard at Sarah as she approached. A few steps closer, Sarah recognized Cindy Dorsett, the leader of a high school clique that had flamed her on Facebook after she'd become Class H.

Cindy stepped in front of Sarah on the sidewalk, blocking her path. "You've got a lot of nerve showing your face today, Evans." Cindy said as the others in her group closed around Sarah menacingly. "I think the cops might want to talk to you."

Sarah fought an urge to run. Any sign of guilt now might incite these wannabe vigilantes. She stepped closer to Cindy, locking her in a stare. "What's your problem, Dorsett?"

"Where's your little Pancho?" Cindy said, lowering her eyes. "Helping his daddy in Toledo?"

"Fuck off," Sarah said, walking past her without looking back.

After putting some distance between herself and the group Sarah exhaled slowly in relief. Not that she feared being arrested. In fact, she was planning on it. But there was no way she'd give Cindy Dorsett the satisfaction of turning her in. However, the confrontation had underscored something important. She needed to know more about what had happened in Toledo—for her own sake as well as those inside the walls.

Arriving at her mother's house, Sarah walked to the back of the bi-level home. After peering through the garage windows to make sure her mother was at work, she retrieved the spare key always kept under a flower pot on the back patio and went inside.

On the wall by the back door, the alarm system keypad chirped softly, a reminder to enter the security code. Sarah ignored it and walked into the kitchen. She was not hungry but knew she needed to eat to keep up her strength, a habit she'd acquired from her days as a soccer player.

The phone rang as Sarah finished making a peanut butter sandwich. It was a call she'd been expecting: the security company checking on her unauthorized entry. Sarah knew the security people would dispatch the police if no one answered the phone after four rings.

Ignoring the phone, Sarah carried her sandwich into the living room, turned on the television and flipped through the channels until she reached CCN. On the 24-hour news channel, Vice President Melvin Bates was reading from a prepared speech, the tapering spire of the Washington Monument framed dramatically in the background.

"...to all those who have appeased the terrorists, to all those who have preached multiculturalism and lacked faith in our way of life, to those in power who failed in their duty to punish the terrorists, to all of those I say: You share the blame for what happened in Toledo."

The broadcast cut to a studio where the ebony face of Simon Potts appeared at an anchor desk. "This startling speech by Vice President Melvin Bates has left Washington in shock. In an unprecedented move, the vice president has publicly broken ranks with the White House during a national crisis and appears to be blaming the Nixon administration for the attack on Toledo. For a congressional reaction, we're now joined by—"

The slam of a car door drew Sarah's attention away from the broadcast. Parting the living room curtains, she saw a police cruiser parked on the street and two black-clad Santa Clarita officers approaching the house. Sarah closed the curtains and smiled. Everything was going according to her plan.

TOLEDO—Day 2

GENEVA, SWITZERLAND

Shortly after 4 a.m., Margaret Zane Garcia rolled over in bed and noticed her husband was gone. Sitting up, she saw a sliver of light under the bedroom door. Ramon was up again—for the second night in a row.

After slipping into her robe, Maggie found Ramon in the kitchen, fully-dressed, pouring a cup of coffee. "What are you doing up at this hour, love?" she asked.

"I'm expecting a call," Ramon said wearily before gulping down the coffee.

"You need to get dressed to answer the phone?"

"It's a call I can't take at home."

Margaret nodded. After three decades of marriage to a man in the movement, she'd grown used to Ramon's odd hours and need for discretion. Still, the last two days had been abnormal, even by Ramon's standards. Usually a man who slept soundly, this terrible business in Toledo had left him restless and irritable. "You need to get some rest, Ray. You look more ragged than a beggar's boots."

"I'll be fine," he said heading for the chalet's door. "See you in an hour or so."

The September air was chilly but Ramon arrived sweating and out of breath after the two block walk to the Hotel Charmilles. Entering the hotel lobby, Ramon dropped heavily into a leather couch near a pair of phone booths along the wall.

A few minutes later, one of the pay phones rang and Ramon looked at his watch. As usual, Fuller was right on time. Ramon entered the phone booth and picked up the receiver. "Major, I want you to know how appalled I am by this tragedy. The cruelty of a war can—"

Fuller cut him off. "Look, I don't have much time. I need to be sure Perez doesn't have any more weapons."

"It's not likely, Major. Perez has no more money," Ramon said, then added, "All the same, it's time to terminate that son-of-a-bitch. Do you still have a tail on him?"

"No. We put all our resources on Cardona."

"Where is Cardona now?"

"Dead. One of our agents took him down before the bomb went off."

"I suppose Cardona would have been worth questioning, but frankly, that's the only good news I've heard all day."

"Garcia, I know you've been trying to help. But there's something more you can do. If I can tell my superiors where I'm getting my information, that would good for your side, too. Right now, the Hispanic Republic is going to take the blame for Toledo. Not many on our side are buying your denials."

"Do you really think your government would clear us publicly?"

"I can't guarantee what my government will do. But I will promise you this. Free me from my word and I'll go to the media and tell them myself."

Ramon closed his eyes, considering Fuller's offer. If a U.S. Army officer vouched for them in the media, it might clear the Hispanic Republic of blame for Toledo. But the exoneration would come with a steep price. The publicity would likely expose Claude Durand's connection as a source of their funding. Claude had warned he'd stop backing them if his role became public. *Am I willing to risk half our income to clear our name?* Ramon asked himself.

"I'll get in touch through our online channel if I decide to do that, Major," he said before hanging up.

Ramon walked slowly out of the hotel lobby, shoulders slumped, feeling very old. This was a bad day for their cause. *Shit, it's a bad day for everybody*, he reminded himself. He was not going to sleep much again tonight—and Fuller's offer would only add to his insomnia.

TOLEDO—Day 4

From *Witness To History,*
© 2067 by Simon Potts

The attack on Toledo drew expressions of sympathy, shock, and indignation from around the globe. Within twenty-four hours, every media source on the planet had run the stunning photo taken by a boater of the mushroom cloud billowing above the shore of Lake Erie. Not since the 9-11 attacks had the United States experienced such universal support and condolences. In Paris, American flags appeared from many windows. The gesture was soon copied in other cities around the world.

The mood at home was quite different.

A terrified and war-weary U.S. public wanted a scapegoat— and Vice President Melvin Bates had given them one: the president. A Gallup poll taken four days after the Toledo attack showed most Americans blamed the White House for its handling of the insurgency. The congressional calls for Nixon's impeachment did not take long—nor did the demands for reprisals against the quarantine zones.

In a statement to the press, U.N. representative for the Hispanic Republic of North America, Ramon Garcia, said, "We deplore this appalling and mindless attack. The Latino Liberation Front is a rogue organization and does not represent all Hispanics." Garcia's comments stalled a resolution by Canada and Great Britain to expel the HRNA from the United Nations. Garcia's denial, however, did little to quell U.S. anger.

In a prepared response not cleared with the White House, Vice President Melvin Bates told reporters, "The American people are not going to buy the hollow claims of innocence by terrorists seeking to avoid our righteous wrath."

—Simon Potts

TYSONS CORNER, VA

"Thank you, Captain. I appreciate the update on Miss Jacobs," Fuller said into the phone before hanging up. There was still no word on Sarah's disappearance.

Fuller walked into his apartment's small kitchen, searching for another bottle of bourbon. Finding a near-empty fifth on the cluttered counter, he poured himself a shot and downed it in a gulp. He was helpless to do anything about Sarah until the investigation was over and he could leave town.

After another belt of bourbon, Fuller returned to the living room with the bottle and slumped onto the couch. Searching for the TV remote, he rummaged through the coffee table's accretion of newspapers, junk food wrappers, magazines, empty bottles, and dirty glasses. Turning on the TV, he propped his feet on the coffee table, kicking some of its flotsam onto the floor.

Flipping through the channels was pointless. Every network was carrying the same live C-SPAN feed of the congressional hearings. Representative Joshua Collins was at the podium and by his rising cadence, Fuller could tell the six-term congressman from South Carolina was nearing the conclusion of his speech.

"Mr. Speaker, I bring this resolution of impeachment against a president who has ignominiously failed to carry out his duties as commander-in-chief. George Whitehead Nixon's negligence in dealing with the terrorist threat has led to the greatest calamity in the history of this nation. The lives of more than twenty thousand Americans demand this president be removed from office."

The congressional chamber broke into a roar of approval—a standing ovation from most of its members that lasted well over a minute. As the view cut to the floor of the House, many representatives shook their fists angrily into the camera, making sure their constituents at home did not miss their outrage. Several tore up photos of Nixon.

Fuller muted the broadcast and woozily reached for the bottle of bourbon. Discovering the fifth was empty, he dropped it on the floor.

Tears suddenly blurring his vision, Fuller covered his face and wept.

He felt the room slowly spin, whirling around the gnawing ache in his chest, an emptiness that seemed to consume him from the inside like a black hole. He'd known the feeling before, but never this bad. The last time had been almost four years ago.

He'd led a convoy into Quarantine Zone B in Los Angeles after the Marcha Offensive. On their way out, the Panchos had lured him into a trap. Ten men under his command had lost their lives when their transport vehicle was destroyed by a volley of RPG fire. He'd watched helplessly as the Bradley exploded, incinerating everyone inside. At that moment, all he'd felt was anger. The remorse would come two days later while lying in his bunk, enveloped by darkness. Only then had the despair and grief of those ten lost lives finally hit home.

Today, that hollow misery had returned.

Looking back at the moment the bomb had exploded, his memories of the incident were vivid. But like the shock of combat, the moment lacked any sorrow.

He'd stared at the big board as the icons for all the teams he'd deployed into the Toledo area blinked like a digital clock after a power failure. Drury and Sonya were silent. No one made eye contact. The deaths of tens of thousands of unsuspecting men, women and children was too much to comprehend. He wanted to feel worse but could not compel his mind to fathom the extent of the tragedy.

"What should we do, Major?" Drury finally asked.

Fuller rose. "I need to inform Tanaka."

After calling the director from his office, Tanaka's response left Fuller stunned.

"I gave you every resource you needed based on the information you provided me, Fuller," Tanaka said defensively. "The blame for this isn't going to fall on me—or the president."

"We'll have plenty of time for blame later, sir. Right now, we need to contact FEMA and coordinate relief efforts. I'd like your permission to do that immediately."

"Yes. Yes, of course," Tanaka said, recovering his composure. "I'll inform the president about what's happened right away."

For the next two days, Fuller had been too occupied to dwell much on his guilt. His situation room had become a round-the-clock clearing house of information for FEMA as they coordinated evacuations and emergency responders. He and his team had scrounged what little sleep they got on couches in the room.

Two days later, with his knowledge of the attack dispersed to other agencies, Tanaka had sent him home with a warning. "Until we figure out how to handle this, you're confined to your apartment, understand? In the meantime, if you so much as walk near a reporter, I'll have you in Leavenworth."

For two sleepless days since then, he'd been at home, tortured by questions that would not go away. Should he have told Tanaka about his pipeline to the Panchos? Would it have made a difference? Consumed in a devil's brew of guilt and grief, he'd retreated into the solace of liquor and junk food.

Now, with time to reflect, the enormity of his failure was sinking in.

There was no way to salvage his career now—and he no longer cared. Under the heat of the congressional inquisition ahead, Tanaka would implicate him and Drury would crack. But that would make no difference. His real punishment had already been meted out.

More than twenty thousand people had died. Had it happened because he'd been too proud to break his word—to an enemy, no less? In his head, he heard their screams of pain, saw the flesh melt from their bones, felt the grief of those who'd seen loved ones die. The weight of his shame pressed down on him like an ocean, suffocating him under its pressure. Could he live with this disgrace?

Fuller rose from the couch and stumbled into the bedroom. Opening the drawer to the nightstand, he took out the M9 and stared at its cold, blue-black finish.

Carrying the pistol into the bathroom, he looked at himself in the mirror. *Have you betrayed your country, Major?* he asked himself. *Do you deserve to live? Go ahead. Make your case.*

Before he could answer, there was a knock at the door.

Fuller waited without moving. After another round of knocking, a voice called out from behind the door.

"I know you're in there. Please open up, It's Sonya."

Placing the pistol under the sink, he walked to the living room and answered the door.

"This is way out of line, Lieutenant," Fuller said, trying

to sound sober. "Junior officers don't come calling on their superiors at home."

"I've been trying to reach you by phone. We need to talk. May I come in?"

"There's nothing we need to talk about."

"Please. Hear me out. There are some things we need to discuss—and they shouldn't be said in the hallway."

Fuller waved Bailey inside. "Fine, but keep it brief," he said after closing the door. "You can tell your handlers at the Pentagon that I acted on my own. They're in the clear from any blame. I'll put it in writing if you like."

Bailey looked puzzled. "I don't understand what you're saying."

"Don't insult me by acting innocent, Sonya. You think I didn't know you were assigned to spy on me from the first day you showed up?"

"You're a bright man and an excellent officer, but respectfully Major Fuller, you're drunk and full of shit."

"Lieutenant Bailey," Fuller said, his voice suddenly formal. "Do you deny participating in a surveillance on me by any governmental organization?"

"I am not spying on you for anybody, Major," she answered sharply. "You want that in writing?"

Fuller stared at her for a moment. "All right. So let me guess," he said over his shoulder as he walked to the window and scanned the street four stories below. "You're worried about what Tanaka's going to put in his investigation about your performance."

"It's not me I'm worried about. Tanaka's going to throw you under the bus, Mike," she said, moving next to him by the window. "You did everything you could to warn him. This is not your fault."

"So what? You think that's going to bring back anyone who died?"

"No. But if a slimeball like Tanaka stays in power and you get drummed out of the service, then the chance of more Americans dying goes up."

Fuller turned and faced her. "It's not that simple, Sonya. My hands aren't clean."

"I was there, Mike. I saw how you handled that crisis. What could you have done differently?"

"That's the question I keep asking myself," he said, staring at the floor. "And there's a reason the answer's not so simple...I deliberately kept Tanaka in the dark about my source on Perez and Cardona."

"Why?"

"I gave someone my word."

"You shouldn't be ashamed of that. Look, I won't pretend to know a lot about this spook stuff but it seems to me Tanaka should have trusted you. He was wrong for not taking the threat seriously, not you. I think Tanaka was more worried about making a political mistake than protecting the American people. Besides, if you hadn't brought Tanaka the information on Perez and Cardona, we wouldn't have had any shot at all of stopping them. You shouldn't blame yourself, Mike," she said, putting a hand on his shoulder. "You're much too good a man to lose."

A place inside Michael Fuller stirred that had been dormant for a long time. Beneath the shell of anger, guilt and loneliness, a surge of tenderness flickered in his chest. "You better go," he said.

"I don't think so, Mike. Something tells me you shouldn't be left alone."

"What if I order you to leave?"

"Then you'll need to put me on report for insubordination," she said, slowly wrapping her arms around his waist. "I'm not going anywhere."

Fuller was dumbfounded as he felt a stirring in his groin and tears form in his eyes.

SANTA CLARITA, CA

Sarah touched the bandage on her forehead and winced. Fortunately, one of the guards had stepped in before things got worse. The unprovoked beating in the exercise yard yesterday had come from a fellow prisoner.

Since word had spread among the women in the county jail that she was Class H, Sarah had become a target. Now she sat alone in a small cell wearing the orange jump suit issued prisoners in protective isolation.

The beat down had been more humiliating than painful. In those first moments following the assault, she'd almost weakened and called her mother, something Sarah had avoided since being locked up. Although her mother had showed up at the jail several times before, Sarah had refused to see her.

Not calling Mike Fuller had been a tougher decision. Mike was no doubt worried about her. But a call from a Class H detainee fitting the description of his missing hostage might get Mike in trouble. Better to leave well enough alone.

Footsteps on the steel floor of the corridor drew Sarah's gaze to the entrance of her cell. "You have a visitor," the burly brunette guard said, unlocking the iron-barred door.

Sarah studied the man in the business suit and brief case entering her cell. He was in his mid-twenties and looked like most people's image of a Latino: dark-eyed and olive-skinned with high cheekbones. "This is your lawyer," the guard said before locking the door behind the man and walking away.

Sarah rose warily from the bunk and stood against the

wall. "I didn't ask for a lawyer. What are you doing here?"

"I was appointed by the court. My name Ajitkumar Singh. Most people call me Jay. May I sit down?" he said pointing to a corner of her bunk.

Sarah nodded but remained standing. "Why are you in my cell? Visitors are supposed to talk to us by phone behind a window."

"I'm your attorney. Our conversations are private. And, by the way, I'd advise you to keep your voice down, Sarah. They can't wiretap your cell. But anything the guards can overhear can be used as evidence against you, and believe me, they're going to be listening. So, please. Will you sit down so we can avoid that?"

Sarah sat on the bunk but kept her distance. "What do you want?"

"I was told you haven't made any attempts to contact anyone since you were arrested and refused to see your mother. That's very unusual."

"Is that against the law?"

"Look, Sarah. I'm here to help you—and you're going to need it," Jay said. "They're charging you with a violation of the Terrorist Arraignment Act."

"The needle law? You've got to be kidding. I'm just Class H and got caught outside the walls. Don't they have to prove I actually helped a Pancho to charge me?"

"Normally, yes. But right now, federal prosecutors are out for blood. The White House is pushing the Justice Department to fast track grand juries and slap the needle law on anybody in the legal system who's Class H."

"Okay, so maybe they'll charge me. But they'll still have to prove it."

Singh pulled a manila folder from his bulging briefcase and scanned a few of the pages. "I know this might be painful to discuss but I need to mention it because it's going to come up in your hearings," he said, flipping through the papers. "You apparently got pregnant while being held by the Panchos. After giving birth, you voluntarily classified your child and yourself as Class H and returned to the Los Angeles Quarantine Zone. On the day Toledo was attacked, you were caught forty miles outside the walls acting suspiciously."

"I didn't even know about Toledo."

"What were you doing in Santa Clarita?"

"I came back home to get some things."

"Sarah, I have to be blunt. That story is not going to play very well with a grand jury right now. People are angry and they're looking for someone to blame," the lawyer said closing the folder. "Things are so bad, even public defenders with Class H clients are getting death threats. The state bar just filed a petition to conceal our names."

Sarah leaned her head against the wall and closed her eyes. She didn't want to die, but that wasn't the most devastating blow. Her dream of being reunited with her son and Pedro was suddenly very dim. "What are my chances?"

"I can stall the prosecutor for a while by filing motions. This bloodlust might die down—if the Panchos don't launch any more attacks."

"And if they do?"

"Then it's going to be very bad—for all of us."

TOLEDO—Day 6

OUTPOST BRAVO, CA

"The colonel wants to see you after you've stowed your gear, Major," the soldier said, opening the Humvee's passenger door.

Michael Fuller chucked his duffel bag into the back seat and stepped inside the vehicle. "Thank you, corporal," he said closing door. The sour-sharp smell of sweat, cordite and cigarettes in the Humvee let Fuller know he was no longer in the world of abstract conflicts. He was back where the metal hit the meat.

As the driver pulled away, Fuller studied the desolate landscape around him and was surprised by the feeling washing over him: relief. Most officers would have seen this assignment back to Outpost Bravo as a reprimand. But punishment was not the only reason Tanaka had sent him back to his old unit in Southern California.

Reporters could not travel to this remote outpost without written permission. With the impeachment hearings underway, the Nixon people wanted him as far from the media as possible. The move was shrewd, too. The posting fit his military résumé, making it seem less like an attempt at a cover-up. Not surprisingly, Sonya was transferred to the high-security missile base in Fort Greely, Alaska. He'd not heard about Drury's fate but imagined he was in a similar media gulag.

Parting from Sonya had been hard after so many years alone. They'd promised to see each other on their next leave. But with the military at DEFCON 2, who knew when that would be? All the same, if she hadn't come to his apartment last week, he might have cashed in his chips. That night, and in those that followed, he and Sonya hadn't just shared the best sex of his life. She'd convinced him the way to put things right was to serve his country. Coming back here fit the bill pretty damn well.

Being back in California also had another benefit. He could do more to help Sarah Evans.

After Sarah had gone missing, he'd called Monica Evans and learned her daughter was in custody and facing a needle law charge. Sarah had refused to see her mother. Maybe she would see him if he showed up at the jailhouse. There had to be a way he could prove Sarah's innocence.

"This your first time in Pancho land, Major?" the driver asked.

Fuller shook his head. "Second time to the dance," he said, then looked at the private's divisional patch. The soldier was from the Third Infantry, one of the divisions transferred from the Middle East. "How's this compare to the sandbox?"

"You know, Major. At first, it didn't make much difference. Hunting Hajjis or hunting Panchos is pretty much the same old shit. But since Toledo, our people are charged up. You wouldn't believe how many volunteers we get for patrol these days."

Fuller stared out the window, troubled by the soldier's reply. He knew the the leaders of the Hispanic Republic had done everything possible to prevent the attack on Toledo. All the same, until the mistrust ended between his side and theirs, they were in for more pointless bloodshed.

TOLEDO—Day 11

From *Witness To History,*
© 2067 by Simon Potts

The demise of President George Whitehead Nixon was remarkably swift.

Before Nixon II, every U.S. president had enjoyed widespread popular support during a military crisis. Nixon's political base, however, was unlike any other president's.

Nixon's moderate views had garnered tepid support among hard-line Republicans. Only after selecting Melvin Bates of the far-right Nationalist Party as his running mate at the GOP convention had Nixon managed to wrest the nomination from a weakened sitting president, Carleton Brenner. That precarious political balance of moderates and hardliners had carried Nixon into the White House.

But Melvin Bates would bring that fragile balance crashing down to earth.

By publicly criticizing the president following the Toledo attacks, Bates destroyed all support for Nixon among the far right. The Democrats pounced on Nixon as well, leaving the president with the slim support of moderate Republicans.

Spurred by polls showing the Nixon's approval ratings plummeting to single digits, the House of Representatives passed articles of impeachment in nine days. The Republican-controlled Senate, whose members served longer terms, was not so easily swayed. Deadlocked at fifty-fifty over the resolution, the tie-breaking vote fell to the Vice President.

In a move that stunned Washington, Melvin Bates voted in

favor of impeachment. Two days later, he was sworn in as the new president of the United States.

Melvin Bates assumed power of a nation teetering between despondency and rage.

He wasted little time tipping the scales.

—Simon Potts

THE BATES PRESIDENCY

THE BATES PRESIDENCY—Day 1

From *Witness To History,*
© 2067 by Simon Potts

Two days after taking office, President Melvin Bates ordered all troops and law enforcement personnel around the San Antonio Quarantine Zone to withdraw. Six hours later, a lone B-2 bomber took off from Whiteman Air Force Base in Missouri, swept in from the north, and released its payload over the San Antonio Quarantine Zone.

The bomber carried a neutron weapon.

Detonating ten thousand feet above the ground, the new-generation neutron bomb showered the ground below with a blast of radiation so intense it immediately destroyed all biological tissue within a two-square-kilometer kill zone. Called a "landlord bomb" in military circles, the high-radiation weapon left most buildings intact.

As the plane turned north, heading for home, It left behind more than fifteen thousand dead. Twice that many were exposed to lethal doses of radiation and would die within a few weeks.

Before the bomber landed, President Bates made a television appearance from the White House.

"Citizens of America, today, in response to the barbaric terrorist attack on Toledo, I ordered an air strike on the San Antonio Quarantine Zone with a neutron weapon.

"Let this act of justice send a message to the cowards who attacked us. We will not lie down meekly while you slaughter our people, trample our laws, and abuse our freedom.

"To those citizens near the San Antonio Quarantine Zone, rest assured you are not in any danger. The radiation from this special weapon is limited in range and duration. Obey your local authorities. They will provide guidelines to keep you safe.

"Public and private property in the San Antonio area has not been damaged, most especially that precious symbol of American independence, the Alamo. The high tech weapon deployed today is designed to inflict damage only to our enemies, not to our people, our property, and our national treasures.

"The days of coddling the terrorists in the Quarantine Zones are over. The politics of appeasement led to the tragedy in Toledo. We must not repeat that mistake.

"As your commander-in-chief, I assure you that our nation will not be caught off guard again. I have ordered our military forces to remain on Defense Condition 2, a state of readiness that will allow us to protect the American people from another attack of this magnitude.

"The Holy Scriptures say 'an eye for an eye and a tooth for a tooth.' I promise the craven evildoers who destroyed Toledo that if they dare attack us again, they will feel our righteous wrath once more."

—Simon Potts

THE BATES PRESIDENCY—Day 2

GENEVA, SWITZERLAND

Approaching the city center in his chauffeured Audi, Ramon Garcia stared at the placid waters of Lake Geneva. His mind, however, was far from calm.

Bates' bombing of San Antonio had forced Ramon into the most troubling moral quandary of his life.

The headlines about San Antonio in most U.S. newspapers were not surprising. OUR RIGHTEOUS WRATH led the front page of the Washington Post. AN ACT OF JUSTICE headlined the Wall Street Journal. Even the New York Times caught the fever with AN EYE FOR AN EYE. Except for a handful of academics and civil rights groups, the bombing of San Antonio was being widely applauded in the United States.

Across the rest of the globe, a different attitude prevailed.

Most of the sympathy for the U.S. following the Toledo attack had evaporated. Angry demonstrators filled the streets in hundreds of cities. Cartoons in foreign newspapers portrayed Melvin Bates as Adolph Hitler, Genghis Khan, and the Grim Reaper amid piles of skulls.

National leaders on every continent were denouncing the use of a neutron weapon against a civilian population—and for placing U.S. forces on a hair-trigger response status.

"Toledo was an attack by a lunatic who managed to get a nuclear bomb. The attack on San Antonio was the act of a lunatic with the most powerful nuclear arsenal in the world. Melvin Bates is a menace to mankind," China's prime minister had stated.

"We will defend ourselves with every means at our disposal," countered President Bates in a White House press conference. "Anyone who threatens us does so at their own peril."

Along with the media coverage, there were moves underway at the U.N. that would bolster the Hispanic cause. Iran had filed a motion to charge President Bates with crimes against humanity. Just as importantly, the resolution by Canada and Great Britain to censure the Hispanic Republic of North America was dropped.

In light of these developments, Ramon had made a gut-wrenching decision. He would not reveal their cooperation with Fuller and risk losing Durand's money. There was no need. Bates had taken the heat off their cause.

The decision still made his stomach churn. Coldly calculating public opinion about these tragedies made him feel like a vulture circling over the bodies of the dead. But like a soldier, he had to put aside his feelings and focus on his goal. The media was a battleground they could not afford to lose—and the end of Durand's funding would be a severe blow to their cause. There was only one consolation to his conscience. His meeting today would hopefully bring the hand of justice to Octavio Perez.

"We're at the Café Leman, Mr. Garcia," the driver said in German-accented English as he stopped the Audi at a small bistro.

"Thank you, Carl. I'll call when I'm ready to leave," he

said before stepping out of the car.

Inside the near-empty café, Ramon took a table near the large half moon-topped window and ordered a latte. His meeting today had been inspired by something Fuller had revealed almost in passing: Miguel Cardona had been killed before the detonation in Toledo. Mulling this over later, Ramon realized Cardona's death held an opportunity.

Shortly after the waiter brought his latte, Ramon saw the man he'd been waiting for enter the café. The head of security at the North Korean legation to the United Nations was short, stocky and wore an expensive suit. He strode purposefully across the room and sat beside Ramon. After the usual exchange of greetings, Ramon got down to business.

"I'm very worried about my former UN delegate, Octavio Perez. One of his aides, Miguel Cardona, has been secretly detained by the Americans in connection with the Toledo bombing. In private, Octavio is very nervous and making some outlandish claims that your government funded the attack. I know this is ludicrous, of course. But Octavio says that if the Americans come after him, he's going to implicate your government in the Toledo bombing. Now, I know your government would never do such a thing. So I thought it would be best to inform you so you can have some evidence ready to prove your innocence."

The security officer rose to his feet and bowed. "Thank you for bringing this matter to our attention, Señor Garcia. We will resolve this unfortunate business."

LOS ANGELES QUARANTINE ZONE B

"Hold still, Pedro," Rosa said as she unwrapped the bandages on her son's leg. "You squirm as much as Daniel when I'm trying to change him."

Perched on the kitchen table as his mother tended to his leg, Pedro flinched again when she brushed against the injury. "I don't think your medicine is doing much good," he grumbled.

Carefully pulling away the last of the dressings, Rosa examined the bullet wound. "You're healing fine, m'hijo. It's only been two weeks. These things take time."

Pedro looked away. "Fine. Just finish up. I want to get to Ramon's library."

"You've been spending a lot of time there, m'hijo," Rosa said, applying a homemade garlic salve to the wound.

"Is there something wrong with reading?"

"Pedro, I could not be happier about your new interest in books," Rosa said as she wrapped fresh bandages around his leg. "I just wish you showed as much attention to your son."

Pedro looked at Daniel, swaddled in a woven basket on the kitchen counter. "Not much I can do for him that you and the wet nurse don't do already."

"You can hold him, talk to him, tell him you love him."

"What difference would that make?"

"Children need love as much as food," Rosa said as she finished the bandaging. "M'hijo, you've been hurt—and I'm not just talking about this bullet wound," she said. "But that's not this child's fault."

Pedro rose from the table. "I don't want to talk about this, mamá," he said before hobbling out of the room.

Rosa walked to Daniel's basket and stroked the baby's head. Like all of God's works, Daniel's arrival had been a mixed blessing.

Sarah had been brave to come back and share this beautiful child with them. Then Sarah had shown ever greater courage when she left Daniel behind to save

Pedro. But Rosa could see how much Sarah's sacrifice was shaming her son. Already tight-lipped, Pedro had become distant and irritable.

Worst of all, Pedro was avoiding his son.

Rosa was sure Daniel reminded Pedro of Sarah's sacrifice. Perhaps Mano could talk some sense into Pedro. No one knew better than her husband how a war could drive apart a father and a son.

THE BATES PRESIDENCY—Day 5

GENEVA, SWITZERLAND

"Did you enjoy the kimchi, Mr. Perez?" the petite envoy seated across the table asked.

"Not bad," Octavio Perez said, finishing up the spicy Korean dish. "This can't touch jalapeños for heat, though."

"There's no better place for authentic kimchi in the city."

"Well, the joint could sure as hell's use some atmosphere," Octavio said gesturing with his fork around the room. The Kang House Restaurant was a stark and dimly-lit eatery in Geneva's backwater Jonction district. *This pretty little number from the embassy sure perks the place up though*, Octavio thought. He'd always fantasized about sex with an Asian woman. This might be his lucky day.

"I want to thank you once again for meeting on such short notice, sir. I must go now."

"Already? Isn't there more we need to talk about?" Other than selecting an entrée, their brief lunch conversation had been about the prospects of a cultural exchange program between North Korea and the Hispanic Republic.

She smiled demurely. "I think we've covered everything for now. Goodbye, sir," she said before paying the waiter and leaving the restaurant.

Octavio watched her leave in bewilderment. The reason for this secret meeting had seemed clear when he'd received the invitation through his encrypted web link with the North Koreans. After the job they'd pulled off in Toledo, he imagined the chinos would be offering more money for another nuke. *To hell with them*, he thought. *I can still run with this from here.*

Their bold stroke in Toledo had succeeded beyond his dreams. They'd managed to oust the moderate Nixon and bring Bates into power. It was only a matter of time before the hard-line Bates turned the entire world against the United States. Already, Bates' attack on San Antonio had gotten their side off the hook for Toledo. But that was only the beginning.

Once he raised the money for the Russian mafia hit, Ramon Garcia would become a martyr. The thought of publicly praising his rival as a hero of their cause slain by the evil gabachos was especially delicious. Octavio would then take his rightful place at the head of their movement.

The only loose end was Cardona. He'd not heard from Miguel in nearly two weeks. Maybe the kid had failed to get away from the bomb in time. *Too bad.* Miguel would be hard to replace but he'd served his purpose. Octavio left the restaurant still buoyant, rubbing his bulging belly in satisfaction.

On the sidewalk, he scanned the street for a taxi and spotted one parked in front of a hotel just over a block away. Walking toward the cab, he saw the car begin to pull away. Octavio broke into a jog, his hand raised above his head. "Taxi! Taxi!" he called out.

A sharp pain below the rib cage made him double over. After two faltering steps, Octavio's heavy body crashed to the pavement.

Fighting for breath, Octavio clutched at this throat, as if his hands could somehow force air into his lungs. Desperate now, he tried to call for help. Unable to expel any air, only a pathetic gurgle escaped his gaping mouth. *Dear God, I'm...* Perez never finished the thought as his vision blurred and eventually went black.

The emergency medics who arrived a short while later had seen this scenario too many times before. An overweight middle-aged man, dead from cardiac arrest.

SANTA CLARITA, CA

Escorted by the guard, Sarah walked along the line of inmates, each seated at a shallow cubicle facing a heavy plate glass window. The drone of their voices echoed in the room as they spoke to visitors through wall-mounted phones. Several of the overall-clad women glared over their shoulders at Sarah as she passed.

This was Sarah's first time in the visitor area and the place was unsettling. The long room pulsated with a mix of desperation and despair. Confined in a world of steel and subjugation, the visiting area gave prisoners a bittersweet taste of what lay outside: familiar faces, news of family, gossip about friends—normal life going on without them.

"Here," the guard said dryly, gesturing toward an empty plastic chair with her truncheon.

Through a window laced with metal wire, Sarah saw the face of Michael Fuller. He smiled at first, then looked startled as he noticed the bandage on her forehead and bruises on her face. "Who did this to you?" he said into the telephone.

"Don't worry, Mike. The staff is treating me okay." Sarah answered from her side of the glass. "I'm just not real popular with some of the prisoners right now."

Fuller nodded. "Things are getting ugly everywhere," he said. "Sorry I didn't come to see you sooner. I had a hard time getting away. Anything you need?"

"No, but I'm glad you came."

"You should see your mother next time she comes. She's worried about you."

Sarah laughed bitterly. "It's more like she's worried what the people at her church will think."

"Don't sell your mother short, Sarah."

She covered her eyes, her voice growing hoarse. "My son and his father... his parents... they're the only people I want to see besides you, Mike. But I don't think that's going to happen," she said, her lower lip quivering.

"It's okay, Sarah. I'm going to get you out of here. But you'll need to help me. Will you do that?"

Sarah looked up, her eyes red. "What do you want me to do?" she asked cautiously.

"Well, to start with, I need to know your lawyer's name. I asked the court but they wouldn't tell me."

Sarah pulled Singh's card from the pocket of her coveralls and held it against the glass. "Most people call him Jay."

Fuller entered the information into his vu-phone, then said, "I know things look bad, Sarah. But I'll get in touch with your lawyer and tell him I'll be a character witness at your hearing. That will kick your case out of the prosecution mill they've set up since Toledo. After a while, this posse mentality is going to die down and someone will throw out your case."

Sarah felt a glimmer of hope for the first time since learning she'd been charged with the needle law. "You really think so?"

"You sit tight and keep a low profile. We'll have you out of here."

"Thanks, Mike," she said, a smile warming her face. "Getting me out of trouble is getting to be a habit for you."

Fuller smiled back. "I needed some help the first time around. But we've got a home field advantage on this one."

THE BATES PRESIDENCY—DAY 6

LOS ANGELES QUARANTINE ZONE B

The large metal door opened with a familiar screech.

Pedro looked up from his book and saw his father enter the one-time meat locker that now housed Ramon Garcia's library.

"I thought I'd find you here," Mano said, closing the door behind him. He stood silently for a moment, as if searching for something to say. "What are you reading?" he asked finally.

Seated in one of the room's two upholstered chairs, Pedro held out a worn hardbound copy of *The Art of War*. "The name caught my eye."

"This was one of the first books I read from Ramon's library," Mano said, taking the book and gently thumbing its pages. "Sun Tzu was a genius. What he wrote about war two thousand years ago still applies today." Mano handed the book back to his son. "I wish it didn't."

Pedro studied his father. The big man rarely made idle talk—except when forced to air his feelings. If this conversation was going to be difficult, he did not want to prolong it. "I don't think you came to talk about books, papá."

"You're right, m'hijo," Mano said, lowering himself into

the other chair. "Look, I'm glad to see you reading. But your mother is worried about you. She says you're paying more attention to your books than to Daniel."

Pedro looked away, unable to face his father. *What kind of man feels ashamed to be around his son?* he wondered. But he could not escape the truth. Every time he looked at Daniel it reminded him that Sarah had traded her life for his—a debt of honor that remain unpaid. Adding to his shame was the memory of Isabel. She'd given her life for him as well. But these were things he could not say aloud. "Even if I could walk, what else is there to do except read? It's like our movement's gone to sleep since Toledo."

"Our cause is important, Pedro. But don't make the same mistake I did," Mano said, placing his hand on Pedro's shoulder. "Don't let this war come between you and your son."

Mano's words took Pedro back to his childhood. He remembered the many times his father had gone away for days, never saying goodbye or explaining why he'd left. Now that he was a rebélde, Pedro understood his father's reasons. But back then, he'd been hurt and confused.

Pedro nodded. "I see what you mean, papá."

"Daniel needs you, m'hijo. You can be a good father and serve our cause, too. Remember that."

"I will," Pedro said hoarsely, trying to keep his emotions in check.

"Good," Mano said pulling the satellite phone from his pocket, "because Ramon says he's got something important to talk about—with both of us."

Pedro felt his gloom lifting. The thought of helping their cause again was something he'd not imagined doing until his leg had healed. Being asked to take part in the call was also a rise in status, something his wounded confidence needed right now. "When?" he asked eagerly.

Mano looked at his watch. "Right now," he said dialing the phone.

GENEVA, SWITZERLAND

Taking another sip of wine, Ramon studied his reflection in the blood red merlot.

This was a horrible war.

Most of those who'd died in Toledo and San Antonio had never asked to be involved or even cared why both sides were even fighting. They'd died all the same.

Their struggle had seemed so noble and clean when he was a young aide for Cesar Chavez. They were standing up for dignity and justice. They were the forces of light opposing the powers of darkness. Fifty years later, the light of their cause was much dimmer, clouded by a thousand compromises.

Today, he would have to pretend to feel something he did not. Ramon was heartsick over the deaths they'd already provoked—and those still to come. But Mano seemed to be wavering in his resolve and Ramon would need to inspire his comrade to carry on the struggle.

He didn't need this misery. Between his money and Maggie's, he could live out his days in comfort, be one of those old men tooling a Jaguar convertible along the Riviera coast, comb-over flapping in the breeze. But he could not walk away from the obligation to his people.

This is the price of leadership, Ramon told himself. The words did little to assuage his restless guilt. The recurring pains in his stomach and indigestion were signs of that burden.

When the satellite phone rang, Ramon crossed the chalet's living room and answered it. "Good to hear from you, Mano," he said, trying to sound hearty. "Is Pedro with you?"

"Yes, you're on the speaker with both of us."

"Excellent. I asked Pedro to take part in the call because our movement's just had a windfall and we'll need both of you to take advantage of it."

"We could use some good news about now, viejo," Mano replied.

"Well, let me start with something that will brighten your day... Octavio Perez is dead."

Mano was silent for a moment. "I never celebrate a death. But Perez had it coming. How did it happen?"

"He had a heart attack four days ago. Died before they could get him to the hospital."

"Perez was fat and out of shape. It's not surprising."

"Yes, that cause seems very reasonable," Ramon said dryly, "but I think it might have been something he ate."

"What do you mean?"

"The Swiss authorities never questioned it, but Octavio had lunch in a North Korean restaurant just before he died."

"Something tells me you were involved in Octavio's lunch order," Mano said. "In any case, we don't need to worry about the Latino Liberation Front getting their hands on another nuke."

"Better than that. Without Octavio, El Frente is out of commission—and that changes the whole ballgame, Mano. We can unify our movement again, and thanks to Bates, we're finally getting the muscle to do it. Several countries have approached me with offers of weapons—automatic rifles, light mortars, even anti-air missiles. We'll be getting communication equipment, too. First, though, we'll need to set up training bases in Mexico so former soldiers like you can show our people in the zones how to use them."

"That's good news. Once we complete our self-sufficiency projects, we'll be ready to fight again."

"We can't wait, hermano. We need to go on the offensive right away."

"We're not ready yet. The water purification projects aren't complete and we're way behind on producing our own energy."

"That won't matter. If things go right, our allies will provide those things."

"And if things don't go right?"

"We have to take that risk. Mano, we need to act now. If we can reunify our movement and provoke Bates into another attack—"

"A lot more people will die," Mano interrupted. "Bates is dangerous, Ramon."

"Yes, he is. That's precisely why we need to move now. Bates outraged the world when he bombed San Antonio. We can use that in our favor if we can lure Bates into attacking another nation."

"How would we do that?"

"We can launch some sorties from Mexico. Bates is itching to flex his muscles, and we can give him the chance. He'll take the bait, Mano."

"I don't like dragging another country into our fight."

"I've spoken to the Mexican legation. They're with us, Mano."

"All right. Assuming we do this, what's Pedro's role?"

"We'll need to move on two fronts at the same time in Southern California. That means having another field commander besides you we can trust."

"Ramon, the assignment of tactical leaders is my decision. We have older fighters with more military experience than Pedro."

"I recognize the decision is yours, Mano. But Pedro is like his father, unwilling to accept defeat. We need that quality more than we need military experience."

"In other words, you want to send my son because he's more willing to die."

"That's not what I mean," Ramon answered, knowing it was not the full truth.

Pedro spoke up for the first time. "I can do this, papá."

"Pedro, you can't even walk yet," Mano said to his son.

"These operations are going to take months to coordinate, Mano. Pedro should be recovered by then," Ramon said. "Try to understand, hermano. We're going to be equipped to fight the Baldies like never before. The people of San Antonio paid for those weapons with their lives. We need our best team on the field."

"Please, papá. Let me do this," Pedro added softly.

After a long pause, Mano spoke. "All right. I'll consider Pedro as a commander," he said reluctantly. "But I'll need to know more details about the operations."

For the next half hour Ramon sketched out the strategy of their operations in San Diego and the Imperial Valley as Mano and Pedro offered tactical opinions. "If we succeed, we'll be on the doorstep of an autonomous region," Ramon concluded before ending the call.

Returning to the kitchen, Ramon poured out the last of the merlot and held up the goblet in a toast.

"To the success of our cause... we've never had a brighter opportunity," he said to the empty room then drained the glass.

The wine tasted bitter.

SANTA CLARITA, CA

The three people in the courthouse conference room were locked in stony silence.

Seated beside her lawyer, Sarah watched the gray-haired prosecutor across the table as he studied her file, peering down through the reading glasses perched on his nose. Reaching into a bulging briefcase, he fished out a folder which he nonchalantly flipped through and then put away.

Jay Singh finally broke the silent impasse. "Well, what's it going to be, Karl?"

The prosecutor thumbed through the papers again and leaned back in his chair. "The way people feel right now, I can get a needle law conviction with any jury in the country on this case."

"Don't try to bluff me, counselor," Singh said, tapping his ballpoint on the table. "I've got a U.S. Army officer willing to vouch for my client's character—and for chrissake, look at her. Does she look like a jury's idea of a Pancho?"

"There's some pretty strong evidence for a needle law case here," the prosecutor said, patting the papers in front of him.

"You've got—let me see," Singh said, leafing through his legal pad, "fifty-four other needle law cases coming up and we both know they'll all be slam dunks. You're going to make your head count, Karl. But if you go to court with my client on a needle law charge, I guarantee you'll be tied up for weeks—even if you get lucky and win. Are you willing to risk your conviction total for this one case?"

The prosecutor slowly scratched his chin. "If she takes six months on the Q&A charge, you've got a deal."

"Can you give me a minute with my client?"

"You've got two minutes—exactly," he said before stepping out of the conference room.

"What's a Q&A charge?" Sarah asked once they were alone.

"A Quarantine and Relocation Act violation—basically it's being Class H and getting caught outside a zone. Normally, they'd just put you back inside the walls. But the old bastard's going to stick you with the six-month max if he has to plea bargain. We still got lucky, though. Nesbitt is near retirement and he's not looking to use your gravestone as a step up the ladder."

"You mean I can go back to the zone in six months?" Sarah asked, her eyes brightening.

"I've already drawn up the papers," Singh said, putting the document in front of her. "Just sign here."

Sarah felt a rush of euphoria as she put her name on the sheet. It might take six more months in jail but she would live to see her son and Pedro again.

THE BATES PRESIDENCY—Day 22

DILLARD, TEXAS

The white SUV cruised north on a stretch of I-35 that cut through the Texas countryside with mind-numbing straightness. Riding beside the driver, Simon Potts unpacked his camera and began shooting some B-roll of the flat landscape dotted with low shrubs and trees.

Leaning out the window, Simon trained his camera on the vehicles trailing their SUV. Receding into the plain behind him was a line of white trucks and semis, the letters "UN" painted prominently on their doors.

In the vehicle with him were four French U.N. Blue Helmets whose icy demeanor seemed to convey that all journalists belonged in the same phylum as tapeworms. Although an interview with the soldiers was unlikely, Simon still considered himself lucky.

He was the only member of the media in this U.N. relief convoy to the San Antonio Quarantine Zone.

He'd wrangled this reporting plum through Ramon Garcia. Knowing that the publicity served his cause, Garcia had forgiven Simon for the tough interview and pulled some strings at the U.N. to get him in. The network had refused to send him on the assignment at first. But after threatening to quit, the suits at CCN had relented, allowing Simon to work alone in the field again.

Once the convoy arrived in San Antonio, Simon would be the first journalist inside the zone since the neutron bomb three weeks earlier. As a bonus, he was riding in the lead vehicle—although Simon was sure this "privilege" was the Blue Helmets' way of keeping him on a short leash.

Since the neutron bomb had been dropped, the White House had placed a media blackout on the San Antonio Quarantine Zone, claiming radiation levels were too high. But amateur videos of the disfigured men, women, and children had still reached the outside world through social media, stirring a wave of indignation.

Unlike the massive rush of aid sent to the victims of Toledo, the Bates administration had done little to help the countless cases of radiation exposure in San Antonio.

After several nations threatened a boycott of U.S. goods in protest, Bates had been pressured by Congress into allowing this United Nations humanitarian aid column. Traveling north from Mexico, the convoy was bringing food, water and medical teams to the area.

As Simon panned his camera toward the front of the convoy, the window behind him exploded.

"What the hell?" Simon shouted. "What's going—"

"Quiet!" Colonel Roux ordered from the back seat before speaking a long stream of French into his radio. A voice speaking French answered him over the RF. Then someone spoke in Spanish.

Simon continued taping until the officer had finished. "Colonel, please tell us what's going on?"

"Some shots have been fired at our convoy. Two other vehicles have been hit," the French officer said with an accent that sounded like he may have prepped at Eton.

"What do you plan to do?"

"As a precaution, the convoy is going to get off the

highway and stop at a town ahead,"

"Is this an organized attack?"

"No, it's not likely. But we cannot take a chance."

Potts turned his camera toward the road ahead and focused on a green exit sign that read "Dillard." Then, from a corner of the frame came a blur of motion.

Simon followed the movement with his camera and gasped in shock. Rising from the low embankment along the edge of the highway, a large farm tractor with a long fertilizer tank in tow was crossing the highway directly ahead of them.

"Colonel!" the driver called out as he instinctively hit the brakes.

With screeching tires, the SUV went into a slide as the driver swerved to avoid a collision. Simon stopped recording and braced himself as the vehicle plunged into the brown grass alongside the highway and came to a stop.

While the colonel barked orders into his radio in French, Simon panned his camera toward the convoy behind them. The neat line of vehicles was now scattered like a train wreck along the highway. Ahead of them, the man driving the tractor jumped out the vehicle and ran, leaving the highway blocked.

Then the gunfire started.

Simon ducked behind the door as the distant *pa-pa-pop* of automatic weapons was joined by a chorus of shouts from the Blue Helmets. The door opened and a hand grabbed him by the collar.

"Come with me," one of the soldiers said, pulling him outside.

Simon grabbed his camera. "Where are we going?"

"The colonel wants all non-combatants over there," the soldier said, pushing him toward a low spot in the median of the interstate. Already, Simon could see other civilians being shepherded to the area by the peacekeepers.

Simon ran in a crouch, his head hunched into his shoulders, as the sound of the gunfire continued. When he reached the low spot, Simon dropped onto the grass next to a doctor he'd met earlier at their staging area.

"Is the U.S. Army attacking us?" the Belgian doctor asked. Over a dozen men and women around the physician turned to hear what Simon would say, their eyes hopeful this American journalist might have an answer.

"It can't be the army," Simon told them. "Even Bates wouldn't be that stupid. These have to be vigilantes."

As the sporadic firing continued, the Blue Helmets formed a rough circle around the civilians, hunkering behind the vehicles, weapons ready but silent. Simon knew U.N. rules prevented them from firing back indiscriminately into the trees and shrubs giving cover to their attackers.

The colonel was crouched next to the lead vehicle, still speaking on the radio when Simon saw his head snap and a splatter of red explode onto the SUV's white door—a split second later came the sharp crack of a sniper rifle. The colonel fell, still holding the phone.

This is bad, Simon realized. Without a leader, their convoy would be adrift, unsure how to respond to this ambush.

An intense barrage of gunfire erupted—the heaviest so far. Simon stopped recording and pressed his body against the grass, trying to make himself a small as possible. Suddenly, an orange flash flooded his eyes and the ground under his body shook like a wave passing beneath him. The sonic shock of a horrific *BOOM* rattled his chest cavity.

Simon covered his head, heart thundering in his chest.

He lay still for a moment, wondering if he was alive or dead. When he finally looked up, the fertilizer tank the tractor had towed into their path was shrouded in billowing orange flames.

One of soldiers ran to their group and dropped to the ground beside them, the whites of his eyes wide around green pupils. "I'm Lieutenant Desmond," he said, short of breath. "We have sent for help. You will be evacuated."

"How are we getting out of here?" Simon asked.

"The Mexican government is sending helicopters."

"What about asking the Americans for help?"

"We called the local authorities. The sheriff told us this was a federal issue and not his jurisdiction. Sorry, but I must get back to my men," the officer said and scrambled away.

For the next twenty minutes, the civilians huddled in fear as the gunfire continued. "Over there," someone said, pointing toward the south, as a distant thumping rose. "It's the helicopters." A cheer went up as two dragonfly shapes appeared just above the horizon, heading in their direction.

Simon sighed with relief and began recording the scene. Then he noticed something strange. A fuzzy gray arrow appeared over their heads, streaking toward the choppers. *It's a missile*, Simon thought in horror as the projectile closed on its target.

The helicopter on the left disappeared into an orange and black fireball. The people around Simon gasped in horror as the faint rumble of the distant explosion reached them. The other chopper hovered for a moment then turned away, heading back toward Mexico. But it was too late. A second missile appeared, striking the remaining aircraft in the rotor, sending it spiraling to the ground in a fiery crash.

The Belgian doctor shook his head. "This is senseless."

Simon recorded his reaction, sure he'd just captured footage that would soon lead news shows across the planet.

For the next three hours, the members of the convoy were kept pinned down until a Texas National Guard unit was deployed to clear the area. By then, the death toll among the U.N. peacekeepers had reached three. After being escorted by U.S. troops back to Mexico, Simon finally learned the full extent of the drama he had witnessed.

Placed on DEF-CON 2 alert, surface-to-air missiles from Randolph Air Force Base had been automatically launched, downing the Mexican helicopters five minutes after they crossed into U.S. airspace.

Counting the Mexican helicopter crews and the U.N. Blue Helmets, a total of nine had died in the abortive U.N. aid convoy. Perhaps even worse, the much-needed relief had never reached the injured in San Antonio.

Outside the borders of the United States, the incident was almost universally condemned as a failure to protect a humanitarian effort and an excessive use of force.

President Bates was unrepentant. "Our borders cannot be crossed at will by another nation's military craft," he said during a White House press conference. "I will not apologize for exercising the right to defend our territory."

Coming on the heels of U.S. air raids against the insurgents across its southern border, Mexico closed down its U.S. consulates, withdrew its ambassador from Washington and severed all diplomatic relations with the United States.

As the geopolitical machinations unfolded, Simon realized there had been only one winner in this tragic incident. More nations were coming forward to provide the Hispanic Republic with weapons, training and supplies in their struggle with the United States.

This new surge of support would be employed by the rebels three months later in a series of shocking attacks that would come to be known as The Halloween Offensive.

THE BATES PRESIDENCY—Month 3, Day 31

IMPERIAL VALLEY, CA

Approaching the crest of the craggy slope, Pedro raised his palm. "Take a break," he said to his unit and walked on to the summit alone. Just ahead, lay the end of the jagged hills they'd been traveling through for the last five days, the Chocolate Mountains, a desolate sierra once used as a gunnery range for the U.S. Navy's aircraft.

Near the horizon, he saw the green checkerboard of California's Imperial Valley sprawling against the shore of the landlocked Salton Sea. In between, was a flat stretch of desert Pedro had been dreading since he'd led his band of twelve out of Los Angeles. Crossing that barren expanse would leave them without cover from the Army's lethal attack helicopters until they reached the tree-lined bank of the Alamo River nearly six kilometers away. If caught in the open by the choppers during the hour-long trek, they faced certain death.

Pedro was counting on the diversionary attacks begun yesterday by his comrades against the Marine Corps Air Station south of Yuma to lure away most of the local helicopters and troops. Still, he was taking no chances. He returned to his unit and waited with them in the shade of some boulders. When the sun was near its peak, he stood and called out, "All right. Let's move."

"Now, Comandante?" Julio Gomez asked. "We're going to cross the desert in the hottest part of the day?"

"Shadows are smallest at midday."

The husky youth nodded without complaint, shouldered his backpack, and helped his younger brother, Elian, to his feet. *They're still eager*, Pedro noted silently. *I hope I can bring them all home.* He'd never led a group this large so far outside the zones before. The tactical plan behind this risky mission had come during their conference call with Ramon six weeks earlier.

"The weapons we've been getting finally give us the luxury to think a few moves ahead," Ramon had said over the satellite phone. "If our cause is going to succeed, we have to chase the farmers out of the Imperial Valley. It's the last concentration of Anglos in southern California."

His father had been skeptical at first. "I hope you're joking," Mano said.

"No, hermano. I'm quite serious. The Imperial Valley could be a sticky issue in our negotiations for an autonomous region. As long as that colony of Anglos remains between us and the Mexican border, we've got a hole in the middle of our territory. The good news is that very few of them are left—not more than thirty-thousand according to my sources."

"Why not wait until we're stronger?"

"We won't have a better time. The day is coming when our allies will support us with land forces from Mexico. It'll be easier to clear a corridor for them now before more Baldies arrive. Oh, and another thing... I realize you wouldn't have it any other way, but we need to do this without a bloodbath. We can't afford to look bad in the world press."

"How can this possibly work, Ramon? You're not only

asking me to uproot thirty-thousand people, you're asking me to conduct an operation over two hundred kilometers away from Los Angeles... a lot of it over open country. The Anglos aren't going to give up easily. That's some of the most productive land in the world."

"You're right, but those mega-farms were built on cheap labor. With all their low-paid workers locked up in the zones, the Imperial Valley farmers are struggling to make money. They're hanging on by a thread, Mano. If we can make a big chunk of that land useless, we'll snip the last strand.

"How are we supposed to do that?"

"The Imperial Valley is really a desert. The only thing making it fertile is the network of irrigation canals and pipelines. If we destroy the watering system—and scare the hell out of the farmers into the bargain—the Anglos may decide they can make a better living somewhere else. I can help you pinpoint the key junctions in the irrigation system."

"You seem to know a lot about the Imperial Valley."

"I was there with Cesar Chavez in '69. We traveled all over the valley during the farm workers strike. That's where I cut my teeth as an activist."

"The Imperial Valley is a big place, Ramon. It would take hundreds of people trained in demolition to do much damage. We can't sneak a group that size out of the zone at once, much less march them five days without getting caught."

"You won't need that many people. You can do the job with a dozen. The key is El Centro. It's the last real town left in the area. If you disrupt the farms and infrastructure around El Centro, everyone left in the area will pull up stakes. I've got a shipment of Semtex and timers on the way to you for the job."

"You make it sound easy, Ramon. We both know better."

"I didn't say it would be easy, hermano. I said it was important."

Since that day, Pedro and his father had been planning this operation. He'd even made a scouting trip to the area once his leg had healed enough to travel. Now, entering the flat expanse of sun-baked clay that seemed to stretch into infinity, he wondered if this long shot would work.

Pedro scanned the hard blue sky as he led his band into the open desert. He was looking for something he did not want to find: the angry-hornet outline of attack helicopters.

In the furnace-like heat, Pedro soon fell into a half-trance, the tempo of his stride and his labored breathing creating a hypnotic rhythm. After three-quarters of an hour, the thin green blur in the distance became a tree line. They had a good chance of making it now.

Then he heard it. A far away roar, rapidly getting louder. "Everybody down!" Pedro ordered as he threw himself to ground. "Keep still."

Running was out the question. They would never make the tree line in time. Their only hope was to lie motionless and pray they weren't spotted.

Shielding his eyes against the glare, Pedro caught sight of two silver specs low in the sky and exhaled in relief. They were jets, taking off from Naval Air Facility El Centro. The planes had already reached an altitude that made it impossible to spot people on the ground. Pedro knew the heat was taking its toll. He should have recognized the difference between the sound of a jet and a helicopter immediately. *Was my father right? Do I have enough experience for this mission?* he wondered, rising to his feet.

"False alarm," he called out, brushing the dust from his fatigues. "Let's get moving,"

When they finally reached the tree line, Pedro crossed the Alamo River and marched his band another three hours, finally making camp for the night along the banks of the New River. As usual, there would be no fire. After another cold supper of cornmeal paste and chicken jerky, they pitched the small stealth-cloth tents that would mask their infrared heat from any night patrols and crawled inside.

Although exhausted from the day's march, Pedro could not sleep. As usual whenever his mind was idle, his thoughts turned to Sarah. No news of her fate had reached him. But every day since her arrest, Pedro had been haunted by a recurring image. He saw Sarah alone in a small cell, waiting for the day they would strap her to a cross-shaped bed and inject the poison in her vein. Trying to shake the tormenting image, he turned his mind to the details of his mission.

The success of their plan depended mostly on their infiltrators. Knowing these hastily trained agents would soon be operating on their own worried him most. Mano and Pedro had spent days combing the Los Angeles zones for Hispanics who could blend in outside the zones. They had not been easy to find. After burying himself in the books in Ramon's library, Pedro now understood why.

While most Mexicans were mestizos—a blend of native and European heritage—among the nation's upper classes, fair-skin, light eyes and Caucasian features were not uncommon. However, the elite of Mexican society was seldom among those who migrated to the United States, creating the scarcity of white Hispanics in most of the quarantine zones of the U.S. Southwest.

Another racial group they knew could blend in outside

the zones was Afro-Latinos. But they were hard to find in the L.A. barrios as well—although Pedro now knew there was no shortage of blacks in Latin America.

From Ramon's history books he'd learned that by the end of the fifteenth century, Spanish weapons and diseases had wiped out most of the indigenous population in the Caribbean and parts of South America. Needing labor for their sugar and coffee plantations, the Spaniards had imported millions of African slaves, creating large concentrations of Spanish-speaking blacks that continued to the present day. Pedro had been astonished to discover that in today's Western Hemisphere, Afro-Latinos outnumbered English-speaking blacks. Yet few people in the U.S. ever pictured someone black—or white—when they thought of a Hispanic.

Their mission depended on this ignorance.

After screening nearly twenty volunteers, Mano and Pedro had selected nine with the looks and language skills to go unnoticed outside the zones. Two had quit during the rigorous training they'd prepared, leaving seven. Pedro had wanted more infiltrators but Mano had convinced him a weak link would jeopardize the mission—and their lives.

An hour before dawn, Pedro gathered his undercover operatives. "I know I've told you a dozen times, but I'm going to tell you again... wait until you hear our shelling before you place the charge on your objective, understood?" The seven first-time agents nodded solemnly, trying to appear brave. "Vayan con Dios," Pedro said and began sending them off a few minutes apart to their respective targets.

Pedro then led the remainder of his unit south along the tree-lined bank of the New River, constantly alert for patrols and farmers as they skirted the deserted town of Brawley. After midday, they reached the first firing position Pedro had selected during his scouting expedition. "We'll set up our mortars here," he said, choosing a sharp curve in the riverbank that gave them cover on three sides. As the crews began assembling the light artillery, Pedro was impressed by their calm precision. They were eager students who regretfully had little else to learn. When the two mortar batteries were ready, Pedro checked his watch.

In twelve minutes, the assault on the Imperial Valley would begin.

Reynaldo Arias stumbled into the alfalfa field beside the road and vomited again. Since leaving Pedro and the others several hours ago, his stomach had been churning in fear. Each step he'd taken from the security of the group seemed to drain his courage. For most of the morning, Rey had recited Pedro's directions to his target again and again, a familiar mantra that helped control his terror. "Follow Rutherford until you get to Butters, then turn north until you reach Williams." Now, finally within sight of his destination, Rey wondered if he'd have the nerve to complete his mission.

The area around the irrigation pipe junction he was supposed to destroy was deserted. In fact, he'd easily evaded the only human he'd run into since leaving camp, a lone farmer in a combine rig harvesting some kind of grain many kilometers back.

Everywhere Rey looked in this flat landscape, he saw signs of a human hand: rectangular fields, arrow-straight roads, irrigation canals, and endless lines of pipe. Someone had built all this—yet everything was still and lifeless. And there lay the root of Rey's fear. He had the terrifying sensation that at any moment, the people who had vanished from this land would suddenly reappear.

I should have never volunteered, he told himself. *I don't have the cojones for this.* Under the needle law, the Semtex and detonator he carried in his backpack were a death sentence—and Ray did not want to die. But as he thought about his unhappy life, he wondered why.

Born in Miami to Columbian parents, Reynaldo Arias had come to Hollywood after high school hoping to make it show business. After the Quarantine and Relocation Act, Rey was interned in Quarantine Zone A. He had not seen his family since that day.

His father, a doctor, had brought his wife to the U.S. fleeing the civil war in Columbia's Choco province. In Miami, they'd started a family in a Puerto Rican neighborhood where their African features and Spanish language were not exceptional. Acceptance, however was elusive. The Puerto Ricans were clannish, often shunning the Columbians. Living near Miami's sizeable black neighborhood, Liberty City, Afro-Latinos like the Arias family were expected to choose an allegiance: "Are you Black or Hispanic?" The question had haunted Rey—and been the cause of many brawls.

Rey was glad his family had moved to the United States, a land infinitely wealthier and safer than Columbia. But his feelings toward the U.S. had always included a kernel of resentment passed down from his father.

Rey's father had taught him that in 1903 the United States had fomented the Columbian insurrection that led to the new nation of Panama, a country that had eagerly sold the Norteamericanos the rights to build their canal. This long-standing resentment, combined with the hardship he'd suffered under the Quarantine and Relocation Act, had led Rey to say yes when Pedro had recruited him. But there had been more to Rey's decision.

He secretly hoped volunteering for this mission would win him a measure of respect and acceptance inside Quarantine Zone A. Although Hispanics across the United States had put aside their differences under the pressure of the Quarantine and Relocation Act, prejudices still persisted. The harsh fact was that many in the zones still looked down on black Hispanics.

A distant rumbling interrupted Rey's thoughts. He looked behind him and froze in terror. A Baldie convoy was approaching.

Rey thought of diving into the chest-high alfalfa, but it was too late. The Baldies had surely seen him. His only hope now was that the soldiers would assume he was a dreg. As the camo-painted vehicles drew closer, Rey felt his knees tremble.

The lead Humvee slowed and came to a stop. Rey's heart thudded in his chest. They were so close he could see the blue eyes of the Baldie manning the machine gun on top of the vehicle.

"Yo, dude. What you doing here?" the soldier called out.

Recognizing the soldier's hip-hop affect, Rey answered in kind, a skill from his dramatic training. "Trying to cop a gig, m'man."

The soldiers in the Humvee seemed to be conferring. Several agonizing seconds passed. Then, without another word, the Humvee roared away. As the rest of convoy rolled by, Rey noticed they were mostly trucks. It was a supply column. A combat patrol would have searched him. Next time, he might not be so lucky.

Once the convoy was out of sight, Rey hurled his backpack into the alfalfa and broke into a run, making a beeline through the field toward the brown mountains from which he'd come. After sprinting several minutes in the midday heat he slowed to a walk, gasping for breath.

In the distance, he heard the dry-cough explosions of mortar shells.

Whoomp. Whoomp.

Seconds later, they fired again.

Whoomp. Whoomp.

Rey knew the Baldies would begin closing in on Pedro and his mortar teams soon. Pedro and the others were risking their lives, drawing the soldiers away so he and the other infiltrators could complete their missions. A wave of shame washed over Rey. If he fled now, no one would ever know, but his hopes of gaining respect in the zones would be a fraud. He could never face Pedro knowing he'd panicked like a coward. As another round of shells fell, Rey realized he had come too far to run away now. His nausea fading, he returned to his road and retrieved his backpack.

Minutes later, Rey reached the irrigation pipe junction they'd chosen as his target. With trembling fingers, he placed the explosive charge on the pipeline as Pedro had trained him and set the timer. With the bomb armed and ticking, Rey hurried away.

Pedro studied the runway at Naval Air Facility El Centro through his binoculars. On the tarmac, twin geysers of smoke and dirt shot into the air as their mortars struck again. After four volleys they had not hit any planes, but that wasn't essential to their plan. Pedro wanted to stir up the hornet's nest—and the hornets were about to swarm. The base was hurriedly fueling its fighters. In a matter of minutes, the jets would be in the air.

"Cease fire," Pedro called out. "Pack up your mortars and get ready to move."

Pedro watched the sky over the base as the young crews behind him coolly took apart their weapons. The success of this mission—and possibly their lives—now hinged on intelligence gathered by Ramon about the U.S. military.

Ramon had discovered all U.S. military facilities were now equipped with FireFinder radar. Under normal circumstances, the base would have tracked them by now and launched a hail of shells on their position. But thanks to Ramon's foresight, Naval Air Facility El Centro had no artillery to fire back. Most of the Marine battalion assigned to defend the base, including their mortar units, was in Yuma repelling the rebel attacks there. A single company of Marines now guarded the base, supported by a squadron of F-18E Super Hornet fighters in for training.

In their battle-ready configurations, the planes carried a devastating arsenal. However, Ramon had uncovered a glaring weakness about NAF El Centro: The facility was now used strictly for air-to-air combat training. The planes at the base were not armed to attack targets on the ground. Other than their limited ability to spot for the ground troops, the planes were a toothless threat.

"We're ready, Comandante." Julio Gomez reported, hoisting his backpack.

"All right, let's move."

Pedro led them south along the tree-lined riverbank. They would travel closer to the safety of the Mexican border sixteen kilometers away before firing another salvo. Jogging along the soggy clay, Pedro expected the ground units defending the base to soon join the planes in pursuit of his mortar teams. He wanted to draw all the remaining manpower of the Imperial Valley south, away from the infiltrators.

Six planes were in the air now, guided by FireFinder

toward the spot where they'd last fired their mortars, nearly a kilometer back. The planes swooped in low, the roar of their engines filling the air.

"Stay under cover," Pedro yelled. He'd learned from his father that even at their slowest speed, the F-18Es traveled much too fast to spot a human in the heavy vegetation along the river. After moving south another kilometer, his mortar teams would set up and fire again.

A thundering boom suddenly drowned out the jet engines. Pedro turned and saw an orange fireball billowing into the air along the river. The lead plane had fired a rocket.

Ramon had been wrong. The planes had missiles that could attack ground targets. Pedro swallowed hard, knowing the odds of the game had just changed. Their chances of leaving the Imperial Valley alive had just grown very slim.

Whooop. "DANGER. IMPROPER ANGLE." *Whooop.* DANGER. IMPROPER ANGLE," warned the mechanical voice inside the F-18F as Lieutenant Jacob Haller banked his plane into a steep dive.

"You're out of your fucking mind, Jake!" the radar intercept officer in the plane's rear seat yelled into the radio. "You can't fire an air-to-air missile at a ground target."

"Just get ready to shoot that Sidewinder when I tell you, Dutch," the pilot replied.

Buffeted by the near-vertical dive, the plane trembled and bounced. Undaunted, Haller tweaked the joystick until the bend in the riverbank pinpointed by FireFinder was lined up in the windshield's crosshairs. "Fire," he said calmly.

Haller held the nose steady for another second and watched the smoky trail of the missile streak toward the riverbank, then yanked back hard on the stick. The jet shuddered, its metallic skin groaning as Haller pulled out of the dive only a few hundred feet above the deck.

Watching the fireball rise on the ground behind him, Haller heard his flight commander's voice over the radio. "Blue Leader to Blue Five. What in the hell was that, Jake?"

"I just figured out how we can hit the Panchos, Skipper. We disable the heat-seeking sensor on the Sidewinders and fire them line-of-sight."

One after the other, the planes swooped down, fired their missiles, and pulled away. Although half a kilometer from Pedro's team, each thunderous strike shook the trees above them. The young faces huddled around Pedro seemed anxious and shaken. He'd assured them the planes would be unable to fire at the ground. "We're OK as long as we stay under cover," he yelled over the cascade of explosions. "They don't know where we are."

After several passes by the planes, Pedro noticed something strange. Many of their missiles were going astray, missing the riverbank completely. Before he could decide what to make of this, one of the jets swerved in his direction after pulling out of its dive. Flying low, the fighter drew closer, its deafening roar growing louder by the second. Had the plane spotted them? It wasn't likely, but he couldn't take the chance. "Everybody down!" Pedro yelled and dropped to the ground.

The jet was nearly on them now. Pedro's chest throbbed from the rumble of its engine. He steeled himself, fighting the urge to run. As the jet passed over them, Pedro instinctively covered his head. Looking up, he sighed with relief as the plane streaked harmlessly away. His relief evaporated when he saw Elian Gomez throw off his pack and start a frenzied sprint into the empty field beside them.

"Elian! Get back here!" Pedro shouted. If the planes spotted him, Elian would probably be killed—and also give away their position. Elian glanced back, his face a mask of terror, and kept running.

Elian's brother Julio rose and shed his backpack. "I'll get him," he said and broke into a run after Elian.

"Stop, Julio! Come back!" Pedro yelled, knowing two bodies moving in the open would be easier to detect from the air. Pedro watched helplessly as Julio closed on his brother and wrestled him to the ground about two-hundred meters away. Miraculously, the planes had not spotted them.

"Stay down! Don't move!" Pedro screamed at the pair, gesturing frantically. Unable to hear Pedro above the roar of the planes, Julio began dragging his panic-stricken brother back toward their position in the trees. Pedro realized their entire unit was now in grave danger.

"Listen, up!" he called out to the rest of his people "Start moving south, now. You'll be safe as long as you stay under the trees. Carmen is in charge," he said, nodding to his oldest remaining team member. "Wait for me at the next bend in the river. If I'm not there in ten minutes, don't stop again until you cross the border."

The rumbling of an approaching jet drew Pedro's eyes skyward. One of the planes was bearing down on Julio and Elian, tilting steeply toward the ground. A missile hissed away from the fighter and exploded fifty meters from the brothers.

Unhurt, Julio and Elian began a mad dash toward Pedro.

A second plane swooped down at the pair and fired, missing them by less than twenty meters. To Pedro's amazement, the boys staggered for a few steps but continued running.

"Spread out!" Pedro yelled, fanning his arms outward as a third plane began its pass. Now a hundred meters away, the brothers saw Pedro's gesture and created some space between them as they ran. The plane launched its missile and Pedro watched in horror as the rocket traced a smoky line directly toward the boys. Elian disappeared in the flash of the fireball. Only a few steps away, Julio's body broke apart as the blast hurled him to the ground. Pedro dropped to his knees and covered his face.

Another rocket struck nearby. The shockwave rocked Pedro, its heat singeing his skin, but he remained motionless. *I should never have taken this mission*, he thought bitterly. *Two more have followed me and died.*

At that moment, Pedro wanted to lay there and wait for the planes to finish him as well. Then he remembered the others moving south along the river. They would need his help to escape alive.

A missile exploded in the trees thirty meters north. Pedro knew the aviators would blanket the tree line with rockets now, hoping to take out more of his people. Running in a crouch, he darted along the trees until he found a cluster of boulders along the riverbank and wedged his body between them. A missile struck the river not far away, showering him in a fountain of water and mud. For interminable minutes, the planes roared overhead, blindly firing rockets into the wooded stretch.

Pressing his body against the wet clay, Pedro wondered

how much longer he could lead people into battle. He'd seen so much killing and death. *The worst point will come when you feel nothing at all*, he reminded himself. By force of will, he buried his doubts. He could not abandon the others.

Pedro looked at his watch. The planes had been pressing their attack for over five minutes. Soon, they would have to return to the base to rearm. When the roar of the engines faded, Pedro retrieved the brothers' backpacks and began jogging south toward his unit. The ground troops from the base would be coming after them soon and he knew the Baldies would not find it hard to pick up their trail. They would need all his skills—and a lot of luck—to make it across the border.

———

Rey's terror was returning. He walked faster, trying to put more distance between himself and his target.

Something had gone wrong. The distant thunder of the battle had been going on for way too long. According to their plan, Pedro's mortars would fire no more than eight salvos. The persistent explosions in the distance told Rey the Baldies were fighting back—hard.

He checked the cheap digital watch Pedro had given him and the other infiltrators. Their charges were scheduled to detonate in two minutes. Rey wanted to run but Pedro had warned him it would be a dead giveaway. So he walked on hurriedly, squinting at the sun's glare off the irrigation canal beside the road.

Ahead, Rey could make out the blue shore of the Salton Sea, the salty body of water where the canal beside him drained. In fact, all the irrigation canals in the Imperial Valley emptied into the Salton Sea—and that held the key to their plan.

Rey looked at his watch again. Less than a minute remained.

He anxiously scanned the flat landscape around him. With no one in sight, he stopped and turned back toward his target. Thirty seconds. Twenty seconds. Ten seconds. Five seconds. *Babaroooom.*

The explosions came in quick succession, almost a sustained roar. In the distance, a series of black clouds appeared over the rectangular fields. Moments later, a geyser of brown water erupted from each cloud as the pipelines vented their pressure. After a few seconds, the fountains tapered off.

Rey turned his eyes to the canal beside the road. The foam on the brown water that had been flowing toward the Salton Sea slowed, stopped, and then began flowing the other way. In a matter of minutes, the cloudy water moving toward the fields was replaced by clear blue water from the Salton Sea.

"Yes, it's working! It's working!" Rey said aloud, laughing with glee.

The sudden loss of pressure from their explosions had created a siphon effect. Soon, a huge section of cropland in the Imperial Valley would be flooded with the salt-filled water of the Salton Sea. With all the farmers taking shelter from the attacks and the Baldies chasing Pedro, no one would be around to stop it.

Walking toward the mountains that would lead him home, Rey remembered what Pedro had said, although he still didn't understand it fully: "Like the Romans did to the Carthaginians, we'll plow salt into their fields."

From the safety of Mount Signal on the Mexican side of the border, Pedro stared at the Imperial Valley surrounded by his exhausted comrades. It would be months before they knew if this mission would succeed in driving out the Anglos. Only one thing was certain: The cost had been high. He'd lost three more young lives to the Baldies on their way out, five dead in all. The chances were slim that all their infiltrators would make it back alive. Pedro hoped the mission was worth the price they'd paid in lives—and the dying was far from over. Right now, his father and their fighters were risking their lives engaging military targets across the country.

He knelt and lifted a handful of the mountain's gritty soil. Unlike many on his side, he was no longer fighting for land. He wanted to win this war so his son could live in peace, unrestrained by walls—and maybe, against all the odds, be reunited with Sarah. He let the dirt slip away between his fingers. "What you did today will not be forgotten, hermanos," he said to his group, rising to his feet. "But there's more to be done. It's time to start back."

SAN DIEGO, CA

Rear Admiral Joseph Rossi smiled as a photo of his four-year-old grandson dressed in a pirate costume appeared on his computer monitor. *Taking after grandpa*, his daughter had captioned the digital photo she'd e-mailed him. Rossi glanced at the stack of paperwork on his desk, hoping he could finish up in time to accompany his grandson this evening for his first Halloween. Sighing, he returned to work.

While reviewing the base's latest operational readiness report, his desk phone rang. "What is it, Ensign?" he said into the receiver.

His aide's voice was shaky and tense. "Admiral, I have the commander at Imperial Beach on the line. He says they're being shelled," The Imperial Beach Outlying Airfield at the southernmost edge of the base housed Coronado's seven active helicopter squadrons.

"Put him on the line—and then get Commander Blake in my office."

A few seconds later, a calmer, older voice said, "Admiral, we've got mortars hitting our tarmac. One chopper's already taken damage. I'd guess it's some kind of light ordnance. Maybe 81 millimeters."

"This could be a misfire from the elephant cage, Doug. Our cowboys in special ops can get a little carried away during exercises."

"I don't think so, Admiral. The shells are coming in from the south."

"From Mexico?"

"Yes, sir."

"It sounds like we've got Pancho trouble."

"The Panchos haven't used mortars before, Admiral."

"I doubt Mexico's decided to reclaim California, Doug. Get a flight of Cobras in the air to take out those mortars. In the meantime, move the rest of your choppers up to North Island. I'm going to alert NORTHCOM and deploy our FireFinder."

"We may need to move into Mexican airspace, Admiral."

"You're cleared," Rossi assured his chopper commander. Under the new DEF-CON 2 rules of engagement, the U.S. military was authorized to cross international borders in hot pursuit.

After sending a message to his superiors at the U.S. Northern Command about the attack, Rossi called the Marine colonel commanding the base's FireFinder unit and ordered him to scan toward the south. The directionally-limited radar designed to track the origin of incoming artillery normally faced west, toward the ocean.

As he hung up, Rossi's aide handed him a written reply from NORTHCOM:

MILITARY BASES ACROSS U.S. UNDER ATTACK. C-IN-C HAS AUTHORIZED DEF-CON 1.

Rossi stared at the message, stunned. No U.S. president had ever placed our forces at DEF-CON 1. It meant the United States was under attack by a foreign power.

Rossi called his aide and said, "Get the Nimitz out of the harbor." In port for routine maintenance, the aircraft carrier USS Nimitz was the centerpiece of the Pacific Fleet, one of the most valuable weapons platforms on the planet. He could not risk this asset.

When Commander Blake arrived, Rossi handed the Base Defense Officer the NORTHCOM message.

Blake read the note and exhaled slowly. "Holy shit, Admiral."

"I've put the Nimitz out to sea. What's the status of our fixed wings?"

"We've got a flight of Hornets from North Island out on air patrol. Right now, they're probably a hundred fifty klicks over the Pacific. All our other aircraft are wheels down."

"Put another flight of Hornets in the air for local support and have all other operational aircraft fueled and ready for takeoff. I want our birds ready to fly if Pancho decides to lob any more shells."

Blake snapped open his vu-phone and began to dial, then stopped and said, "What about our other surface ships?"

"They've only fired light mortars."

"I know they can't ding our tin cans with those, but I'd

like to get our support ships out of the harbor."

"Do it. But I want our floating firepower to stay close. We may need it."

"Should we turn our FireFinder toward the coast, Admiral?"

"It's already done. They're scanning south."

"What about the east, sir? The Quarantine Zone's just across the bay."

"I realize that, Blake. But we know for certain we've got an enemy with mortars to the south. We have to deploy against our most immediate threat."

"Aye, sir," the officer said and began punching numbers into his vu-phone.

While Blake relayed his orders, Rossi got a call from the Imperial Beach commander. "The shelling stopped as soon as we put our Cobras in the air, Admiral, but there was something strange. When my birds flew in, they spotted a mortar position just south of the border and took it out with a couple of Hellfires. As they came in to mop up, they found the position was a decoy, a bunch of dummies and some pipes."

"Keep searching the area, Doug. The real mortar crew is still out there. I've turned the FireFinder in your direction and put a flight of Hornets in the air. If the Panchos decide to fire again, we'll be ready."

"Thanks, Admiral. But I think the beaners are done for the day. They know they're messing with the big dogs now."

———

Mano steadied himself against the window frame and focused his binoculars on North Island Air Station across the channel of San Diego Bay. From the top floor of this abandoned downtown high rise, he could see the runways crisscrossing the north end of the fan-shaped island. Arriving in a long line, helicopters from Imperial Beach were landing near the squadrons of fighters and transport planes already parked along the tarmac. The crowded airstrip was a hive of activity as fuel and ammo trucks clustered around the aircraft.

When the last of the choppers had landed and their rotors spun to a stop, Mano turned on his satellite phone and said, "Fire."

Seconds later, a puff of smoke appeared on the runway, followed by a distant boom.

"Ten degrees west," Mano said into the phone and another puff materialized, this time near one of the fighter jets.

"Two degrees north."

The fuel vehicles were moving away from the planes now, knowing they'd been targeted. A puff of smoke engulfed the jet in Mano's binoculars. When the cloud cleared, the broken remnants of a charred fuselage lay on the tarmac.

"Five degrees west," he said, aiming for the next fighter in the neat line.

The fourth mortal shell narrowly missed the jet, striking a fuel truck hurrying past. The explosion began as an orange ball of flame on the ground and billowed upward into a black, lollipop cloud.

"Cease fire and get out of there," he said. Their time was up. The base's counter-battery radar would lock in on his mortar crew if they fired from their position inside the Quarantine Zone much longer.

Climbing down the building's stairwell, his task done, Mano felt no relief. The base's FireFinder radar might not pinpoint their exact firing position, but he had no doubt they'd know their mortars came from inside the walls of the zone. Would the base commander fire back blindly into an area crowded with innocent civilians?

He'd risked the hazardous journey to San Diego with the mortar crews he'd trained for nearly a month. But in the next few moments, they faced the part of their plan that frightened Mano most.

———

WHOOMP.

Rossi felt the concussion through his feet an instant before he heard the booming cough of a mortar shell. Rushing to the window, he saw a fading cloud of smoke above a black pothole in the tarmac two hundred meters away.

"Admiral! Get down!" Blake yelled, already on his belly.

Ignoring Blake, Rossi picked up the phone. "Ensign, call the FireFinder commander and tell him to switch his radar east, *now!*" he said, then turned to Blake. "Scramble the aircraft on the runways. They're sitting ducks out there... and clear the trucks out, too." Blake uncovered his head and began making calls from the floor.

WHOOMP.

Another mortal shell exploded and Blake dropped his vu-phone, pressing himself harder against the ground. "Sorry... Sorry... " he said, scuttling after the phone.

WHOOMP.

"Dammit!" Rossi shouted as he watched the next shell land—a direct hit on an F18.

"This has to be coming from the Quarantine Zone, Admiral," Blake called out. "Small mortars don't have the range to reach us from anywhere else."

Goddamned Congress, Rossi fumed to himself, *Every base should have at least two FireFinders.*

WHOOMP.

The room glowed orange for an instant before a deafening boom made Rossi duck and cover his ears. He looked out the window and saw a fuel truck in flames.

The desk phone rang and Rossi answered it.

"Admiral, I have the FireFinder commander on the line," his aide announced.

"Put him through."

"Admiral, I've got my unit facing east and ready to track the next incoming round."

"Good. We'll forward the coordinates to fleet command for counter battery fire. Stand by."

They waited wordlessly, anxious to hear the next shell.

After several minutes of silence, Blake slowly rose to his feet. "I think the shelling has stopped, sir."

"Commander, keep your radar tracking east," Rossi said into the telephone. "Call me immediately if they open fire again."

"Aye, sir," the Marine said and disconnected.

Rossi sat down, rubbing his balding head. "They're cagey bastards, I'll give them that. The attack on Imperial Beach was a feint to pack North Island with aircraft and give them more targets."

Blake stared through the window at the smoking wreckage on the runway. "Admiral, we both know those mortar shells came from the Quarantine Zone across the bay. I request your permission to lay a carpet barrage on the area."

"Request denied, Commander."

"Admiral, they took out a sixty-million-dollar aircraft. We can't let them get away with that."

"Everybody in that zone isn't a Pancho, Blake. Our job is to fight our nation's enemies. That's not a license to slaughter civilians."

"After Toledo, they're all the enemy, sir."

Rossi stared at the top of his desk. "If all of us come to believe that, we'll never win this war."

THE HALLOWEEN OFFENSIVE

From *Witness To History,*
© 2067 by Simon Potts

Launched on October 31st, the rebel's Halloween Offensive marked several new milestones in the suddenly resurgent conflict.

The concerted attacks on over thirty military and strategic targets from coast to coast seemed to signal an end to the era of terror against civilians by the Latino Liberation Front. The leadership of the Hispanic Republic had retaken the initiative of the insurgency.

In one of the most daring attacks, the rebels flooded large tracts of farmland in California's Imperial Valley with polluted, salt-laden water siphoned from the Salton Sea by explosives, destroying crops and damaging the soil.

The October 31st assaults also marked the first time the insurgents had attacked with light artillery. Rebel mortars had destroyed several aircraft on the tarmac of the U.S. Navy base in San Diego. Remnants of exploded shells recovered across the country revealed the rebels' 81mm mortars were so widely used throughout the world it was impossible to determine their supplier.

During the Halloween attacks, the U.S. launched aerial counter-strikes against rebel forces on Mexican soil. Mexico's president called the action "reckless and provocative," to which President Bates replied, "If you harbor terrorists, expect to be treated like one." The United Nations Security Council issued a statement condemning the "serious violation of sovereign territory by the United States."

More significantly, it was the first time a U.S. president had raised the nation's defense status to DEF-CON 1. "The United States is now in a state of war," Melvin Bates announced.

"Let this serve as notice to our enemies that any attacks against us will be met with swift and severe retaliation."

Most Americans had hoped the San Antonio bomb would destroy the insurgents' will to fight. The Halloween Offensive proved them wrong.

Public polls taken after the rebel assaults detected a drop in public confidence for Melvin Bates. The president, however, remained steadfast in his convictions. "We want peace. But woe to those who wage war against us."

—Simon Potts

THE BATES PRESIDENCY—Month 4, Day 7

SANTA CLARITA, CA

Sarah jogged eight paces, turned and ran eight paces back, completing the first lap of the day in her exercise area. Running inside this barren concrete space had been disorienting at first. The blank gray walls stretched two stories high, taller than the space was long. Looking at the narrow strip of sky overhead made you feel trapped in a hole shaped uncomfortably like a grave. All the same, Sarah treasured the five hours a week she was given outside her six-by-eight foot cell.

The steel door at the end of the concrete box opened as Sarah tallied her eleventh lap, much too soon for the hour she was allotted. But instead of a guard, Jay Singh entered.

"Welcome to the dog run," she said, as he stepped inside.

Singh looked around and smiled weakly. "Not exactly Club Med, is it?"

"It beats ducking shit."

"What do you mean?"

"I used to get my exercise break in a fenced area next to the prison yard. But after the Halloween attacks, someone threw her feces at me. When the guards took her away, it nearly started a riot. So now I exercise in here."

"You're very brave, Sarah."

"I've only got three months to go. I can stand anything for that long."

"Well, I'm afraid that's not certain anymore," Singh said, nervously rubbing his face. "That's why I'm here."

Sarah's eyes narrowed. "I signed the plea bargain, Jay."

"Yes, but your prosecutor has retired and his replacement's presented new evidence which lets her reopen your case. This new prosecutor's young and trying to make her bones on Nesbitt's cold cases. Her name's Andrea Gordon."

"What's this new evidence?"

Singh opened his briefcase, pulled out a deposition and handed Sarah the document. "Seems one of your mother's neighbors, one Cindy Dorsett, says you menaced her shortly before you were arrested."

"That's absolute bullshit. Cindy confronted me."

"Unfortunately, Gordon doesn't care. She just wants a reason to reopen the case. Old man Nesbitt skimmed off all the easy needle law convictions after Toledo. So you are the proverbial bottom of the barrel. But after the Halloween attacks, Gordon figures she's got a good chance to nail you and win some points with the new Bates people at the Justice Department."

Sarah raised her head and stared at the narrow patch of sky above. This new prosecutor surely had a family and loved ones, people who she cherished. But to Gordon she was a huntsman's trophy, a piece of meat served to a public hungry for revenge. "Can we beat this?" she asked finally.

Singh exhaled slowly. "I'll be honest, Sarah. Any jury we select right now is going to be angry about the Halloween attacks. Our best bet will be to stall the trial until things cool off."

"Stall? For how long?"

"As long as we can. Look, I know you want to get back to your son. But our first priority is to keep you alive. I've already filed for an extension on the trial. We'll be in court two weeks from today," he said knocking on the steel door to summon the guard. "I'll be back to see you before then."

After Singh was gone, Sarah slumped against the wall and closed her eyes.

For the last three months, two visions had sustained her through the slow torture of solitary confinement. One was the moment she first hugged Pedro. The other was holding her son once again. Already, the visions were beginning to fade.

THE BATES PRESIDENCY—Month 4, Day 18

From *Witness To History,*
© 2067 by Simon Potts

As the United States continued to plummet in world opinion, support and military aid for the rebel cause soared. Volunteers from every nation in Latin America flocked to Mexico, with many slipping across the border to join the fight in the Quarantine Zones. Two long-time adversaries of U.S. interests in the region, Venezuela and Bolivia, secretly provided military advisors to staff the new rebel training bases in northern Mexico. Supply depots for the insurgents sprung up in a number of other Latin American countries as aid poured in from the rest of the world.

Later in the year, an incident in the Caribbean would ratchet up the tensions between the U.S. and its southern neighbors.

During a training exercise north of Puerto Rico, the newly commissioned Argentine aircraft carrier A.R.A. Guillermo Brown launched six unarmed fighters. Led by a rookie flight commander, the inexperienced pilots vectored toward the Florida coast during drills and unknowingly entered U.S. radar space.

With the U.S. military on hair-trigger status, Homestead Air Force Base near Miami scrambled a flight of F-35 fighters. One hundred kilometers from the unknown radar blips, the U.S. warplanes challenged the bogeys by radio. The Argentine planes, using a narrow-band radio frequency, were unaware of the fast-approaching U.S. jets. With no response to their challenge, the F-35s launched a barrage of missiles that downed four of the Argentine planes.

When the two surviving Argentine fighters reported the attack from an unknown source, the captain of the Guillermo Brown radioed Buenos Aires for instructions and powered up his anti-aircraft missile system as a precaution. The F-35s detected the telltale radar signature of the carrier's SAM system and launched a volley of Penguin anti-ship missiles at the threat. Less than an hour later, the Guillermo Brown was at the bottom of the sea, most of her crew of 1,300 lost.

With the world in shock over the tragic accident, the White House argued the U.S. fighter pilots were simply following the DEF-CON 1 rules of engagement and offered no apologies. Following Mexico's example, Argentina severed diplomatic relations with the United States.

The enmity between the U.S. and its southern neighbors would soon worsen.

—Simon Potts

SANTA CLARITA, CA

Sonya Bailey yawned, sat up in the bed and raised her arms in a cat-like stretch. "How about some breakfast, Mike? After last night, I think you'll need to get your strength back," she said with a sly smile.

"My friend Mr. Beam is joining me for breakfast," Michael Fuller answered, grabbing a near-empty fifth of bourbon from the motel room nightstand. After rubbing his bloodshot eyes, he drained the rest of the bottle.

Laying back down, Sonya placed her head on Fuller's chest. "You still seem stressed, Mike."

Fuller slowly stroked her cheek. She'd brought passion and tenderness back into his life. *How can I complain after that?* he wondered. All the same, so many things still remained unresolved—especially with Sarah who was now back on trial for her life. Someday he'd tell Sonya about his connection with Hank Evans' daughter. But for now, it was best to be discreet.

After a moment Fuller smiled. "I'm glad you're here," he said, looking into her eyes. "Not much else good to say."

Sonya sighed, letting her gaze drift toward the ceiling. "I thought getting shipped out of D.C. was a raw deal at first," she said. "But it's worked out better for both of us."

"Define 'better' for me, will you?"

She laughed softly. "What's your problem with the brass this time?"

"This insurgency is being handled just as stupidly at the tactical level as it is back in Washington."

"Have you tried suggesting changes?"

"Yeah, quite a few times. They all get shot down."

"Like what?"

"Well, they turned down my plan to take out the Pancho's Iglas."

"You forget I'm a desk soldier, Mike. What's an Igla?"

"It's a shoulder-fired rocket. Goddamn thing is heat-seeking and can hit anything in flight out to five thousand meters. We quit flying over the zones after the Panchos got their hands on them and took down two of our choppers."

"Sounds like the local brass is scared to lose any more birds."

"Absolutely. If they just had the balls to put a few choppers in the air at once, we could take out their Iglas right after they launched. But that's a risk the brass doesn't want to take. Now the Panchos have gotten bolder. They're not afraid of our choppers anymore and it's changed the whole tactical picture," he said, shaking his head. "Of course, you can't completely blame the local commanders. There's no smart way to do something stupid."

"You told me that might happen."

"Yeah, and it pisses me off when I'm a swami about it. The Panchos are just about on equal footing with us now, Sonya. They ambush us. We ambush them. Everywhere is no-man's-land. We have to fight to keep supply lines open to our bases and they do too. It's a total cluster fuck."

"I'm sorry I asked, Mike. I didn't mean to get you worked up."

"Don't apologize. It's my fault for talking shop."

"We need to start meeting somewhere else, someplace where this war is far away."

Fuller looked at his watch. "Your plane doesn't leave for another four hours—let's see if we can't find something better to do till then," he said smiling.

Sonya playfully slapped his arm and grinned. "Major Fuller, you're a beast."

THE BATES PRESIDENCY—Month 5

From *Witness To History,*
© 2067 by Simon Potts

In the fifth month of the Bates presidency, U.S. relations with Latin America reached a new low.

The growing rift widened when a U.S. reconnaissance satellite detected the presence of two rebel training camps in the deserts of northern Mexico. On the president's orders, the U.S. Air Force launched air strikes against the facilities, destroying most of the buildings and killing an undisclosed number of insurgents. When Mexico's president publicly condemned the action as "a violation of our sovereignty," President Bates warned, "We will protect ourselves from these breeding grounds of terror near our borders. The terrorists will not find a safe haven in the bosom of Third World despots." When asked by reporters if the U.S. would ever attack rebel camps and supply facilities in any country in the world, Bates replied, "As president, it is my sworn duty to defend our homeland. Anyone, anywhere, supporting the terrorists plaguing our nation can expect to feel our wrath."

Following the air strikes and Bates' statement, the Organization of American States formed a military coalition for the first time in its history. In a treaty similar to the now-defunct NATO, the Spanish-speaking nations of the Western Hemisphere allied themselves in a mutual defense pact called the Alianza Latinoamericana. Although not mentioned by name in the treaty, the implication was clear: The ALA's primary adversary was the United States.

Not long thereafter, the People's Republic of China was drawn into the escalating tensions when a ship from a Chinese fishing fleet working the California Current for tuna was sunk by a U.S. Coast Guard cutter. The cutter's tired crew, on round-the-clock battle stations for weeks, had mistaken the tightly clustered group of fishing vessels for an approaching military formation.

Meanwhile, the insurgency in the Quarantine Zones was nearing all-out war. Supplied with more sophisticated weapons and the training to use them, the rebels were now launching raids outside the walls. Much of the Southwest was now a free-fire area for the U.S. military. The regions around the Quarantine Zones were a battle-scarred no-man's-land of ambushes, shelling, and firefights. With each passing day, the likelihood of mainstream Americans ever moving back into these areas grew dimmer.

—Simon Potts

THE BATES PRESIDENCY—Month 6

Margaret Zane Garcia placed a serving of yellow cake with white icing on the corner of her husband's desk. "I used your mother's recipe this time. So don't start griping again about my tres leches not being as good."

Ramon smiled weakly. "Thanks, Maggie. I'll eat it later," he said pressing his abdomen. "I'm not hungry."

"Your stomach hurting again?"

"Nothing serious. I'll be fine."

"Ray, I know you're pressed for time right now, but you need to eat, love. I never thought I'd say it, but you're getting too thin."

"My mother told me this would happen when I married a gringa. 'You can never make those women happy, Ramon.' Wise words from a woman who never finished the fifth grade."

"And divorced three husbands," Maggie added. "I think Doña Marcela knew more than her share about being dissatisfied with men.

Ramon laughed. "Well, at least mamá knew when to leave her man alone so he could get some work done."

"All right, patrón. Your obedient wife needs to get her hair done anyway," she said heading for the chalet's door. "I'll see you for dinner."

Once he was alone, Ramon retrieved the satellite phone from a desk drawer and dialed Manolo Suarez. "Is Pedro with you," he asked after Mano answered.

"We're both here," Mano's voice said from the speaker.

"Do we have casualty figures from our Mexican training bases yet?"

"We were lucky, Ramon. The planes destroyed the buildings but most of the trainees were out on joint maneuvers. We'll rebuild."

"That's good news. We've had a break here in Geneva, too," Ramon said, trying to ignore the pain in his belly. "All the zones have voted and we finally have another U.N. representative."

"It's taken long enough. Who is it?"

"Mario Luis Arroyo."

Pedro spoke up. "Excuse me, Don Ramon, but I've never heard of him."

"That's not surprising, Pedro. Mario was a dark horse. He started a machine tool company in Dallas and got very rich before it was all taken away by the Q&R act. Apparently, he still knows how to make connections and swing deals. After each zone voted for their favorite son, Mario was everyone's second choice."

"I hope he can help our cause," Mano said.

"I think he will. Mario's made a lot of business contacts all over the world. I've heard he's a drinking buddy of the Chinese envoy to Switzerland."

"You diplomats get all the rough duty."

"Respect your elders, Mano. You're setting a bad example for your son," Ramon quipped.

"Any more news about Sarah Evans, Don Ramon?" Pedro asked. "We've been listening to the BBC on the short wave here but they're not reporting on her case."

"Unfortunately, needle law cases in the States have

become as common as shoe stores in a shopping mall," Ramon answered. "But I've been keeping up with Sarah through the web." Ramon paused, reluctant to break the bad news. "Her case has been reopened, Pedro."

"You mean she's back on trial?" Pedro asked anxiously.

"I'm afraid so," Ramon said, touched by the young man's pain. "Pedro, I'm going to make you a promise. Sarah is the mother of your son and she sacrificed herself to save one of the key members of our cause. We are not going to abandon her."

"Thank you, Don Ramon."

"There's another piece of business I need to share with you, something that could raise our status in the diplomatic community," Ramon said. "The Alianza Latinoamericana has offered us a deal. If we supply them with intelligence on the U.S. military, they promise to bring us into the alliance as a government in exile."

"When?" Mano asked.

"They can't recognize us publicly right now. The ALA officials are afraid it might provoke the U.S. into an attack—and they're not ready for that just yet."

"Can we trust them?"

"We're not risking a lot by helping them. Most of the intelligence they need can be done from a safe distance. They want us to keep tabs on which military vessels are in port, the types of aircraft deployed at air bases, and reports on any large troop movements."

"There is no 'safe distance,' Ramon. I'll admit, traveling outside the zones is safer than it's ever been but there's still a risk. Our people are in danger anytime they leave the walls."

"This is worth the risk, Mano. It's not the same as full U.N. recognition, but becoming a signatory to the alliance gives us more legitimacy—and it's backed by military muscle. It's an important diplomatic step."

"How long will all these diplomatic steps take, Ramon? When do we get our lives back?"

"I don't know, hermano. All I can tell you is the journey to a homeland has always been a long one. The Zionists struggled more than thirty years before they established the state of Israel—and the Palestinians had been battling them to get it back ever since."

"That's not very encouraging."

"I don't believe in God, Mano, but I do believe in destiny. I think this struggle is our destiny and we can't walk away from it. Yes, we have a long fight ahead before we're free—and a lot of us may not live to see it. But right now, you and Pedro need to take charge of the surveillance for the ALA. The future will take care of itself."

Mano exhaled slowly. "All right. Send me a list of the military facilities they want us to monitor over the netlink. I'll start recruiting teams for the job."

"Gracias, hermano. I knew I could count on you," Ramon said, ending the call.

I should have told them, Ramon thought as he put away the phone. *They have a right to know.* But Mano still seemed hesitant and edgy. The news might have increased his friend's doubts, something that could cost lives in the deadly challenges Mano faced.

Maybe you're just making excuses, old man, he told himself. He'd not even broken the news to Maggie yet.

He'd asked the doctor to be blunt and the oncologist had pulled no punches. The prognosis for the pancreatic cancer they'd uncovered gave him less than six months.

OUTPOST BRAVO, CA

"Here they are, Major," Sergeant Wilkins said, pointing to the two bodies on the motor pool floor with his rifle. "They both had AK-47s. We turned the weapons over to Ordnance already."

"How much ammunition were they carrying?" Fuller asked.

"Four clips apiece."

"Looks like the Panchos aren't hurting for weapons these days," Fuller said, moving closer to the teenagers lying face up on the concrete. Investigating Pancho KIAs was the duty he dreaded most about his new assignment to battlefield INTEL. They were usually so damned young.

He checked the bodies for gang tattoos and found none. In another time, these kids might have been productive citizens instead of enemies.

"How long ago did you take down these two, Sergeant?" Fuller asked, searching through their blood-drenched clothes.

"A couple of hours."

Fuller rose to his feet and faced the squad leader. "Where?"

"About eight klicks from here, near the east bank of the San Gabriel."

"I'd like to go back there."

"You've got to be kidding, Major," the soldier answered. "Back in Hajji land, the INTEL officers just checked to see if the bad guys matched any of the bounty pictures."

"There might be a tunnel somewhere in the area where you ran into these two."

"Look, Major, we brought these bodies back to the base so you wouldn't have to face a bullet."

"Thanks, Wilkins, but I think it's worth a look."

"Major, you know everyone's pulling out at 1700 hours, right?"

Like everyone at Outpost Bravo, Fuller knew all patrols around the zones were being suspended for twenty-four hours beginning Christmas Eve, a move the base commander had implemented to help raise morale.

"Don't worry, Sergeant. I'll get your squad back to base in time."

Wilkins exhaled slowly. "Major, can I have word with you—alone?"

"All right."

Wilkins waited until his men were outside before he spoke. "Major, I know you've seen combat," he said, his voice dry and tired. "Back in the world, they don't know what it's like out here. My guys have been on patrol two days and they're wiped out. I'm worried somebody's going to get sloppy and get themselves hurt. It's Christmas Eve, sir. Can you cut my guys a break?"

"We're soldiers, Wilkins. We don't get to choose which orders to obey."

Wilkins' face hardened. "Major, I don't need a speech about God and country, okay? I did three tours in the sand box—and this fucking Pancho land ain't any different. Americans don't live here anymore and this shithole's not worth getting any of my men killed on Christmas Eve. If you want my stripes, you can put me on report."

Fuller studied the young sergeant. Wilkins was standing up for his comrades, putting their safety above the risk of demotion. *In his shoes, I'd probably do the same*, Fuller realized. Still, this was a challenge to his authority. As an officer Fuller knew an army would implode without discipline. But he also understood that soldiers were human and each of us had a breaking point. Wilkins seemed dangerously close.

"Sergeant, if there is a tunnel out there, I doubt the Panchos will move it in the next twenty-four hours," Fuller said evenly. "You and your squad will report back here to me at 1400 hours tomorrow."

Holding back a smile, Wilkins raised his hand in a salute. "Yes, sir."

Back in his quarters several hours later, Fuller rehashed the encounter as he lay in bed, unable to sleep despite a heavy holiday meal and a half bottle of bourbon.

Americans don't live here anymore, the young sergeant had said. The words were telling.

To veterans like Wilkins who'd spent years battling insurgents overseas, the Panchos were just another foreign enemy. These young soldiers had grown up with the insurgency as a fact of life. They no longer saw the quarantine zones as part of their country.

Fuller rose and poured himself another glass of bourbon, his mind drifting to a conclusion he did not want to reach.

Our politicians had squandered the chance to end this insurgency. We'd treated our own citizens like enemies, tried to control them with bullets when we should have used beans. The needle law and free-fire areas had made us the Panchos best recruiter. In the end, we'd created a foreign nation inside our own borders.

Now, short of genocide, there was no way left to win.

THE BATES PRESIDENCY—Month 6, Day 7

SANTA CLARITA, CA

The high walls of the courtroom were paneled in polished walnut, even the U.S. seal behind the judge's chair was carved in the same dark wood. The somber opulence reminded Sarah of her father's coffin.

Seated beside her lawyer at the defendant's table, Sarah was clad in orange overalls, her hands manacled to a chain around her waist. The prosecution had requested the restraints at the start of the trial, asserting Sarah's violent behavior in jail made her a risk to the jury. Singh had objected. But the judge had overruled, leaving Sarah with two strikes against her with the jury from the very first day. Now, after nearly three months of legal stalls by Singh, the trial was coming to a close.

Surprisingly, Andrea Gordon's closing argument had been brief and halfhearted, giving Sarah hope. Singh had then presented the defense's closing arguments, stressing the lack of any real evidence and Fuller's testimony of Sarah's character. As Singh returned to the defendant's table, he snuck a wink at Sarah. The case was looking hopeful.

Andrea Gordon then rose from prosecutor's table. "Your honor, I'd like to present a rebuttal."

"I object, your honor," Singh called out. "The defense always has the closing arguments.

"There is precedent for a rebuttal from the prosecution, Mr. Singh," the judge answered. "Objection denied."

"Thank you, your honor," Gordon said, giving Singh a sidelong glance of triumph. "The defense has argued that we have no real evidence the defendant is guilty of aiding and abetting the enemies of the United States. Yet Sarah Evans listed her child as Class H, revoking her rights as a citizen, and willingly returned to Quarantine Zone B in Los Angeles. Seven days later—the day of the heinous attack on Toledo—we find the defendant in Santa Clarita, unwilling to explain why she was there."

"Objection," Singh said, rising to his feet. "Your honor, my client gave an explanation of why she was in Santa Clarita."

"Sustained," the judge replied.

Gordon smiled wryly. "Let me rephrase that, your honor. The defendant has failed to provide an explanation for why she returned to Santa Clarita that someone older than six would find credible."

Several people in the courtroom laughed.

The judge rapped his gavel. "Any more outbursts and I'll clear the gallery."

"I apologize for the outburst, your honor," Gordon said with a slight bow of the head. "But it *is* hard to believe that a young woman with no known military experience or security training could make her way undetected over thirty miles of territory patrolled by the world's best troops. Are we expected to believe she had no help? And what reason does Sarah Evans give us for being thirty miles outside the quarantine zone on the day of the Toledo attack? 'I came back to get some more of my things' she tells us. Are we to believe it's mere coincidence that she chose to do that on this particular day? The defense has failed to answer any of these questions."

Gordon paused, then gestured toward Sarah. "It's hard to imagine the kind of pressure to betray her country this young woman endured while under the thrall of the terrorists. We've seen trained, battle-hardened soldiers crack under similar circumstances. But as the Halloween Day attacks have proven once again, these terrorists will exploit any opportunity to harm us. We cannot let pity for the defendant allow us to lower our defenses and lose more American lives. Ladies and gentlemen of the jury, I realize it's a difficult task before you. But I hope you will do your duty as Americans and send a message to the terrorists that we will no longer tolerate their aggression without dire consequences."

The prosecutor returned to her seat and the judge dismissed the jurors. Sarah watched the twelve men and women leave without making eye contact, knowing her fate was now in their hands.

A buzz rose from the gallery after the judge adjourned the court. Looking behind her, Sarah saw the trial's largest crowd yet. A few of the onlookers making notes appeared to be reporters. Most of the others simply glared at her coldly.

Singh patted her hand. "This is the hardest part."

"How long will the jury take?"

"The longer the better. If they go more than a couple of hours, the judge will move you to a holding area."

Sarah closed her eyes, replaying the details of the testimony in her mind, wondering what the jury would think. After less than an hour, the jury returned to the courtroom and the bailiff reconvened the trial.

"How do you find the defendant?" the judge asked the jury's foreman.

"Guilty, your honor," she answered soberly.

Several people in the gallery cheered.

THE BATES PRESIDENCY—Month 6, Day 8

GENEVA, SWITZERLAND

Mano walked down the hospital corridor still feeling awkward in his new clothes. After years of jeans or fatigues, the sports coat and slacks felt like an alien skin grafted onto his body. The sense of dislocation was not hard to understand. Over the last four days, he'd traveled from the dangerous and gritty world of the zones to the glittering, orderly commotion of Geneva.

In a habit from his days as a GI flying overseas, he'd hoarded a pack of airline pretzels in his coat after the 22-hour flight from Tijuana. For most aboard the plane, the processed meals the attendants had served were an unappetizing expedience. For Mano, they were an exotic feast consumed with a large helping of guilt. All the same, his time on the plane had not been a happy one despite the first class seat Ramon had arranged.

The fact their cause could now manage airfares and fake travel documents was a sign of the progress they'd made. But despite these luxuries—or perhaps because of them—this trip had only deepened Mano's doubts about continuing their struggle.

Would the people in the zones ever see abundance like this? Would his sons and their children ever know a day of peace? Mano knew the future for his people was uncertain if they quit fighting. But would it be any worse than the harsh reality of the present? After months of agonizing, he still had no answer.

At a junction in the corridor, Mano stopped to navigate the hospital's multi-lingual signs. Turning right, he passed the entry for what he deciphered was the Palliative Care Unit. In the ward's third room, he spotted Ramon.

His old friend lay on the bed, partly covered in a blanket. Maggie sat reading in a chair nearby. Ramon's face was gaunt and jaundiced, his withered chest heaving as he labored to breathe. When Mano entered the room, Ramon's half-closed eyes grew brighter.

"What a surprise," Ramon said, his voice weak and raspy. "I figured a naco like you would get lost on the way to Geneva and wind up circling Bombay on a cycle taxi."

"I'm glad to see you're feeling well enough to insult your visitors."

Maggie rose, managing a smile. "Thank you for coming, Mano," she said, hugging his broad shoulders.

"I'm grateful to you both for arranging this trip."

"Sit down, Mano" Maggie said, pushing another chair closer to the bed. "We have a lot of catching up to do."

"What's the latest on Sarah?" Ramon asked.

"Everything we planned is on schedule—for now. I'll know for sure when I get back."

"This Sarah reminds me of Jo sometimes," Ramon said, growing wistful. "They both look fragile on the outside, but inside, they're tougher than leather."

For the next hour, they reminisced about their early days with Josefina Herrera, marveling at how far Ramon had come from his job a bookstore clerk in East Los Angeles. When the talk came to the present, Mano's mood became somber, something that Ramon did not miss.

"Maggie, I'll bet you're probably craving a biscotti from

the café across the street," Ramon said smiling.

Maggie smiled back and stood. "If you'd dropped that hint any heavier, it would have broken my toe," she said before leaving the room.

Once they were alone, Ramon touched Mano's arm. "Something's been troubling you for a while, hermano. I think it's time you told me about it."

"I didn't come all this way to talk about my problems."

"Look, I know you'd rather be waterboarded than tell anyone how you feel. But let's be honest. We 're not going to get many more chances to talk, Mano. Tell me what's been bothering you."

Mano rubbed his face and sighed. "Ramon, this war has been going on a long time. But what does our cause have to show for it? I've seen a lot of people die—including two of my children. At what point does all this death and misery stop being worth it?"

"I don't have the answer to that, hermano. Each of us has to reach that bargain in his own heart. But there's something I'm certain about," Ramon said, trying to sit up. A spasm of coughs wracked him but Ramon refused to stop. "You... won't... quit," he said, gasping with each word.

Mano patted his arm. "Lay still, Ramon."

"No. Listen to me," he said grabbing Mano's sleeve. "Right now, we need you in the field. But the day will come when you'll lead all our people."

"That's crazy, Ramon. I'm not a diplomat. I don't know anything about politics or the media."

"Those are the skills of leadership, Mano. Skills can be learned." The coughing wracked Ramon again. "What... What makes a leader is in a person's soul. The good ones care more about others than about themselves. And I've never known anyone more selfless than you, Mano."

"You're tired, Ramon. We can talk about this later."

"I don't have much time left, Mano—and I'm not going to let you leave until we've settled this. Our cause is going to need you as a leader. You need to understand that."

"Arroyo is a good man. You said so yourself."

"Mario Luis is the right leader for the moment. He has the skills you lack right now. But the day we're a nation and Arroyo has the power to truly govern, he'll fail us. Like so many small time politicians, he sees government as a way to get richer." Ramon stopped to catch his breath. "The day we're a nation, we'll need someone who'll set an incorruptible foundation. George Washington did that for the United States. You can do the same for the Hispanic Republic."

"Ramon, this is way beyond—"

Ramon waved weakly, cutting him off. "I know you don't want to do this, Mano. This will be the biggest sacrifice you'll ever make. But your people need you and you can't let them down." He extended a bony hand toward Mano. "Give me your word. Promise me you'll lead our people when the time comes."

Mano exhaled slowly, then gently clasped his hand. "All right. You have my word," he said softly. "Now lay back down and rest."

"You've made a dying man happy, Mano. I hope you'll stick around and watch how an agnostic leaves this world," he said with a faint smile, his eyes growing glassy. "I promise you, it won't be long."

True to his word, Ramon Garcia never saw the sunrise.

THE BATES PRESIDENCY—Month 6, Day 11

SANTA CLARITA, CA

Ajitkumar Singh sat on the edge of the jailhouse bunk, his hands folded tightly. "You need to stay strong, Sarah. This isn't over yet. I've already filed for an appeal," he said, trying to comfort her. "However, there's a step the government's going to take that may seem a little scary." He paused and nervously adjusted his necktie. "They're going to move you to the penitentiary in Victorville."

Seated on the other side of the single bed, Sarah felt her legs tremble but managed to control her voice. "That's where they have the execution chamber, isn't it?"

"Yeah, but don't worry. I'll keep working on your case. I just may not get to see you as often. Victorville's about eighty miles away."

"When are they moving me?"

"Sometime in the next five to ten days. The Marshal's office won't be more specific."

Sarah lowered her eyes. "Will you please tell Mike Fuller?"

"Sure, sure" he said, rising to his feet. "Look, I've got to go. I'm due in court. You going to be okay?"

She nodded without looking up.

"This isn't over yet, Sarah. We've still got some cards to play," Singh said, stepping to the door. "Guard," he called out down the corridor. "I'm ready to go."

Singh stared wordlessly at his wingtip shoes as he waited. After an uneasy silence the guard arrived and let Singh out, locking the door behind him with a metallic clank. Sarah listened to their footfalls fade on the steel floor of the corridor.

She stared through the bars at the rust-stained wall beyond. Singh's act had not been very convincing. No one had ever beaten a needle law rap—and after the Toledo and Halloween attacks, her chances were less than zero. They both knew that. There was no point in pretending—but both of them had all the same .

Her stomach was suddenly queasy, like someone falling from a cliff and waiting in horror to hit the ground. She was going to die. The only question was when.

Sarah felt the cavernous terror only those certain of death ever know. The world would go on. The sun would rise and set. People would laugh, fight, love, work, play, sing. Nothing would stop—except you. Then Sarah thought of her son.

She would not see Daniel grow up, never see him walk or listen to his first laugh. She would be less than a memory to her son, just a face in a photograph, an object of curiosity like a long-dead ancestor. He would never know how much she loved him. That hurt her more than the fear of death.

And Pedro.

Yes, she'd managed to save him. But now she would die without ever seeing him again.

THE BATES PRESIDENCY—Month 6, Day 12

SEATTLE, WA

Thelma Bailey pushed the screen door open with her hip and carried the tray of drinks out to the front porch. "It's really nice having both of you visit," she said to her daughter and Michael Fuller sitting together on the porch. After placing the tray on a small table before them, Thelma handed Fuller one of the tall glasses. "I sweetened your tea the way my husband used to like it, Michael," she said smiling wryly. "Sonya tells me you're partial to a touch of bourbon."

"Thanks, Mrs. Bailey," Fuller said with a guilty grin as he accepted the glass.

"You're welcome," she answered. "But if you don't stop this 'Mrs. Bailey' business, I'm going to thump you for making me feel like an old woman."

Fuller laughed. "All right. That's a promise, Thelma."

"Good. Now, you two go on and visit for a while. I've got some phone calls to make," Thelma said before going back in the house.

"Seems like your mother keeps pretty busy," Fuller noted.

"Yeah, after daddy passed and I went away to school, the church was all she had. It shocked the hell out of me when she used those church connections to get elected to city council."

"The people we love can surprise us sometimes. We don't always know them as well as we think."

Sonya took a sip of tea and leaned her head back on Fuller's shoulder. "Have you ever thought about going into politics?"

Fuller laughed softly. "You'd have better luck asking a Palestinian to join B'nai B'rith."

"I'm not kidding, Mike," Sonya said sitting up. "You're always telling me how the government's fucked up this whole Hispanic issue."

"Sonya, I'm a soldier. What I don't know about politics could fill a library. What I *do* know about politics, I totally detest."

"I thought being a soldier meant making sacrifices to defend your country."

"I've done that," Fuller said suddenly somber. "I'm still doing it."

"But you're not going to change much as long as you're taking orders from fools and glory hounds. You've said so yourself."

"Maybe so," he said looking away.

"Mike, I know you'd give your life in the line of duty. So I can't see why you'd refuse to serve your country as a civilian just because you find politics distasteful."

"Be realistic, Sonya. Even if I tried to run for office, where would I start? I live on a base in the middle of Pancho land."

"Our congressman here in King County is retiring next year," Sonya said, trying to suppress a smile. "If you have an apartment in the area, you'll meet the residency requirements."

"You can't be serious."

"My mother can turn out enough votes to get you nominated. I think your message will get you elected, Mike. There are a lot of progressive voters in this area. If a soldier comes forward with a message of peace, he will not lose."

"You had this planned all along, didn't you?"

Sonya put her arms around his neck and brushed her lips against his. "I care as much about our country as you do, Mike. I'm just trying to make sure we have the best people leading us."

THE BATES PRESIDENCY—Month 7, Day 17

NEAR ACTON, CA

They'd passed the last vestiges of Santa Clarita several miles back: the bare concrete foundations of an unfinished housing tract clinging to the scrubby hills like gravestones. From the back seat of the squad car, Sarah looked out the window and reached a grim realization as they approached the San Gabriel mountains. This was the last time she would see the city where she'd grown up.

Almost everything good she could remember had taken place in Santa Clarita... learning to ride a bike with her dad, her first day of school, slumber parties, soccer games, even the birth of her son. Now, she was being escorted by U.S. Marshals on a trip that would never take her back.

Slowly, a trickle of tears began their way down her cheeks. Sarah wanted to wipe them away but her hands were secured by cuffs to a chain around her waist. All she could manage was to rub her face against the shoulder of her orange overalls.

From the front passenger's seat, a female Deputy Marshal pushed a cigarette through the steel mesh separating them. "You want a smoke?" the matronly woman asked.

Sarah shook her head.

"These things are bad for you anyway," the woman said to Sarah, putting the cigarette in her mouth and lighting up. "Ted, I need some coffee," she said to the driver.

"You caffeine junkies are worse than crackheads, Eva," the Marshal driving answered smirking.

"And you're an insubordinate asshole," Eva jibed back before picking up the handset on the car's radio. "Chase One this is Queenie."

"Go ahead, Queenie," a voice from the radio replied.

"Hey, I want to stop for some coffee next chance we get."

"We got Acton coming up in about twelve miles. Nothing else in between."

Eva made eye contact with one of the Marshals in the cruiser ahead of them and gave him the thumbs up sign. "Thanks, Chuck. Guess I can last till them," she said, ending the transmission.

"Great," the driver said. "Now we'll need to stop for a piss break before we get to Victorville, too."

"So what, Ted? I don't think our passenger's in any hurry to get there," Eva said, glancing toward Sarah. "Why should you be? Shut up and earn some overtime."

They rode on in silence after that with Sarah leaning against the window, enjoying the sun on her face. Since being taken into custody, she'd only seen the sky during court appearances and the five hours each week she was allowed outdoors in her dog run. *Will this be the last time I see the sky?* she wondered.

The rugged landscape of this mountain pass was familiar to Sarah from childhood visits to her aunt in Barstow. She'd always loved seeing the pink and tan stone layered like a parfait where the roadbed cut through the bluffs. In those days, this had been a busy highway. Now, their two squad cars were the only vehicles in sight.

"Hey, what the hell is this?" Ted said as they crested a ridge.

Looking through the windshield, Sarah saw a black soldier in combat gear waving down the squad car ahead of them. Behind the soldier, one of his comrades held three men at gunpoint before a gaping hole in the highway's retaining wall. The men were swarthy and wearing prison coveralls.

Sarah's eyes widened in shock as she looked closer at one of the men and recognized Pedro.

———

Pedro tried not to look at Sarah. If her reaction tipped off the Marshals, this could end very badly.

The black soldier approached the first cruiser and spoke to the lawman in the passenger's seat. "Could you contact our base, sir? Our radio's out. We blew a tire and went down into the ravine," the soldier said, nodding toward the gap in the guard rail. "We were on a prison run with a load of Panchos to Victorville. We caught these three but five others got away."

"Anybody hurt?" the Marshal asked, getting out of the car.

"No, and nobody's going to get hurt if you don't do anything stupid," the soldier said, pointing his automatic rifle at the deputy's chest. As he spoke, Pedro and the other men produced weapons and surrounded the vehicles, their guns trained on the Marshals inside at point blank range.

"All of you, outside. Nice and slow," Pedro ordered the lawmen. "Keep your hands where we can see them." After the deputies complied, Pedro ordered the Marshals to lie on the ground and had his fighters disarm them. Pedro then opened the back door of the cruiser and helped Sarah out of the car.

"Oh, my God. I can't believe this," Sarah said, trying to embrace Pedro despite the restraints.

"Where are the keys?" Pedro asked the Marshals.

"They're at our destination," Eva answered. "Restraint keys don't travel with our prisoners."

"You're probably lying but I don't have time to argue," Pedro replied. "Chuy, get the cutters."

As Chuy disappeared down the ravine, Eva spoke to Pedro. "You're not helping this girl at all, you know. She's not really a Hispanic and there's a chance she might have been pardoned. Hell, that still might happen if you all clear out right now. But if she goes with you, there's no way any of you comes out of this alive. You're a long ways from home, Pancho."

"I'll take my chances," Sarah said defiantly.

Chuy rose out of the ravine wearing a backpack and carrying the cutters along with several lengths of rope. "Here," he said handing Pedro the metal snips. As Pedro began cutting Sarah free, Chuy handed the ropes to the black soldier. "It's time for you to show our guests to their room," he said smiling.

Reynaldo Arias winked at Chuy then spoke to the marshals. "Please don't get all heroic on us. We don't want to hurt anyone, okay?" he said and began binding their hands behind their backs while the others kept them covered. When Reynaldo was finished, they led the law officers down into the ravine.

Sarah stood silently as Pedro cut away her waist chain and hand cuffs.

"That should do it," Pedro said, removing the last of Sarah's restraints.

Her hands finally free, Sarah embraced Pedro, burying

her head in his chest. She held him tightly for a time, her eyes closed. "I've waited a long time for this."

Pedro tenderly lifted her chin. "We'll have more time later. Right now, we have to get moving," he said, stripping off the prison overalls, revealing a t-shirt and jeans. He then handed Sarah a change of clothes from Chuy's backpack. "I hope these fit. The Marshal wasn't wrong about our chances. We *are* a long way from home."

———

Wheels squealing, the squad car fishtailed right as they made another switchback turn on the narrow mountain road. Sarah caught sight of the cliff they'd almost gone over and swallowed hard. "Do we have to drive so fast?" she asked Pedro in the back seat next to her.

"Speed is our friend right now," Pedro answered. "I'm more worried about the Baldies than Chuy's driving."

"Pedro's right," Chuy added from behind the wheel. "The more distance we put between us and the Marshals back there, the better."

"What did you do with them?" Sarah asked. "They weren't bad people."

"They'll be okay. We tied them up in the shade of a tree down in the ravine," Pedro explained. "Our two Baldies ditched the other squad car a few miles up the road. Someone will see the hole in the guard rail and go down there for a look—but hopefully not too soon."

"How did you get those soldiers to help you?"

Pedro and Chuy laughed. "They're both Latinos," Pedro answered.

"But one guy was black and other one was white—he even had blue eyes."

"Yeah, that's Joaquin. He's from Argentina," Pedro said. "Funny things is, Joaquin barely speaks English."

Chuy began to laugh again. "Blessed Mother, the way Joaquin murders English, if he'd said anything in front of the Marshals, we'd have been busted for sure!"

"So the black guy is a Latino, too?"

"His family's from Columbia."

"I still can't believe this, Pedro. How did you even know where to find me?"

"We've been following your trial. After your conviction, we knew you'd be moved to Victorville—and there's only one highway pass still open through the San Gabriels. Someone at the jail tipped us off on the time they were moving you, although that took some cash."

"You make it sound simple, but I don't think it was."

"No, it wasn't. But we had a lot of help. From top to bottom, people on our side wanted to see you free, Sarah."

Sarah met Pedro's eyes. "I don't know how to thank you," she said, then looked down. "When I heard they were moving me, I was sure I'd..." Sarah words drifted off and she covered her face and wept.

Pedro smiled and stroked her hair. "Hey, we didn't come all this way to make you cry."

Sarah wiped her eyes and smiled back. "How's Daniel?"

"Mamá is taking good care of him," Pedro said beaming. "He's drinking soy milk from a bottle now and eating cornmeal. Started crawling, too. We're going to need shoes for that boy pretty soon. He'll be walking any day now."

"I can't wait to see him," Sarah said, nestling against Pedro and closing her eyes.

The car swerved into another curve, drifting into the gravel lining the road. "C'mon, Chuy. Don't make me out a liar about your driving," Pedro called out to his friend.

"You two better hold on tight. We've still got more than thirty miles to go."

Sarah looked around at the desolate mountain countryside. "Aren't you worried we'll be spotted in this car?"

"Most of the Baldie units are closer to the zones. We caught them by surprise coming this far north. We're safe—for now."

"Yeah, they never thought we'd be crazy enough to try something like this," Chuy added.

Over an hour later, after weaving through a maze of mountain roads lined with pine and fir, Chuy pulled over at the base of a steep peak.

"Why are we stopping?" Sarah asked.

Pedro gently touched her face. "From here on in, we walk."

Once Sarah was out of the car, Pedro handed her a backpack and a rifle.

Sarah put on the backpack but gave the rifle back to Pedro. "I won't shoot anybody. I'm sorry."

"You won't have to shoot anyone. Just think of it as a noise maker to scare away the Baldies."

"I don't know how to use a gun."

"It's easy," Pedro said, handing her the rifle. "Just release the safety here, pull back this charging handle and you're ready to squeeze the trigger," he said, then demonstrated with his own weapon.

"Like this?" Sarah said, repeating his movements.

"Exactly," Pedro said, taking back the rifle. After disengaging the action and resetting the safety, he handed the weapon back to her. "One more thing. Don't fire unless one of us tells you to, okay?" Pedro cautioned.

Sarah slung the rifle over her shoulder. "All right. I can do that."

"Good. If everything goes right, you'll just carry it in case we need a spare."

After pushing the squad car out of sight into a gully, Sarah, Pedro and Chuy hiked to the top of the steep wooded ridge ahead of them. Burdened by the supply pack and the rifle, Sarah was winded as they reached the summit. The view from the top took her breath away as well.

Receding into a hazy horizon was the expanse of what had once been the second largest megacity in the United States.

"Can we see Zone B from here?" Sarah asked.

Chuy stretched his arm toward the southwest. "See that open space? The wall starts about a mile beyond that."

"Seems we could have stayed under cover longer if we'd come out of the mountains over there," Sarah said pointing to the west.

Pedro smiled. "The Baldies know that, too. That's why they put their main fortifications directly north of the zone. We're going to come in through the side door and enter from the east."

"How long before we're back inside?"

"That depends on the Baldies. That's a free fire area down there," Pedro answered then took her hand. "C'mon. We need to keep moving," he said, starting down the slope.

For the next half hour, they trekked down the face of the mountain, moving in safety under the cover of the trees. The slope was gentler on this side of the peak, giving the descent the air of a recreational hike. Chuy discretely walked ahead, leaving Sarah and Pedro alone to talk.

"How do we get inside the wall once we reach the zone?" Sarah asked. "I noticed a lot of the sheriffs' deputies stationed around the gates.

"We'll be going in through a tunnel."

"Is it the same tunnel you brought me through the first time?" Sarah asked, remembering her ordeal as Pedro's captive.

"No." Pedro said, looking uncomfortable.

"Strange, isn't it? After all I went through in the zone, here I am, risking my life to get back in."

Pedro looked into the distance. "We all change our minds."

"You're thinking about your father, aren't you?"

"Yeah, I used to think he was soft."

"What convinced you he wasn't?"

"The way my father acted when I brought you to our house that first night. I'd never seen that side of him before."

Sarah was silent for a moment, then said, "Your father killed Isabel's brother, didn't he? Don't deny it. I overhead your parents talking about it."

"It was an accident. My father just wanted to scare him away."

"Isabel's brother was also your partner when you captured me."

"Who told you that?"

"When you're locked up alone all day, there's a lot of time to think," Sarah said. "The picture by your bed when I brought Daniel to see you—I knew I'd seen that face before. Lying in my bunk, I remembered where. He almost caught me the day you set me free. It was the only time I'd seen him without the mask."

"His name was Angel. I thought he was cool. Then I found out he was just a thug."

"Did Isabel know what her brother really did?"

"She thought he was a hero, fighting for his people."

"I feel sorry for her, but I'll never forgive her for betraying us."

Pedro looked startled. "How did you know that?"

"Who else knew when we'd all be at the church and had a reason to tell the soldiers?"

"You're right. We found out later from a street vendor that Isabel went outside the South Gate to the see Baldies the night before the raid."

"Like I said, jail gave me lot of time to figure things out," Sarah said then paused. "There's something else I figured out," she said, her voice thickening with emotion. "Right now, I'm going where I belong."

They walked on in silence after that until they reached a cluster of empty mansions in the foothills. In the foyer of a neo-French chateau, they ate a hurried lunch of hard-boiled eggs and chicken jerky before moving down into the urban flatlands.

Working as a team, they moved carefully through a vacant landscape of ranches, apartments, strip malls and commercial buildings. Chuy took point, scouting for Baldies while Pedro and Sarah trailed behind. Their progress was slow as they zigzagged from cover to cover.

They continued moving this way for several hours until they approached a residential cul-de-sac below a row of barren hills. Here, Chuy stopped and waved for Sarah and Pedro to come forward.

"What is this up ahead?" Sarah asked as they walked toward Chuy.

"Used to be a city park. It's over a mile across and about three miles wide."

When Pedro and Sarah reached Chuy, the bearded rebel nodded toward the hills. "Around or over?" he asked Pedro.

"How much longer to go around?"

Chuy shrugged. "Two hours, maybe more if we spot any Baldies."

Pedro looked at the sun edging toward the horizon. "The Baldies have the advantage after dark. We better take the short cut."

Chuy nodded and jogged ahead. "Don't follow too close," he called out over his shoulder.

Chuy's heart was thumping as he scrambled near the crest of the hill. He knew there was more than exertion driving the pounding in his chest. Charging blindly up this open slope was dicey, maybe the riskiest thing they'd done all day. Still, if Pedro said go, he'd do it. The kid had balls and brains.

Pedro had planned this entire operation and Chuy was proud to be included. They'd pulled off a feat of cojones they'd still sing corridos about in the barrios when he was an old man of forty. And now, with Gloria expecting their first, he'd have a story to tell his grandkids. The thought made Chuy smile.

Reaching the top of the hill, Chuy got down on his belly and crawled toward the ridge. His smile faded as he peered down the other side.

Coming up the slope less than thirty paces away was a Baldie patrol; eight soldiers in a wedge formation.

The Baldies had not seen him. That much was good. But they would be on him in a matter of seconds. Worse yet, he could not retreat. Once the Baldies reached the top of the hill, they'd catch Pedro and Sarah in the open, halfway up the slope behind him. There was no time left to think. Chuy raised his AK-47 and opened fire.

The burst of gunfire drew Pedro's eyes to the hilltop. He saw Chuy prone and taking cover behind the ridgeline, his weapon pointed down the other side of the hill. Chuy fired again, then glanced toward Pedro and waved his arm, signaling his comrade to retreat.

A chorus of gunshots erupted from the other side of the slope. The Baldies were firing back.

"What's happening?" Sarah asked.

Pedro grimaced, knowing his gamble had been a mistake. "You need to get off this hill," he said, looking back toward the homes about fifty yards below them. "See that blue house? Get there as fast as you can and wait for me."

"I want to stay with you."

"I'll be fine," he said, touching her cheek. "Go on."

As Sarah jogged down the slope, Pedro cocked back his AK-47 and charged in the opposite direction. He'd made the decision to take this route and he would not abandon Chuy.

———

A cloud of dust exploded in front of Chuy as another hail of bullets from the Baldies struck the ridgeline giving him cover. Chuy knew it was only a matter of time before the soldiers flanked him. *Once that happens, I'm done for*, Chuy realized. All he could do now was buy enough time for Pedro and Sarah to get off the hill.

Placing his rifle over the ridge, Chuy fired another unaimed burst toward the Baldies, then looked down the slope behind him to check on Pedro and Sarah. To his chagrin, his friend was running toward him.

Chuy waved desperately at Pedro, signaling him to retreat. Now about fifty paces away, Pedro shook his head and continued up the hill. *Just like his father*, Chuy thought.

Too brave for his own good. Their cause could not lose a man like that.

After taking a deep breath, Chuy looked up at the sky and made the sign of the cross. *If this is how it ends, I have no regrets.*

When Pedro saw what his comrade was doing, he called out. "No, Chuy! Don't!"

Ignoring Pedro, Chuy rose to his feet and advanced over the ridgeline into the open, firing his AK-47 on full automatic mode like a firefighter using a water hose. After three steps, he was hit. Chuy screamed and doubled over, but continued to fire until another volley of bullets cut him down.

Pedro fell to knees, covering his face. He'd made a mistake and his friend had paid with his life. *I don't deserve to lead men like this,* he told himself. Enraged at his failure, Pedro rose to his feet and started up the slope, determined to atone for Chuy's death—even if it meant his own.

Then he remembered Sarah.

If the Baldies captured her, she would be back on trial for her life. Without him to guide her to safety, Sarah was as good as dead. Chuy had given his life to save Sarah and he could not squander that gift. Avenging Chuy's death would have to wait.

Pedro fired a pair of bursts toward the ridgeline. *That should keep them pinned down a while longer,* he told himself, praying he was right as he began sprinting down the hill. He fired twice more on his descent, expecting the Baldies to open up on him at any second.

To his surprise, Pedro reached the blue house undetected.

"Where's Chuy?" Sarah asked as he stepped inside the gutted ranch home.

Pedro looked away. "He's leading the Baldies away from us," he said, not wanting to alarm her. "C'mon. We've got to clear out of here."

A violet cloak of dusk was closing on the tree line across the San Gabriel River as Pedro and Sarah huddled in a patch of reeds, assessing their final obstacle.

"Our tunnel's just on the other side," Pedro explained. "But we've got to be careful crossing. The Baldies always patrol the rivers." He slowly pushed aside the reeds and scanned the area. "You stay here until I get to that clump of reeds by the drainage pipe on the other side," he said, pointing to his destination. "When I signal it's safe to cross, run like your pants are on fire."

Sarah nodded then watched Pedro leave the chest-high reeds lining the levee and start down the incline. Pedro ran hard once he was out of the arundo. There was no cover until he reached the other side, almost a hundred yards away.

Staring anxiously, Sarah followed his progress. Pedro was nearing the edge of the river when she was startled by the tramping of boots behind her.

Turning toward the sound, Sarah saw a line of soldiers not far away moving toward the levee through a parking lot strewn with burned out cars.

Her heart began to race. In a few more seconds, the soldiers would be close enough to see Pedro. Caught out in the open, he'd be slaughtered.

You have to help him, said a strange voice in her head. As if watching herself in a dream, Sarah raised the automatic rifle, switched off the safety and pulled back the mechanism. Then, in what seemed slow motion, she pointed the weapon over the heads of the soldiers and squeezed the trigger.

CRACK-ACK-ACK!

An ear-splitting sound like a jackhammer shocked Sarah back to her senses. The soldiers dove for cover among the cars and Sarah fired again.

CRACK-ACK-ACK!

Sliding out of the reeds, Sarah rolled down the levee, trying to stay out of the soldiers' sight. Getting to her feet at the bottom of the embankment, she broke into a run toward Pedro while pointing toward the levee where she'd seen the soldiers. Halfway across the ankle deep river, Pedro understood her gesture and began firing in that direction.

Sarah ran headlong toward Pedro, the rhythmic huffing of her labored breathing tuning out everything else. Pedro was walking backward, firing bursts toward the spot where she'd pointed as he continued slowly across the river. Sarah's feet splashed into the shallow brown water, closing the distance between them. After a dozen more steps, she caught up with Pedro.

"Keep running!" Pedro said. "When you get to the reeds on the other side, start firing to give me cover."

As Sarah sped toward the other bank, the barking of Pedro's rifle was answered by gunfire from the soldiers. With each stride, she feared a bullet would make it her last. Reaching the levee, Sarah scrambled up the incline, almost dropping the rifle. The reeds at the top of the levee tore at her bare arms as she pushed through them, then turned back toward the river.

Pedro was out of the water, still retreating slowly while

shooting toward the far bank. Sarah raised the rifle and fired in the same direction, less startled by the noise this time.

Hearing Sarah's gunfire, Pedro broke into a run toward her. Sarah fired again and saw what looked like cameras flashing from the other bank. *They're shooting back, she realized.* Another thought quickly followed. *If I can see their flashes, they can see mine.* Sarah moved three steps to the left behind the reeds, then fired again.

Pedro was climbing the levee now. In horror, Sarah saw the dirt around him explode in a half dozen places. The soldiers had spotted him.

She raised the gun and pulled the trigger. Nothing happened. As she desperately examined the rifle, Sarah heard a series of thuds—bullets striking the ground. *They know where I am*, she realized with cold chill.

Pedro suddenly burst through the reeds a few steps away. "C'mon! Let's get out of here! Follow me and stay low," he said, leading her in a crouch toward the loading dock of a burned-out warehouse.

Inside the momentary safety of the building the pair stopped to catch their breath, leaning their backs against the wall, chests heaving. After a moment, Pedro laid his hand over hers. "You did good out there, Sarah."

"Thanks," she answered trembling.

"The worst is over," he said soothingly.

"Won't they come after us?"

"Yeah, but our tunnel is very close. We'll be underground before the Baldies cross the river."

Sarah followed Pedro as he ran to the back of the warehouse and they emerged into an alley lined with commercial buildings. "See that brick building?" Pedro said, pointing toward the only one on the block. "That's our way home," he said, taking her hand and breaking into a run.

Striding alongside Pedro, Sarah felt a strange mix of relief and elation. Finally within sight of their destination, Sarah gave in to the luxury of thinking about her son. Before long, she would be holding Daniel again. Would he remember her?

A low rumbling interrupted her thoughts.

From one of the driveways leading into the alley emerged a military vehicle unlike anything Sarah had seen. The olive green machine now blocking their path was shaped like a shark with a machine gun turret where its fin should be and four wheels on each side.

"Over here!" Pedro said, pulling her behind the cover of a dumpster. "The Stryker may not have seen us."

A burst of machine gun fire raked the steel shell of the dumpster, proving Pedro wrong.

"What do we do? We can't go back," Sarah said, knowing the troops from the river would soon arrive behind them.

For the first time that day, Sarah saw fear in Pedro's eyes. "Give me a minute. Let me think," he said, swallowing hard.

The roar of the engine grew louder. Sarah could smell the exhaust fumes. She knew they were trapped and now the vehicle was closing for the kill.

"I failed you, Sarah," Pedro said grimly. "I'm sorry."

"I had nothing to lose." she answered, touching his cheek.

Pedro looked into her eyes. "I never had a chance to say it, but—"

A blinding flash cut off Pedro's words. Sarah was knocked to the ground by a searing gust as a violent thunderclap boomed.

Dazed, Sarah opened her eyes. The world was a gray fog thick with the smell of gunpowder. Pedro's hand reached for her through the smoke.

"Get up. We need to hurry," he said, helping Sarah to her feet.

Rising from behind the dumpster, Sarah saw the vehicle that had pursued them. Black smoke billowed from the blown out hatches on its charred metal shell.

"What happened?" Sarah asked as they ran past the vehicle.

"Seems some friends have been expecting us. Let's go," he said, taking her hand.

As they sprinted toward the brick building, Sarah saw a tall figure in the doorway holding a weapon that looked like a long hollow tube. She smiled as she recognized Mano.

"Nice shot, papá," Pedro said , clapping his father on the shoulder as they reached the door. "Glad you got back in time to meet us."

"Where's Chuy?" Mano asked.

Pedro shook his head. "He's not going to make this trip."

Mano nodded solemnly. "Everything's ready," he said, waving them inside.

"Good. We've got Baldies on our six," Pedro said as he led Sarah through the door.

The large room was filled with rows of tall machines Sarah recognized as printing presses. At a large four-color unit along the back wall, Mano swung back the side panel on the machine revealing a hollow chamber where the roller mechanism should have been. "Pedro, you go down first and show Sarah the way. I'll close up behind us."

Less than a half hour later, they were inside the wall of Quarantine Zone B.

Rosa kissed Daniel's cheek and gently lowered the sleeping nine-month-old into the crib. He looked so much like Pedro it made her ache with nostalgia. The joy of raising a baby was a treasure spent so quickly.

Poor Sarah, Rosa thought. *She'll never know this feeling.*

The news of Sarah's conviction had hit Rosa hard. Sarah had done nothing wrong. Yet she'd been sentenced to die like a stray dog in a city kennel. Rosa shook her head in despair as she covered the baby. Like her children Elena and Julio—and the many killed in Toledo and San Antonio—Sarah would become one more innocent soul sacrificed to this war.

Rosa sat down beside the crib Mano had made, hoping the sight of her grandson would ease her worries. She was grateful for the brightness Daniel brought into their lives. By cherishing the small blessings that came with each day, Rosa had learned to live with the constant threat of death looming over her family. But the last few days had left her edgy.

Pedro had gone outside the walls four days ago. Chuy had disappeared as well which meant they were probably together, though she was never sure. Then Mano had returned from Geneva with the shocking news that Ramon Garcia was dead. This morning, Mano had let her know he'd be going outside the walls again. In all, the toll of events was unsettling.

The sound of the front door opening brought Rosa to her feet. As she'd done many times before, she made the sign of the cross and offered a silent prayer. *Blessed Mother, if you've brought my loved ones back to me, I give you my humble thanks. If in your wisdom you have not, please give me the strength to face whatever fate you've chosen.*

Donning her armor of faith, Rosa walked into the living room.

The Suarez family had moved again Sarah noticed as Mano led them to the porch of a tiled-roof bungalow near the center of Zone B. Although exhausted, hungry and grimy, when Mano opened the door, Sarah had only one thought: to see her son.

The living room furniture was familiar to Sarah but there was no one in sight as they entered the house.

"Mamá must be with the baby," Pedro said, closing the door behind them.

"I haven't let myself think about Daniel until I knew we were safe," Sarah said. "When can I see him?"

Rosa entered the living room, hands folded on her breast, eyes wide in surprise. "I heard your voice, Sarah, but I couldn't believe it," she said, throwing her arms open.

Sarah rushed to embrace Rosa. "I missed you, mamá," she said, resting her cheek on Rosa's shoulder.

"I missed you too, m'hija," Rosa said, softly patting Sarah's back. "But I know there's someone else you want to see right now." Taking Sarah's hand, Rosa led her to Daniel's room and opened the door. "I'll leave you two alone," she said and slipped away.

Walking to the crib, Sarah's heart swelled as she saw her son.

His face had changed, grown a little longer, features more distinct. The changes reminded Sarah of the months she'd been away, time she'd never recover. I'll never let that happen again, m'hijo, she vowed.

Daniel's eyes were closed and peaceful, oblivious to the turmoil in the world around him. All he knew was love—thanks to his family in the zone. Sarah was grateful for that.

But Sarah's ordeal over the last seven months had

changed the way she saw her son. Sarah now understood more clearly the troubles ahead for Daniel, hardships he'd eventually face alone. Someday he'd learn there were people who hated him simply because of his heritage. The time would come when he would hear his father called a terrorist and his mother a traitor. There would be others who would resent him because in their eyes he would not seem completely Hispanic.

But for now, Daniel knew none of these things.

Sarah wanted his innocence to last forever. And in that innocence, there was a promise of change. Her son had roots in both worlds. Maybe he would see through the hate and anger. Maybe he would find a way to bring peace. Maybe there was a reason to hope.

***

Later that night, after a meal and a bath, Sarah and Pedro stood facing each in the small bedroom. The light of a lone candle bathed the cozy space in soft warm light, a paradise compared to the cold harshness of Sarah's cell during the last seven months.

Clad in Rosa's plushest robe, Sarah slowly stepped closer to Pedro and put a palm on his bare chest.

"Most people get to know each other before they have children. We never got that chance," she said softly stroking his skin. "I don't know what your favorite food is, or how you like your coffee, or even your birthday. But I know something a lot more important. I know what kind of man you are."

Pedro smiled and caressed her cheek. "One thing you'll find out is that I don't like to talk much."

"I know *that* already," she said smiling back. "But you were ready to tell me you loved me—even if it took the threat of death."

"I didn't think you'd remember."

"Hard to forget the first time someone you love says he loves you."

"But I didn't really say it, did I?" he teased, slowly opening her robe.

"We can go back outside the wall and get cornered by some Baldies if that puts you in the mood."

Pedro laughed, then his face softened. "I love you, Sarah," he said then kissed her tenderly.

"I love you, Pedro," she answered, pulling him down on the bed.

Although both were exhausted, neither slept much the rest of the night.

THE BATES PRESIDENCY—Month 9

From *Witness To History,*
© 2067 by Simon Potts

As the U.S. continued to withdraw forces from around the world to contain the growing insurgency at home, its enemies abroad exploited the pullouts.

The first crack in the dam appeared in the Middle East as a devastating wave of suicide bombings and rocket attacks struck the weakened U.S. garrisons around the Persian Gulf. The most serious threat, however, came on the Korean Peninsula. There, a combined force of over one million troops from North Korea and China were massing at the 38th parallel, poised to overrun Seoul.

Rumbles of dissent against White House policies arose in Congress when Virginia Dont, a Minnesota senator, proposed a bill limiting the president's powers to launch nuclear attacks "only under conditions of immediate threat to the nation." The bill never made it out of committee. But it marked the first attempt by Congress to limit the powers of a president some lawmakers believed was growing reckless.

Beset by turmoil at home and abroad, and feeling his once-unquestioned support weakening, President Bates issued a blunt warning during a nationally televised appearance. "God has given this nation a power unlike any other in human history. Those who believe we lack the will to use our nuclear arsenal to defend ourselves are mistaken."

Shortly after the president's speech, the Republic of China petitioned the U.N. Security Council for a treaty to resist the

U.S. threat. "Even a madman will not dare attack all of us. We must unite," China's prime minister Jun Ai Guo argued. The prime minister's message found fertile ground. "Once unleashed, the deadly clouds from nuclear weapons will not respect national boundaries," Germany's chancellor said before the U.N.

Two months later, over one-hundred-fifty nations signed the Strategic Treaty at Russin, a military alliance drafted in a municipality of Geneva. The signatories of the STAR agreement promised mutual protection if the United States launched a nuclear attack against any of its members. Australia, Great Britain, Israel, and South Korea, once-staunch U.S. allies, chose to remain neutral.

The United States stood alone.

—Simon Potts

THE BATES PRESIDENCY—Month 10, Day 4

LOS ANGELES QUARANTINE ZONE B

Except for the gas lanterns replacing the electric lights, Holy Trinity Church had not changed much since the day eight years ago when Mano had wandered inside to pray for work. The young parish priest had sent him to the Cielo Azul Bookstore where he'd met Josefina Herrera and Ramon Garcia. Since then, the fate of his family and the struggle of his people had become one. Mano found it fitting that, today, his son would be married in the place that had changed all their lives.

Beside him in the front pew, Rosa held her grandchild and dabbed at tears of joy as their son stood proudly by his bride. The small church was half-empty but the love of those few at the wedding Mass seemed to fill the void. In a centuries-old gesture, Father Ignacio lifted his palms and said, "Let us pray." When Mano bowed his head, he asked God to give his son the strength to put his family first. Mano knew all too well it was not an easy task.

Mano's infatuation with Josefina Herrera had nearly destroyed their family. Yet Jo had opened his eyes to the plight of their people. He would always be grateful to her for that. Nothing in this life was ever perfect—not even perfectly bad. Accepting that fact was one of the hardest lessons he'd learned.

After the ceremony, the family and guests gathered in Mano's home to share a feast of the simple fare grown within the zones. Mano had never tasted a better meal. Amid the death and the pain, his son's wedding was a moment of peace and plenty.

Sarah smiled serenely as she and Pedro fed each other pieces of cornbread cake in the familiar wedding ritual. The strains of a waltz from a battery-powered disc player brought the new couple to their feet for the traditional wedding dance.

As the pair of nineteen-year-olds swayed uneasily in time to the music, Mano leaned close to his wife so that only she could hear. "They come from such different worlds, querida. I hope this war doesn't drive them apart."

Rosa smiled serenely. "Give them some credit, Mano. Their love may do more for justice and peace than this war ever will."

THE BATES PRESIDENCY—Month 22

From *Witness To History,*
© 2067 by Simon Potts

Twenty-two months into the presidency of Melvin Bates, most of the world stood at the brink of war.

Washington D.C.'s embassy row was a ghost town as nation after nation severed diplomatic relations with the United States. In a game of brinksmanship, each side had upped the military ante, afraid that backing down would provoke a preemptive attack.

Across the Texas border, the U.S. faced eleven combat divisions of the Allianza Latinoamericana deployed in Mexico and supplied by nations of the European Union. Threatening the U.S. west coast was an eight-division STAR expeditionary force being assembled in Zhanjiang, China. Throughout Asia, other armies were being formed by countries eager to employ their surging populations.

The United States was an aging nation, its citizens of military age rapidly declining. Proposals to reinstate the military draft had been shelved after lawmakers calculated the anemic number of new soldiers it would add. The nations aligned against the United States were awash in youth—youth that through sheer numbers could neutralize the U.S. superiority in conventional weapons. Many feared the conflict would not remain conventional, however.

The planet's last superpower faced a vast coalition alone. Desperate and cornered, President Bates had vowed to deploy the fearsome nuclear arsenal of the United States if threatened. One-hundred-fifty-two nations, eleven with nuclear capabilities, would retaliate in a war that threatened to engulf most of humankind. It was a war nobody wanted, yet everyone seemed powerless to prevent.

With the fate of the world teetering on the edge of a sword, the nearly-dormant peace movement in the United States found an unlikely voice in a first-term congressman from the state of Washington. His name was Michael Fuller.

—Simon Potts

THE BATES PRESIDENCY—Month 27

From *Witness To History,*
© 2067 by Simon Potts

Melvin Bates lost his bid for re-election, bringing peace candidate Virginia Dent into the White House in a landslide victory.

As Dent had promised during the campaign, the newly-elected president negotiated a cease-fire with the Hispanic insurgents and issued a pardon for all needle law detainees. This was followed by the scheduling of peace talks.

Delegates from the two sides were convened, along with representatives from other nations including China, Russia and the Alianza Latinoamericana. The conference was widely applauded in the U.S. and abroad as a step back from the brink of a catastrophic global war.

Costa Rica, with its reputation as the "Switzerland of Latin America," was selected as the site for the historic meeting.

Leading the delegation for the United States was a second term congressman with deep experience in U.S./Hispanic relations, Michael Fuller. His counterpart for the Hispanic Republic of North America was Manolo Suarez.

—Simon Potts

THE NOSARA ACCORDS

THE NOSARA ACCORDS—Day 1

NOSARA, COSTA RICA

The two men in business suits ambled side-by-side along the beach, each accompanied by sharp-eyed security teams trailing at a discrete distance. Their shadows stretched long across the white sand as the sun dipped into the shimmering Pacific surf.

"Thanks for meeting me outside channels like this," Michael Fuller said.

Manolo Suarez loosened his tie. "It's a relief to get away from the diplomats."

"You know, the first time we met, you stopped one of your guys who was working me over pretty good with a hose. A couple of hours into the conference today, I began to wonder which felt worse."

Mano laughed. "I didn't think it was possible for a group of people to talk so much and say so damned little."

"Job security," Fuller said, joining Mano's laughter.

The pair walked together wordlessly for a time, gazing at the rugged splendor of the Nosara coast.

"Nice place," Mano said. "Reminds me of a green Baja California."

"Glad you like it. Holding the conference here was the best idea our side came up with. I was hoping the place would give us a chance to talk privately."

Mano was suddenly tense. "I'm not going to cut any deals under the table."

"Relax. I just want to hear about Sarah and Daniel."

"I don't know who you're talking about."

"Habits die hard with old soldiers like us, don't they? You can stop pretending about Sarah. She's off the hook and so are you for breaking her out. Dent's pardon made sure of that. Besides, I've got some skeletons in the closet of my own when it comes to Sarah."

Reassured, a tight smile of pride formed on Mano's face. "Sarah's the same as always. She's insisting Daniel learn Spanish. Problem is, there's nobody left in our families who knows more than a few words."

"How's Pedro?"

"He's doing well," Mano answered. "I read you've started a family."

"Been doing your homework on the opposition, eh?"

"I could ask you the same question."

Fuller grinned. "Look at us. Two old soldiers sparring like politicians. We've come down in the world, Mano."

"That we have, Mike."

Fuller looked out across the water, suddenly serious. "How did we let this happen?"

"You're unhappy about the peace conference?"

"On the contrary. What I mean is how did we let this war get started in the first place?"

"I don't know," Mano shrugged. "I started fighting before I even knew we had a cause. Some skinheads killed one of my sister's daughters in a drive-by."

"Your niece was killed by a few racist scumbags, Mano. How did a man like you turn against his country? You were a Ranger."

Mano exhaled slowly. "My youngest son, Julio was killed by an Army armored column. They didn't even..."

Mano paused, rubbing his face. "Look, Mike. That was a long time ago and I wanted blood for blood. I thought that's what honor demanded. Looking back, there's a lot I'd do differently. But there's one thing I can't change. None of this would have happened if my people hadn't been cornered to begin with."

"Mano, you've got to understand that most Americans had nothing against your people—until the terrorism started."

"And you've got to understand that most of my people never took part in any terrorism." Mano stopped walking and placed his hand on Fuller's shoulder. "Your side and mine let the extremists speak for all of us, Mike. We can't ever let that happen again."

EPILOGUE

From *Witness To History,*
© 2067 by Simon Potts

In November 2066, the Union of the Americas began the first general session of the hemisphere's new economic confederation.

Most historians now credit the path to the Union with the establishment of the autonomous region known as the Hispanic Republic of North America established within U.S. territory by the Nosara Accords.

With borders open to all nations of the hemisphere, the Hispanic Republic became a nexus for the flow of technology and investment to the south along with much needed labor to the north.

Although many thorny issues remained unresolved, most saw the Union of the Americas as a promising step to greater prosperity and peace for the hemisphere. The confederation's headquarters in officially-bilingual Miami symbolized the growing unity between north and south.

The president elected to guide the newly formed confederation was a leader whose pedigree was a key factor of his candidacy: Carlos Suarez, youngest son of Manolo Suarez, the first prime minister of the Hispanic Republic.

Suarez's first act as UOA president was the proposal of a motto unanimously approved by all 35 member nations: "Extremism is our only enemy."

—Simon Potts

Glossary—Pancho Land

Anglo—An informal term for Non-Hispanic Whites.

Baldies—Nickname given to U.S. troops by residents of the quarantine zones. Based on the Spanish word "baldes" meaning bucket. A bilingual pun in reference to the soldiers' helmets (Spanish: baldes) and short haircuts (English: baldies).

carajo—A mild profanity. Typically used the way "hell" and "damn it" are used in English.

chino, chinos—Spanish slang for someone of Asian descent, usually not pejorative.

cojones—Spanish slang for testicles. Used to denote courage much as "balls" is used in the United States. Pronounced: co-HOE-ness

corridos—Mexican/Central American folk songs usually narrating mythic deeds or tragic love stories.

Dalton Gang—Nickname given by U.S. troops to sheriff department personnel guarding the zones.

Dios mio—Translation: My God. Used in same context as the English expression.

El Frente—Informal name for the Latino Liberation Front, a terrorist splinter group of the Hispanic insurgency.

gabacha (female), **gabacho** (male)—A pejorative term for Non-Hispanic Whites used primarily in Mexico.

hermana (female), **hermano** (male)—A comrade in the Latino cause. Translation: "sister" or "brother"

Hispanic Republic of North America—The provisional government of the Latino insurgency recognized by the United Nations with two non-voting representatives.

jéfe—boss, chief, leader. Pronounced: HEF-ay

Latino Liberation Front—A terrorist splinter group of the Hispanic insurgency.

mero—The leader of a street gang.

m'hija, m'hijita (diminutive)—Term of endearment literally meaning "my daughter" but often used for any younger person with close bonds to the speaker. Pronounced: ME-ha, me-HEE-ta

m'hijo, m'hijito (diminutive)—Term of endearment literally meaning "my son" but often used with any younger person with close bonds to the speaker. Pronounced: ME-ho, me-HEE-to

mi amor—Romantic term of endearment. Translation: "my love"

naco—Mexican term for someone or something perceived to be of low social class, sometimes used with racist overtones by fair-skinned Mexicans

Panchos—Nickname used by U.S. troops for Hispanic combatants.

pinche—Expletive used as an adjective, mostly by Spanish speakers of Mexican origin. English equivalent would be using "fucking" as an adjective.

pinche madre—expletive used mostly by Spanish speakers of Mexican origin expressing pain or dissatisfaction. Translation: "fucking mother"

placas—Gang graffiti. Pronounced: PLOCK-us

puta—slut, harlot. Translation: "female prostitute"

puto—effeminate, weak. Translation: "male prostitute"

querida—Romantic term of endearment. Translation: "beloved"

Santa Muerte—Translation: Holy Death. The worship of a sacred figure usually depicted as a skeleton clad in a robe and holding a scythe and globe. Originated in Mexico, the syncretic cult combines the saint veneration of Roman Catholicism with Mesoamerican traditions of death worship.

rebélde—A combatant in the rebel cause. Pronounced: ruh-BEL-day

señora—A term of respect for an elder married female. Translation: "Mrs."

vato—A gang member. Pronounced: BA-to

ve con dios (singular) **vayan con dios** (plural)—Translation: Go with God.

viejo, viejito (diminutive)—Term of endearment for an older close friend or relative. Translation: "old one" Pronounced: bee-A-ho, be-a-HE-to

Discussion questions—Pancho Land

Several characters changed their feelings and views during the story. Which character changed most and what motivated the change?

How would you evaluate the moral compass of each character? Did they act justly or did they simply justify their actions?

Who were the "villains" in the story? What made them "villains"? Who were the "heroes" in the story? What made them "heroes"?

Which character in the story did you identify with most?

What challenges do couples of different ethnicities face in today's society? What unique challenges do children of these unions face?

Did any characters make you aware of the racial diversity of people labeled Hispanic? Is "Hispanic" a race?

Were you surprised to learn of the racial prejudice within the Latino community in the U.S. and in the nations of Latin America? Were you aware of the history of emnity between Spanish-speaking nations?

The terms "Hispanic" and "Latino" exist only within the borders of the United States. Given the diversity of race and culture among Latin American nations, why do you believe many people from Latin America in the United States accept the Hispanic identity?

Did the acceptance of the Hispanic identity contribute to the turmoil depicted in the story?

How would you compare the grievances of the Hispanic insurgency in the story to grievances of other wars of independence such as the American Revolution or the U.S. Civil War?

If you were one of the interned Hispanics, what would you have done differently to change your conditions?

The turmoil in the Class H series parallels similar ethnic conflicts with the Basques in Spain, the Tamils in Sri Lanka, the Chechens in Russia, and the Balkans. Do you believe a similar conflict could ever develop in the United States?

The novel envisions a hemispheric economic confederation in the Americas similar to the European Union. Do you believe such a union would ever be possible? What are the pros and cons of such an economic entity?

The Class H Trilogy
by Raul Ramos y Sanchez

AMERICA LIBRE

In a near-future U.S. torn by civil war, ex-GI Mano Suarez must decide his loyalty to his country--and his wife.

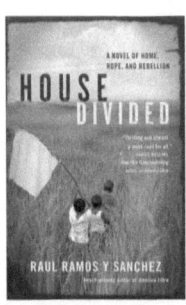

HOUSE DIVIDED

The ethnic conflict that divided a nation now threatens to destroy the family of rebel Mano Suarez.

PANCHO LAND

The Suarez family saga reaches a third generation as the ethnic conflict brings the entire world to the brink of war.

Social Media Connections
Raul Ramos y Sanchez

Facebook

http://www.facebook.com/ClassHTrilogy

When you "like" the Class H Trilogy page on Facebook, you're automatcially entered to win free a signed copy every month. Choose from any of the three novels.

Twitter

@Raul_Ramos

Goodreads

Search for author Raul Ramos y Sanchez

Author's Diary Blog

News and views from the author

www.raulramosysanchez.blogspot.com

About the author

Raul Ramos y Sanchez

Cuban-born Raul Ramos y Sanchez grew up in Miami's cultural kaleidoscope before becoming a long-time resident of the U.S. Midwest. Ramos began the Class H Trilogy in 2004, with the input of scholars from Latin America, Spain, and the United States. The author and his work have been featured on television, radio, online, and in print media across the U.S. and abroad.

Author Highlights:

Books-Into-Movies Award winner from Edward James Olmos of Latino Literacy Now

Best Novel winner - International Latino Book Awards

Violet Crown Awards Fiction Finalist, Writers League of Texas

A USA Today "Summer Reads" author

A LATINA Magazine "10 Hottest Summer Reads" author

Listed among "best Hispanic writers in the beginning of the 21st century" by pop culture search engine ChaCha.com

Number one among 2011 Top Ten Latino Authors - LatinoStories.com

For more information, visit www.RaulRamos.com